Color rose over Miss Hurst's bosom and up her throat to stain her cheeks. It was delicious, Ashe thought, like the flush of pomegranate juice over iced sherbet on a hot day.

She was no wide-eyed innocent if she took the meaning of his glance and words so promptly. But then she was obviously no sheltered Society miss.

How old was she? Twenty-five? Twenty-six? Attractive, bright, stylish but not married. *Why not?* he wondered. *Something to do with her secret lives, no doubt.*

"I would very much appreciate it if you did not mention that we had met before this evening, my lord."

"Members of the *ton* are not expected to be shopkeepers, I assume?"

"Precisely."

"Hmm. Pity my maternal grandfather was a nabob, then." He was unconcerned what people thought of his ancestry, but he was interested in how she reacted.

"If he was indecently rich, and is now dead, there is absolutely nothing for the heir to a marquisate to worry about. Society is curiously accommodating in its prejudices." Her expression was bleak. "At least as far as gentlemen are concerned. Ladies are another matter altogether."

"So I could ruin you with this piece of gossip?"

"Yes—as you know perfectly well..

Tarnished Amongst the Ton
Harlequin® Historical #1137—May 2013

Author Note

When I finished writing *Forbidden Jewel of India,* which was set in India in 1788, I couldn't help wondering what would happen in the future to my hero and heroine, Nick and Anusha Herriard. What better way, I reasoned, than to travel forward in time to the Regency and find out?

This story is the result of that time-traveling, and finds the Marquess and Marchioness of Eldonstone—as they now, reluctantly, find themselves—arriving in London with their son and daughter, Ashe and Sara.

Ashe, I discovered, is not enthusiastic about finding a suitable wife, and I was as surprized as he was by the young lady he encounters on the dockside. The Herriards may be unconventional, but are they let alone Society—going to accept Phyllida Hurst, with her shady background and layers of secrets?

Ashe doesn't know either, but he can't help being attracted—even if it leads to adventures with naughty artworks, a wicked crow and a sinister crime lord. I hope you enjoy reading *Tarnished Amongst the Ton* as much as I did writing it.

LOUISE ALLEN

Tarnished Amongst the Ton

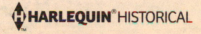

HARLEQUIN® HISTORICAL

Recycling programs for this product may not exist in your area.

ISBN-13: 978-0-373-29737-5

TARNISHED AMONGST THE TON

Copyright © 2013 by Melanie Hilton

Printed in U.S.A.

Other works include Harlequin Historical *Undone!* ebooks

*Disrobed and Dishonored
**Auctioned Virgin to Seduced Bride

Harlequin Books

Hot Desert Nights
"Desert Rake"

Together by Christmas
"A Mistletoe Masquerade"

*Those Scandalous Ravenhursts
††Silk & Scandal
**The Transformation of the Shelley Sisters
†Danger & Desire

**Did you know that these novels are also
available as ebooks? Visit www.Harlequin.com.**

With love for AJH—
and thanks for all the London walking!

LOUISE ALLEN

has been immersing herself in history, real and fictional, for as long as she can remember. She finds landscapes and places evoke powerful images of the past—Venice, Burgundy and the Greek islands are favorite atmospheric destinations. Louise lives on the North Norfolk coast where she and her husband share the cottage they have renovated. She spends her spare time gardening, researching family history or traveling in the UK and abroad in search of inspiration. Please visit Louise's website, www.louiseallenregency.co.uk, for the latest news, or find her on Twitter, @LouiseRegency, and on Facebook.

Chapter One

3 March 1816—the Pool of London

'It is grey, just as everyone said it would be.' Ashe Herriard leaned on the ship's rail and contemplated the wide stretch of the River Thames before him through narrowed eyes. It was jammed with craft from tiny skiffs and rowing boats to those that dwarfed even their four-masted East Indiaman. 'More shades of grey than I had realised existed. And brown and beige and green. But mostly grey.'

He had expected to hate London, to find it alien, but it looked old and prosperous and strangely familiar, even though every bone in his body wanted to resent it and all it represented.

'But it is not raining and Mrs Mackenzie said it rains all the time in England.' Sara stood beside him, huddled in a heavy cloak. She sounded cheerful and excited although her teeth were chattering. 'It is like the Garden Reach in Calcutta, only far busier. And much colder.' She pointed. 'There is even a fort. See?'

'That's the Tower of London.' Ashe grinned, unwilling to infect his sister with his own brooding mood. 'You see, I have remembered my reading.'

'I am very impressed, brother dear,' she agreed with a twinkle that faded as she glanced further along the rail. '*Mata* is being very brave.'

Ashe followed her gaze. 'Smiling brightly, you mean? They are both being brave, I suspect.' His father had his arm around his mother and was holding her tight to his side. That was not unusual—they were unfashionably demonstrative, even by the standards of Calcutta's easy-going European society, but he could read his father and knew what the calm expression combined with a set jaw meant. The Marquess of Eldonstone was braced for a fight.

The fact that it was a fight against his own memories of a country that he had left over forty years ago did not make it any less real, Ashe knew. Estranged from his own father, married to a half-Indian wife who was appalled when she discovered her husband was heir to an English title and would one day have to return, Colonel Nicholas Herriard had held out until the last possible moment before leaving India. But marquesses did not hold posts as military diplomats in the East India Company. And he had known it was inevitable that one day he would inherit the title and have to return to England and do his duty.

And so did his own son, Ashe thought as he walked to his father's side. He was damned if he was going to let it defeat them and he'd be damned, too, if he couldn't take some of the burden off their shoulders even if that meant turning himself into that alien species, the perfect English aristocrat. 'I'll take Perrott, go ashore and make certain Tompkins is here to meet us.'

'Thank you. I don't want your mother and sister standing around on the dockside.' The marquess pointed. 'Signal from there if he's arrived with a carriage.'

'Sir.' Ashe strode off in search of a sailor and a rowing boat and to set foot on dry land. *A new country, a new destiny. A new world,* he told himself, *a new fight.* New worlds were there to conquer, after all. Already memories of the heat and the colour and the vivid life of the palace of Kalatwah were becoming like a dream, slipping though his fingers when he would have grasped and held them. All of them, even the pain and the guilt. *Reshmi,* he thought and pushed away the memory with an almost physical effort. Nothing, not even love, could bring back the dead.

There must be reliable, conscientious, thoughtful men somewhere in creation. Phyllida stood back from the entrance to the narrow alleyway and scanned the bustling Customs House quay. *Unfortunately my dear brother is not one of them.* Which should be no surprise as their sire had not had a reliable, conscientious bone in his body and, his undutiful daughter strongly suspected, not many thoughts in his head either beyond gaming, whoring and spending money.

And now Gregory had been gone for twenty-four hours with the rent money and, according to his friends, had found a new hell somewhere between the Tower and London Bridge.

Something tugged at the laces of her half-boots. Expecting a cat, Phyllida looked down to find herself staring into the black boot-button eyes of the biggest crow she had ever seen. Or perhaps it was a raven escaped from the Tower? But it had a strange greyish head and neck, which set off a massive beak. Not a raven, then. It shot her an insolent look and went back to tugging at her bootlaces.

'Go away!' Phyllida jerked back her foot and it let go with a squawk and went for the other foot.

'Lucifer, put the lady down.' The bird made a harsh noise, flapped up and settled on the shoulder of the tall, bare-headed man standing in front of her. 'I do apologise. He is fascinated by laces, string, anything long and thin. Unfortunately, he is a complete coward with snakes.'

She found her voice. 'That is unlikely to be a handicap in London.' Where had this beautiful, exotic man with his devilish familiar materialised from? Phyllida took in thick dark brown hair, green eyes, a straight nose—down which he was currently studying her—and golden skin. *Tanned skin in March?* No, it was his natural colour. She would not have been surprised to smell a hint of brimstone.

'So I understand.' He reached up and tossed the bird into the air. 'Go and find Sara, you feathered menace. He swears if he's confined to a cage,' he added as it flew off towards the ships at anchor in mid-stream. 'But I suppose I will have to do it or he'll be seducing the ravens in the Tower into all kinds of wickedness. Unless they are merely a legend?'

'No, they are real.' *Definitely foreign, then.* He was well-dressed in a manner that was subtly un-English. A heavy black cloak with a lining that was two shades darker than his eyes, a dark coat, heavy silk brocade waistcoat, snowy white linen—no, the shirt was silk, too. 'Sir!'

He had dropped to one knee on the appalling cobblestones and was tying her bootlaces, allowing her to see that his hair was long—an unfashionable shoulder-length, she guessed—and tied back at the nape of his neck. 'Is something wrong?' He looked up, face serious and questioning, green eyes amused. He knew perfectly well what was wrong, the wretch.

'You are touching my foot, sir!'

The gentleman finished the bow with a brisk tug and stood up. 'Difficult to tie a shoelace without, I'm afraid. Now, where are you going? I assure you, neither I nor Lucifer have any further designs upon your footwear.' His smile suggested there might be other things in danger.

Phyllida took another step back, but not away from assaults on her ankles or her equilibrium. Harry Buck was swaggering along the quayside towards them, one of his bullies a pace behind. Her stomach lurched as she looked around for somewhere to hide from Wapping's most notorious low-life. Nausea almost overcame her. If, somehow, he remembered her from nine years ago...

'That man.' She ducked her head in Buck's direction. 'I do not want to be seen by him.' The breath caught in her throat. 'And he is coming this way.' Running was out of the question. To run would be like dragging a ball of wool in front of a cat and Buck would chase out of sheer instinct. She hadn't even got a bonnet with a decent, concealing brim on it, just a simple flat straw tied on top of a net with her hair bundled up. *Stupid, stupid to have just walked into his territory like this, undisguised and unprepared.*

'In that case we should become better acquainted.' The exotic stranger took a step forwards, pressed her against the wall, raised one cloak-draped arm to shield her from the dockside and bent his head.

'What are you doing—?'

'Kissing you,' he said. And did. His free hand gathered her efficiently against his long, hard body, the impudent green eyes laughed down into hers and his mouth sealed her gasp of outrage.

Behind them there was the sound of heavy footsteps, the light was suddenly reduced as big bodies filled the entrance to the alleyway and a coarse voice said, 'You're on my patch, mate, so that'll be one of my doxies and you owe me.' *One of my doxies. Oh God. I can't be ill, not now, not like this.*

The man lifted his head, his hand pressing her face into the soft silk of his shirt. 'I brought this one with me. I don't share. And I don't pay men for sex.' Phyllida heard Buck's bully give a snort of laughter. Her protector sounded confident, amused and about as meek and mild as a pit bull.

There was a moment's silence, then Buck laughed, the remembered hoarse chuckle that still surfaced sometimes in her worst dreams. 'I like your style. Come and find my place if you want to play deep. Or find a willing girl. Ask anyone in Wapping for Harry Buck's.' And the feet thudded off down the alleyway, faded away.

Phyllida wriggled, furious with the one man she could vent her feelings on. 'Let me go.'

'Hmm?' His nose was buried in the angle of her neck, apparently sniffing. It tickled. So did his lips a moment later, a lingering, almost tender caress. 'Jasmine. Very nice.' He released her and stepped back, although not far enough for her peace of mind.

She usually hated being kissed, it was revolting. It

led to other things even worse. But that had been…surprising. And not at all revolting. It must depend on the man doing the kissing, even if one was not in love with him, which was all Phyllida had ever imagined would make it tolerable.

She took a deep breath and realised that far from being tinged with brimstone he actually smelled very pleasant. 'Sandalwood,' she said out loud rather than any of the other things that were jostling to be uttered like, *Insolent opportunist, outrageous rake. Who are you?* Even the words she thought would never enter her head—*Kiss me again.*

'Yes, and spikenard, just a touch. You know about scents?' He was still far too close, his arm penning her against the wall.

'I do not want to stand here discussing perfumery! Thank you for hiding me from Buck just now, but I wish you would leave now. Really, sir, you cannot go about kissing strange women as you please.' She ducked under his arm and out onto the quayside.

He turned and smiled and something inside her did a little flip. He had made no move to detain her and yet she could feel his hand on her as though it was a physical reality. No one would ever hold her against her will, ever again, and yet she had felt no fear of him. *Foolish. Just because he has charm it does not make him less dangerous.*

'*Are* you strange?' he asked, throwing her words back to her.

There were a range of answers to that question, none of them ladylike. 'The only strange thing about me is that I did not box your ears just now,' Phyllida said. And why she had not, once Buck had gone, she had no idea. 'Good day, sir,' she threw over her shoulder as she walked away. He was smiling, a lazy, heavy-lidded smile. Phyllida resisted the urge to take to her heels and run.

She had tasted of vanilla, coffee and woman and she had smelt like a summer evening in the raja's garden. Ashe ran his tongue over his lower lip in appreciative recollection as he looked around for his father's English lawyer.

I will send the family coach for you, my lord, Tompkins had written in that last letter that had been delivered to the marquess along with an English lady's maid for *Mata* and Sara, a valet for his father and himself. The most useful delivery of all was Perrott, a confidential clerk armed with every fact, figure and detail of the Eldonstone affairs and estates.

Given that your father's rapid decline and unfortunate death have taken us by surprise, I felt it advisable to waste no time in further correspondence but to send you English staff and my most able assistant.

His father had moved fast on receiving the inevitable, unwelcome news. Ashe was recalled from the Principality of Kalatwah where he had been acting as aide-de-camp to his great-uncle, the Raja Kirat Jaswan; possessions were sold, given away or packed and the four of them, along with their retinue, had embarked on the next East Indiaman bound for England.

'My lord, the coach is just along here. I have signalled to his lordship and sent the skiff back.'

'The end of your responsibilities, Perrott,' Ashe said with a grin as he strode along the quayside beside the earnest, red-headed clerk. 'After seventeen weeks of being cooped up on board attempting to teach us everything from tenancy law to entails by way of investments and the more obscure byways of the family tree, you must be delighted to be home again.'

'It is, of course, gratifying to be back in England, my lord, and my mother will be glad to see me. However, it has been a privilege and a pleasure to assist the marquess and yourself.'

And the poor man has a hopeless tendre *for Sara, so it will probably be a relief for both to have some distance between them.* It was the only foolish thing Ashe had discovered about Thomas Perrott. Falling in love was for servants, romantics, poets and women. And fools, which he was not. Not any longer.

His father had done it and had recklessly married for love, which was fortunate or he, Ashe, wouldn't be here now. But then his father was a law unto himself. In any case, a soldier of fortune, which is what he had been at the time, could do what he liked. His son—*the Viscount Clere*, he reminded himself with an inward wince—must marry for entirely different reasons.

'My lord.' Perrott stopped beside a fine black coach with the crest on the side that had become familiar from numerous legal documents and the imposing family tree. It was on the heavy seal ring his father now wore.

Liveried grooms climbed down from the back to stand at attention and two plainer coaches were waiting in line behind. 'For your staff and the small baggage, my lord. The hold luggage will come by carrier as soon as it is unloaded. I trust that is satisfactory?'

'No bullock carts and a distinct absence of elephants,' Ashe observed with a grin. 'We should move with unaccustomed speed.'

'The fodder bills must be smaller, certainly,' Perrott countered, straight-faced, and they walked back to the steps to await the skiff.

'There you are!' Phyllida dumped her hat and reticule on the table and confronted the sprawled figure of her brother, who occupied the sofa like a puppet with its strings cut.

'Here I am,' Gregory agreed, dragging open one eye. 'With the very devil of a thick head, sister dear, so kindly do not nag me.'

'I will do more than nag,' she promised as she tossed her pelisse onto a chair. 'Where is the rent money?'

'Ah. You missed it.' He heaved himself into a sitting position and began to rummage in his pockets. Bank notes spilled out in a crumpled heap on the floor. 'There you are.'

'Gregory! Where on earth did this all come from?' Phyllida dropped to her knees and gathered them up, smoothing and counting. 'Why, there is upwards of three hundred pounds here.'

'Hazard,' he said concisely, sinking back.

'You always lose at hazard.'

'I know. But you have been nagging me about the need for prudence and economy and I took your words to heart. You were quite right, Phyll, and I haven't been much help to you, have I? I even call your common sense *nagging*. But behold my cunning—I went to a new hell and they always want you to win at first, don't they?'

'So I have heard.' It was just that she hadn't believed that he would ever work that sort of thing out for himself.

'Therefore they saw to it that I *did* win and then when they smiled, all pleasant and shark-like, and proposed a double-or-nothing throw, I decided to hold my hand for the night.' He looked positively smug.

'And they let you out with no problem?' The memory of Harry Buck sent shivers down her spine. He would never let a winner escape unscathed from one of his hells. Nor a virgin, either. She blanked the thought as though slamming a lid on a mental box.

'Oh, yes. Told them I'd be back tomorrow with friends to continue my run of luck.'

'But they'll fleece you the second time.'

Gregory closed his eyes again with a sigh that held more weariness than a simple hangover caused. 'I lied to them. Told you, I'm turning over a new leaf, Phyll. I took a long hard look in the mirror yesterday morning and I'm not getting any younger. Made me think about the things you've been saying and I knew you were right. I'm sick of scrimping for every penny and knowing you are working so hard. We need me to attach a rich wife and I won't find one of those in a Wapping hell. And we need to save the readies to finance a courtship, just as you planned.'

'You are a saint amongst brothers.' Which was an outrageous untruth, and this attack of virtue might only last so long, but she did love him despite everything. Perhaps he really had matured as she said. 'You promised me we could go to the Richmonds' ball tomorrow night, don't forget.'

'Not the most exclusive of events, the Richmonds' ball,' Gregory observed, sitting up and taking notice.

'It would hardly answer our purpose if it was,' Phyllida retorted. 'Fenella Richmond enjoys being toadied to, which means she invites those who will do that, as well as the cream of society. We may be sure of finding her rooms supplied with any number of parents looking to buy a titled husband in return for their guineas.'

'Merchants. Mill owners. Manufacturers.' He sounded thoughtful, not critical, but even so, she felt defensive.

'Your sister is a shopkeeper, if the *ton* did but know it. But, yes, they will all be there and all set on insinuating themselves into society. If they think that Lady Richmond is wonderful, just imagine how they are going to enjoy meeting a handsome, single earl with a country house and a large estate. So be your most charming self, brother dear.'

Gregory snorted. 'I am always *charming*. That I have no trouble with. It is being good and responsible that is the challenge. Where have you been all day, Phyll?'

Best not to reveal that she had been looking for him. 'I was in Wapping, too, buying fans from the crew of an Indiaman just in from China.' *And being attacked by a weird crow and kissed by a beautiful man.* As she had all afternoon she resisted the urge to touch her mouth. 'I'll go and put this money in the safe and let Peggy know we're both in for dinner.'

Phyllida scooped up her things and retied her hat strings as she ran downstairs into the basement. 'Peggy?'

'Aye, Miss Phyllida?' Their cook-housekeeper emerged from the kitchen, wiping her hands. 'His lordship's home with a hangover, I see. Drink is a snare and an abomination.'

'We will both be in for dinner, if you please.' Phyllida was used to Peggy's dire pronouncements upon almost any form of enjoyment. 'And Gregory has brought both the rent and the wages home with him.' She counted money out onto the scrubbed pine table. 'There. That's yours for last month and this month and Jane's, too. I'll pay Anna myself.' Jane was the skinny maid of all work, Anna was Phyllida's abigail.

'Praise be,' Peggy pronounced as she counted coins into piles. 'Thank you, Miss Phyllida. And you'll be putting the rest of it away safe, I'm hoping.'

'I will. I'm just going to the shop, I'll be back in half an hour.'

'Rabbit stew,' Peggy called after her as she ran back upstairs. 'And cheesecakes.'

The day that had started so badly was turning out surprisingly well, she decided as she closed the front door, turned left along Great Ryder Street, diagonally across Duke Street and into Mason's Yard. The rent and the wages were paid, Gregory was finally behaving himself over the campaign to find him a rich wife and there were cheesecakes for dinner.

No one was around as she unlocked the back door of the shop, secured it behind her and made her way through into the front. The shutters were closed and the interior of the shop in shadow, but she could see the flicker of movement as carriages and horses passed along Jermyn Street. She would open tomorrow, Phyllida decided as she knelt before the cupboard, moved a stack of wrapping paper and lifted the false bottom. The safe was concealed beneath it, secure from intruders and her brother's 'borrowings' alike, and the roll of notes made a welcome addition to the savings that she secretly thought of as the Marriage Fund.

Gregory's marriage, not hers, of course. Phyllida secured the cupboard and, on a sudden impulse, opened a drawer and drew out a package. Indian incense sticks rolled out, each small bundle labelled in a script she could not read, along with a pencilled scribble in English.

Rose, patchouli, lily, white musk, champa, frankincense... jasmine and sandalwood. She pulled one of the sticks from the bundle and held it to her nose with a little shiver of recollection. It smelled clean and woody and exotic, just as he had. Dangerous and unsettling, for some inexplicable reason. Or perhaps that had been the scent of his skin, that beautiful golden skin.

It was nonsense, of course. He had kissed her, protected her—while taking his own amusement from the situation—and that was enough to unsettle anyone. There was no mystery to it.

Phyllida let herself out, locked up and hurried home.

It was not until she was changing in her bedchamber that she realised she had slipped the incense stick into her reticule.

It was a while since she had bought the bundle, so it was as well to test the quality of them, she supposed. The coating spluttered, then began to smoulder as she touched the tip of the stick to the flame and she wedged it into the wax at the base of the candle to hold it steady. Then she sat and resolutely did not think of amused green eyes while Anna, her maid, brushed out her hair.

She would act the shopkeeper tomorrow and then become someone else entirely for a few hours at Lady Richmond's ball. She was looking forward to it, even if she would spend the evening assessing débutantes and dowries and not dancing. Dancing, like dreams of green-eyed lovers and fantasies of marriage, were for other women, not her. Coils of sandalwood-scented smoke drifted upwards, taking her dreams with them.

Chapter Two

'May I go shopping, *Mata*? I would like to visit the bazaar.'

'There are no bazaars, Sara. It is all shops and some markets.'

'There is one called the Pantheon Bazaar, Reade told me about it.'

Ashe lifted an eyebrow at his father as he poured himself some more coffee. 'It is not like an Indian bazaar. Much more tranquil, I am certain, and no haggling. It is more like many small shops, all together.'

'I know. Reade explained it to me while she was doing my hair this morning. But may I go out, *Mata*?'

'I have too much to do today to go with you.' Their mother's swift, all-encompassing glance around the gloomy shadows of what they had been informed was the *Small* Breakfast Parlour—capital letters implied— gave a fair indication of what she would be doing. Ashe had visions of bonfires in the back garden.

He murmured to his father, 'Fifty rupees that *Mata* will have the staff eating out of her hand by this time tomorrow and one hundred that she'll start redecorating within the week.'

'I don't bet on certainties. If she makes plans for disposing of these hideous curtains while she's at it, I'll be glad. I can't take you, Sara,' the marquess added as she turned imploring eyes on the male end of the table.

'I will,' Ashe said amiably. Sara was putting a brave face on it, but he could tell she was daunted as well as excited by this strange new world. 'I could do with a walk. But window shopping only, I'm not being dragged round shops while you dither over fripperies. I was going along Jermyn Street. That's got some reasonable shops, so Bates said, and I need some shaving soap.'

An hour later Sara was complaining, 'So *I* have to be dragged around shops while *you* dither about shaving soap!'

'You bought soap, too. Three sorts,' Ashe pointed out, recalling just why he normally avoided shopping with females like the plague. 'Look, there's a fashionable milliner's.'

He had no idea whether it was in the mode or not. Several years spent almost entirely in an Indian princely court was not good preparation for judging the ludicrous things English women put on their heads and he knew that anything seen in Calcutta was a good eighteen months out of date. But it certainly diverted Sara. She stood in front of the window and sighed over a confection of lace, feathers and satin ribbon supported on a straw base the size of a tea plate.

'No, you may not go in,' Ashe said firmly, tucking her arm under his and steering her across Duke Street. 'I will not be responsible for explaining to *Mata* why you have come home wearing something suitable for a lightskirt.'

'Doesn't London smell strange?' Sara remarked. 'No spices, no flowers. Nothing dead, no food vendors on the street.'

'Not around here,' he agreed. 'But this is the smart end of town. Even so, there are drains and horse manure if you are missing the rich aromas of street life. Now that's a good piece.' He stopped in front of a small shop, just two shallow bays on either side of a green-painted door. 'See, that jade figure.'

'There are all kinds of lovely things.' Sara peered into the depths of the window display. Small carvings and jewels were set out on a swirl of fabrics, miniature paintings rubbed shoulders with what he suspected were Russian icons, ancient terracotta idols sat next to Japanese china.

Ashe stepped back to read the sign over the door. '*The Cabinet of Curiosity.* An apt name. Look at that moonstone pendant—it is just the colour of your eyes. Shall we go in and look at it?'

She gave his arm an excited squeeze and whisked into the shop as he opened the door. Above their head a bell tinkled and the curtain at the back of the shop parted.

'Good morning, *monsieur, madame.*' The shopkeeper, it seemed, was a Frenchwoman. She hesitated as though she was surprised to see them, then came forwards.

Medium height, hair hidden beneath a neat cap, tinted spectacles perched on the end of her nose. Perfectly packaged in her plain, high-necked brown gown. *Very French*, he thought.

'May I assist you?' she asked and pushed the spectacles more firmly up her nose.

'We would like to look at the moonstone pendant, if you would be so good.'

'*Certainement. Madame* would care to sit?' She gestured to a chair as she came out from behind the counter, lifting an ornate chatelaine to select a key before opening the cabinet and laying the jewel on a velvet pad in front of Sara.

Ashe watched his sister examine the pendant with the care their mother had taught her. She was as discriminating about gemstones as he was and, however pretty the trinket, she would not want it if it was flawed.

His attention drifted, caught by the edge of awareness that he had always assumed was a hunter's instinct. Something was wrong...no, out of place. He shifted, scanning the small space of the shop. No one was watching from behind the curtain, he was certain there were only the three of them there.

The *vendeuse*, he realised, was watching him. Not the pendant for safekeeping, not Sara to assess a potential customer's reactions, but, covertly, him. *Interesting.* He shifted until he could see her in the mirrored surface of a Venetian cabinet. Younger than he had first thought, he concluded, seeing smooth, unlined skin, high cheekbones, eyes shadowed behind those tinted spectacles, a pointed little chin. She caught her lower lip between her teeth and moved her hands as though to stop herself clenching them. There was something very familiar about her.

'How much is this?' Sara asked and the woman turned and bent towards her. Something in the way she moved registered in his head. *Surely not?*

Ashe strolled across and stood at her shoulder as though interested in her answer. She shifted, apparently made uncomfortable by his nearness, but she did not look at him.

She named a price, Sara automatically clicked her tongue in rejection, ready to negotiate. He leaned closer and felt the Frenchwoman stiffen like a wary animal. She had brown hair, from what he could see of the little wisps escaping from that ghastly cap. They created an enticing veil over the vulnerable, biteable, nape of her neck.

'I would want the chain included for that,' Sara said.

He inhaled deeply. Warm, tense woman and... 'Jasmine,' Ashe murmured, close to the *vendeuse*'s ear. She went very still. Oh, yes, this was just like hunting and he had found game. 'You get around, *madame.*'

'My varied stock, you mean, *monsieur*?' She spoke firmly, without a tremor. Her nerves must be excellent. 'Indeed, it comes from all over the world. And, yes, the pendant suits your wife so well that I can include the chain in that price.'

'But—' Sara began.

'You want it, my dear?' Ashe interrupted her. 'Then we will take it.' Interesting, and subtly insulting, that his acquaintance from the quayside assumed he was married. Perversely he saw no reason to enlighten her immediately, and certainly not to pursue this further with Sara sitting there.

What sort of man did she think he was, to kiss and flirt with chance-met women if he had a wife at home? Ashe knew himself to be no saint, but he had been brought up with the example of marital fidelity before him daily and he had no time for men who were unfaithful to their wives.

Which was why he intended to choose with extreme care. This was England, not India, and flouting society's rules would not be excused here. The family were different enough as it was, with their mixed blood, his maternal grandfather's links to trade and his paternal grandfather's reputation for dissipation.

Ashe had a duty to marry, to provide the next heir, to enrich the family name and title with the right connections and the estate with lands and money. He glanced down at his sister, reminded yet again that her own hopes of a suitable, good marriage depended on respectability. But he would be tied to the woman who brought those connections and that dowry with her. There had to be mutual respect or it would be intolerable. Love he did not expect.

'This is your own shop?' he asked as he peeled off his gloves in order to take banknotes from the roll Perrott had provided. He calculated currency conversions in his head, valuing the stock he could see. Even at Indian prices there was a considerable investment represented on the shelves around him.

'Yes, *monsieur*.' She was doggedly sticking to her French pretence. Used to negotiating with hostile Frenchmen in India, he could admire her accent.

'Impressive. I was surprised that the name is the Cabinet of Curiosity, not *Curiosities*.' Without the conflicting stinks of the river and the alleyway the subtle odour of jasmine on her warm skin was filling his senses. His body began to send him unmistakable signals of interest.

'My intention is to provide stimulation to the intellect,' she said, returning him his change. Her bare fingers touched the palm of his hand and he curled his fist closed, trapping her.

'As well as of the senses?' he suggested. She went very still. Her fingers were warm, slender. Under his thumb he felt her pulse hammering. He was not alone in this reaction. *Stimulation to the senses, indeed.*

'To find the treasures here one needs curiosity,' she finished, her voice suddenly breathless. Her accent had slipped a trifle.

'You may be sure you have stimulated mine,' Ashe murmured. 'All of them. I will return, with or without my...sister.'

Her hand tensed in his and as suddenly relaxed. Oh, yes, she was as aware of him as he was of her and the news that he was unmarried had struck home.

'I must wrap the pendant, *monsieur.*' She gave a little tug and he released her. There was no wedding ring on those long slender fingers with their neat oval nails. The hunting instinct stirred again and with it certain parts of his body that were better kept under control when he was supposed to be escorting his sister on a blameless shopping expedition.

Ashe slipped the flat box into his breast pocket, resumed his gloves and waited for Sara to gather up her reticule and parasol. 'You open your shop every day?'

'*Non.* I open as the whim takes me, *monsieur,*' the lady of curiosities said, a little tart now and very French again. He had flustered her and she did not forgive that easily, it seemed. 'I am often away buying stock.'

'Down by the Pool of London, perhaps?'

She shrugged, an elegant gesture that made him wonder if she was, indeed, French. But her accent when they first met had been completely English, he recalled and she had slipped up just now. 'Anywhere that I can find treasures for my clients, *monsieur*. Good day, *monsieur, mademoiselle.*'

'Au revoir,' Ashe returned and was amused to see her purse her lips. She suspected, quite correctly, that he was teasing her.

Phyllida shot the bolt on the door and retreated into the back room. *Him. Here.* As though she had not had enough trouble trying, and failing, to get him out of her head. She spread out her right hand, the one he had captured in his own big brown fist. She had felt overpowered, an unexpected sensation. What was most unsettling was that it was not unwelcome. A strong, decisive man after Gregory's lazy indecision was…stimulating. And dangerous. She reminded herself that for all the charm he was a man and one who probably had no hesitation in seizing what he wanted if charm alone did not work. Men had no hesitation in using their superior strength to take advantage of a woman.

He had been without his devil-bird, but with a charming sister who was, it seemed, as bright as she was pretty. The wretch, after that kiss, to let her think he was with his wife! It did not mean he did not have one at home, of course. Not that she cared in the slightest.

But who was he? He had paid in cash, which must mean he was not one of the *ton*. If he had been, he would have simply handed her his card and expected her to send him an account. Besides, she had never seen him before yesterday and she knew everyone who was anyone, by sight at least. Whoever he was, he was wealthy. His clothes were, again, superb, with that hint of foreign styling. His sister, too, was dressed impeccably and the simple pearls at her neck and ears were of high quality.

A wealthy trader? If he was with the East India Company it might explain his presence at the docks. A ship owner, perhaps.

Phyllida realised she was twisting the chain of her chatelaine into a knot and released it with an impatient flick of her wrist. He was the first person who had connected any of the elements of her complicated life. But provided he was not in a position to link Mrs Drummond, the dealer who scoured the East End and the docks for treasures for the stock of Madame Deaucourt, owner of the Cabinet of Curiosity, with Phyllida Hurst, the somewhat shady sister of the Earl of Fransham, he was no danger, surely?

Except for your foolish fantasies, she scolded herself. She had never enjoyed being kissed before and that caress by the Customs House had been skilled, casually delivered as it had been. The man was a flirt of the worst kind, Phyllida told herself as she jammed the tinted spectacles back on her nose and went to open up the shop again.

And he must flirt with everything and anything in skirts, she decided, catching sight of herself in a mirror. He could hardly make the excuse that he had been so stunned by her beauty he had not known what he was doing. When properly dressed and coiffed she was, she flattered herself, not exactly an eyesore. But yesterday, in a plain stuff gown with her hair scraped back and hidden in that net, she should never have merited a second glance. Which was, of course, her intention. And it had taken him a while, even with those watchful green eyes, to recognise her in today's outfit.

The problem was that she found herself wishing with a positively reckless abandon that her nameless man *would* spare her a second glance. And that kind of foolishness threatened the entire plan of campaign she had set in motion at the age of seventeen and which had cost her so dear. *Idiot*, she lectured herself. *If he looks at you seriously it will be as a mistress, a possession, not a wife.* And marriage was only a dream, not a possibility, for her.

'Bonjour, madame.' She opened the door and dipped a respectful curtsy to Lady Harington, who swept in with a brisk nod. She was a regular customer who obviously had no idea that she had spent quite fifteen minutes in conversation with Phyllida in her respectable guise only two evenings previously at a musicale.

'I have received a small consignment of the most elegant fans from the Orient, *madame.*' She lifted them from their silk wrappings and laid them out on the counter. 'Each is unique and quite exclusive to myself. I am showing them only to clients of discernment.' *And they are very, very expensive*, she decided, seeing the avid glint in her ladyship's eyes. Earning the money to drag them back from the edge of ruin and to bring Gregory into complete respectability was everything. Nothing must be allowed to threaten that.

'Thank you for my present, Ashe.' Sara slid her hand under his elbow as they made their way from St James's Square and turned right into Pall Mall. 'Why did you let the shopkeeper believe we were married?'

'I corrected her soon enough. It is no concern of hers.' *She was interested, though.*

'You were flirting with her.'

'And what do you know of flirting, might I ask? You are not out yet.' One of the problems with being male, single and all that implied was that Ashe was only too aware of the thoughts, desires and proclivities of the other single males who were going to come into contact with his beautiful, friendly, innocent sister. It was enough to make him want to lock her up and hide the key for at least another five years.

'I was out in Calcutta. I went to parties and picnics and dances. Everything, in fact.' She tilted her head and sent him a twinkling smile that filled him with foreboding. 'It is just that you were in Kalatwah and didn't know what I was up to.'

'That is different. It is all much more formal here. All those rules and scandal lurking if we trip up on as much as one of them. Especially for you, which is unfair, but—'

'I know. Young ladies must be beyond reproach, as innocent as babies.' Sara sighed theatrically. 'Such a pity I am not an innocent.'

'What?' Ashe slammed to a halt, realised where he was and carried on walking. If he had to take ship back to India to dismember whoever had got his hands on his little sister, he would. 'Sarisa Melissa Herriard, who is he?' he ground out.

'No one, silly. I meant it theoretically. You don't think *Mata* is like those idiotic women who don't tell their daughters anything and expect them to work it all out on their wedding night, do you? Or leave them to get into trouble because they don't understand what men want.'

Ashe moaned faintly. No, of course their mother, raised as an Indian princess, and presumably schooled in all the theory of the ancient erotic texts, would have passed that wisdom on to her daughter as she reached marriageable age. He just did not want to think about it.

He had been away from home too long and his baby sister had grown up too fast. On board ship he hadn't realised. She had been her old enthusiastic, curious self and there had been no young men to flirt with except the unfortunate Mr Perrott, so Ashe had carried on thinking of her as the seventeen-year-old girl he had left when he went to their great-uncle's court. But she was twenty now. A woman.

'Then pretend, very hard, that you haven't a clue,' he said.

'Of course,' his oh-so-demure little sister said. 'So, were you flirting?'

'No. I do not flirt with plain French shopkeepers.'

'Hmm. I'm not so certain she *is* plain,' Sara said. 'I think she would like to appear so. Perhaps because she has trouble with rakish gentlemen like you.' They stopped before a rambling pile of red brick with two scarlet-coated guards standing in front. 'What on earth is that?' she asked before Ashe could demand why she considered him rakish and how she would know a rake if she saw one.

He had been doing his homework. 'St James's Palace. It is very old.'

'It is a sorry excuse for a palace, in my opinion—the most junior raja can do better than that.' Sara wrinkled her nose in disapprobation.

'Come on, we'll go through to the park.' Ashe took her past the guards before they could be arrested for *lèse-majesté* or whatever crime being rude about the sovereign's palaces constituted.

'So, are you looking for a mistress?' she enquired as they went through the improbably named Milkmaids' Passage and into Green Park.

'No!' *Yes*. But he certainly was not going to discuss that with his little sister. It was far too long since he had been with a woman. There had been women after Reshmi—he was not a monk, after all—but the voyage had lasted months and the ship might as well have been a monastery.

'You will be looking for a wife, though. *Mata* said you would be. At least there are lots more women in London to fall in love with than there were in Calcutta society.'

'I have no intention of falling in love. I need to find a wife suitable for a viscount.' And one who was heir to a marquisate at that.

'But Father and *Mata* made a love match. Oh look, cows wandering about. But they aren't sacred, are they?'

'Shouldn't think so.' He spared the livestock a glance. 'Not unless the Church of England has developed some very strange practices. Look, there are milkmaids or cow herds or something.

'Our parents met and fell in love before they knew Father's uncle had died, making grandfather the heir,' he reminded her. '*Mata* even ran away when she found out before the wedding because she did not think she would make a good marchioness.'

'I know, but it is ridiculous! She is clever and beautiful and brave,' Sara said fiercely. 'What more could be needed?

'She is the illegitimate daughter of an East India Company merchant and an Indian princess—not the usual English aristocratic lady, you must agree. She only agreed to marry Father and to take it on because she loves him—why do you think he stayed in India until the last possible moment?'

'I thought it was because he and his father hated each other.'

That was one way of describing a relationship where a bitter wastrel had packed his own seventeen-year-old son off to India against his will.

'Father made his own life, his own reputation, in India. He never wanted to come back, especially with *Mata*'s anxieties, but they know it is their duty.' He shrugged. 'And one day, a long way away, I hope, it will be mine. And I'm not putting another woman through what our mother is having to deal with. So much to learn, the realisation that people are talking behind her back, assessing whether she is up to it, is well bred enough, watching for every mistake.'

'I had not realised it would be that bad. I am an innocent after all,' Sara said with a sigh. 'I will do my best not to add to their worries.' She flashed him a smile. 'I can be good if I try. And I suppose if you find the right wife she will be a help to *Mata*, won't she?'

'Yes,' Ashe agreed, wishing it did not feel so much like buying a horse. 'She can take on some of the duties of chaperon for you once we are married. And a suitable bride will have social and political connections.' He knew little about English politics as yet, but the intrigues of an Indian court seemed simple in comparison to what he had read.

'I want to find someone like *Mata* found Father. Poor Ashe.' Sara squeezed his arm companionably. 'No love match for you.'

He should have answered faster, made a joke of

it, because Sara knew him too well. 'Oh, was there someone?'

'Yes. Perhaps. I don't know.' He was mumbling. He never mumbled. Ashe got a grip on himself. 'It never got that far.'

'Who?' When he didn't answer she asked, 'At Kalatwah?'

Reshmi. The Silken One. Great dark eyes, a mouth of sinful promise, a heart full of joy and laughter. 'Yes.'

'You left her?'

'She died.' *Two years ago. It was impossible,* he had known it was doomed from the start and finally he had told her, far too abruptly because he didn't want to do it. They said it was an accident that she had trodden on a *krait* hidden in the dry grass and he tried to believe that it *was* chance, that she would never have chosen to kill herself in such a ghastly, painful way. But his conscience told him that she had been too distracted, too full of grief to be as careful as she normally was.

It was his fault. Since Reshmi he had organised his liaisons with clinical care, generously but with no misunderstandings on either side. And no attachments either.

'It was a long time ago, I don't think of her now.' He tried not to, because when he did there was still the ache of her loss, the memory of the sweetness of her lips on his. The guilt at having had so much power over another person's happiness and having failed her.

He would never find it again, that almost innocent feeling of first love. It had been cut short, like an amputation, and that, and the guilt, was why it hurt. He would never be that young, or foolish, again, which was a mercy because love seemed to hurt both parties. How would the survivor cope with the pain if one of his parents outlived the other?

Sara leaned into him and rested her head against his shoulder for a moment, too sensitive to ask more. After a moment she said, 'Look, they are milking the cows. Is that not truly incredible? Right by the palace!' She let go of his arm and ran across the grass, laughing, so he strode after her over the green grass, shaking off the heat and colours of India. That was the past.

Chapter Three

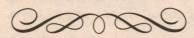

'How elegantly your daughter dances, Mrs Fogerty.' Judging by the amount of money lavished on Miss Fogerty's clothes and the almost painful correctness of her manners, *elegant* was likely to be a very acceptable compliment to her doting mama.

'Why, thank you.' The matron simpered and made room on the upholstered bench to allow Phyllida to sit down. Her efforts to recall to whom she was speaking were painfully visible, but Phyllida did not enlighten her. 'Her partner is an excellent dancer.' Mrs Fogerty watched Gregory closely.

'The Earl of Fransham? Yes, indeed. A very old family.' Phyllida waved her exquisite fan gently and allowed Mrs Fogerty a good look at the antique cameos she was wearing. All part of her stock, although now when she wanted to sell them she would have to go to another dealer or they might be recognised.

'You are related to him?' The older woman was avid for details.

'A connection.' If it came to serious courtship, Phyllida was resigned to fading completely into the background. 'Large estates, of course, and the most magnificent country house.' *With dozens of buckets under the drips, death watch beetle in the roof and pleasure gardens resembling the darkest jungle.* 'Although,' she lowered her voice, 'like so many of the really old noble families, the resources to invest are sadly lacking.'

'Indeed?' Mrs Fogerty narrowed her eyes and regarded Gregory's handsome figure and impeccable tailoring with sharpened interest. To Phyllida's delight she had picked up on the hint that the earl was in the market for a rich wife and was not in a position to be picky about bloodlines.

Mr Fogerty, a self-made Lancashire mill owner, was high on her list of wealthy parents in search of an aristocratic son-in-law and Emily Fogerty seemed bright and pleasant, although perhaps not strong-willed enough to deal with Gregory. She was not the only one under consideration, however, nor her favourite. After a few minutes of conversation Phyllida excused herself and drifted off in search of Miss Millington, the sole child of banker Sir Ralph Millington and her ideal candidate.

'Phyllida Hurst!' The Dowager Countess of Malling stood close to the main entrance of the Richmonds' ballroom.

'Ma'am.' She curtsied, smiling. The old dragon scared half the *ton* into instant flight, but she amused Phyllida, who knew the kind heart behind the abrasive exterior. 'May I say what a very handsome toque you are wearing?'

'I look a fright in it.' The old lady patted the erection on her head and smiled evilly. 'But it amuses me. Now, what are you up to these days, my dear?'

She was some kind of connection of Phyllida's

mother and had done a great deal to mitigate the damage of her parents' scandalous marriage and make the Hurst siblings acceptable to the *ton*, so Phyllida always made time to relay gossip, have her gowns criticised and enquire after the Dowager's pug dogs, Hercules and Samson.

'Shall we sit down, ma'am?'

'And miss all the arrivals? Nonsense.' Lady Malling fetched Phyllida a painful rap on the wrist with her fan. 'Give me your arm, child. Now, who is this? Oh, only Georgina Farraday with her hair even blonder than normal. Who does she think she is deceiving?' The set had just finished, the music stopped and her voice cut clearly through the chatter.

Phyllida suppressed a smile. 'I dare not comment, ma'am,' she murmured.

'Pish! Ah, this is more interesting. Now *that* is what I call a fine figure of a man.'

Phyllida had to agree. The gentleman standing just inside the entrance was in his late fifties, but she doubted he had an inch of spare flesh on his lean, broad-shouldered body. His hair was silver-gilt, his evening dress was cut with an expensive simplicity that set off his athletic frame and on his arm was a striking golden-skinned woman with a mass of dark brown hair piled in an elaborate coiffure.

'He is certainly handsome. And so is his lady—see how beautifully she moves. She must be foreign—Italian, do you think?' And indeed, the curvaceous figure in amber silk made every other woman in the room look clumsy as she came forwards, a faint smile on her lips, head high. There was something faintly familiar about the couple, although surely she would have remembered if she had seen either of them before?

'Of course,' the dowager said with a sharp nod of satisfaction as she made the connection. 'Not Italian, Indian. That, my dear, must be the Marquess and Marchioness of Eldonstone. He hasn't been in the country for forty years, I should think. At outs with his father, for which no one could blame him. Now the old reprobate is dead they have come home.

'The wife, so they say, is the child of an Indian princess and a John Company nabob. Interesting to see what society makes of her!'

'Or she of society.' The marchioness looked like a panther in a room full of domestic cats. A perfectly well-behaved panther and a collection of pedigree cats, of course, but the fur would fly if they tried to tweak her tail, Phyllida decided, admiring the lady's poise.

Then the couple came further into the room and she gasped. Behind them were the man from the dockside and his companion from the shop. His sister. No wonder the older couple had looked familiar. Their son—for surely he could be nothing else—had his father's rangy height and broad shoulders, his mother's dark brown hair and gilded skin. The daughter's hair was the gold her father's must once have been and she moved with the same alluring sway as her mother, a panther cub just grown up. The moonstone pendant she had bought from Phyllida lay glowing on her bosom.

Her shock must have been audible. Beside her the dowager chuckled richly. 'Now that will be the viscount. The heir to a marquisate and those looks to go with the title—there is a young man who will cause a flutter in the dovecotes!'

'Indeed,' Phyllida agreed. *Indeed!* 'The daughter looks delightful, do you not think?' She felt momentarily dizzy. She had dreamt about this man and here he was, in all his dangerous splendour. Dangerous to a spinster's equilibrium and even more dangerous to a spinster with secrets.

'Pretty gel. Got style. They all have. I doubt it is *London* style though, which is going to be entertaining,' the old lady pronounced. 'I shall make myself known. Coming, my dear?'

'I do not think so. Excuse me, ma'am.' Phyllida disengaged her arm and began to sidle backwards into the throng, all gaping at the newcomers while pretending not to.

Oh, my heavens. Phyllida sat down in the nearest empty alcove and used her fan in earnest. He—the Viscount Whatever—was a member of the *ton* after all and, with a sister obviously ready to be launched, the family would be here for the Season. He would be everywhere she went, at every social event.

Was there any hope that he might not recognise her? She strove to collect herself and think calmly. People saw what they expected to see—she had proved that over and over again as she served society ladies in the Cabinet of Curiosity. He had never seen her wearing anything other than the drabbest, most neutral day dress, and never with her hair exposed.

Phyllida studied her reflection in the nearest mirrored surface and stopped herself chewing her lower lip in agitation. That was better. There was nothing to connect the elegantly gowned and poised young lady who moved so easily in fashionable society with either the flustered woman he had kissed on the dockside or the French shopkeeper.

And going into hiding for the rest of the Season was not an option, either, there was a match to be made. Phyllida unfurled her fan with a defiant flourish and set out in search of Miss Millington and her substantial dowry.

She would circulate around the room in the same direction as the Eldonstone party and that would ensure she never came face to face with, as her *alto ego* Madame Deaucourt would doubtless call him, *Le Vicomte Dangereux*. At least he hadn't brought his devil-bird to the ball—that would have caused a stir, indeed.

'There would not appear to be any difficulty in attracting young ladies to you, Ashe,' his mother said with her wicked chuckle.

'I fear I am only getting the attention of Father's rejects,' he murmured in her ear. 'You are going to have to do something soon or he will be carried off by saucy widows and amorous matrons.'

'Nonsense, Nicholas can look after himself.' Anusha Herriard put her hand on Ashe's forearm and nodded to where Sara was the centre of an animated group of young ladies with an attendant circle of hopeful men. 'As can your sister, I think.'

Lady Richmond had begun the introductions, but the Herriards had soon found themselves absorbed into the throng with one new acquaintance introducing them to the next. 'This is a crush,' Ashe grumbled under his breath. 'At least at Kalatwah all one had to deal with was the odd assassination attempt and treacherous French diplomats.'

'You go and flirt with some young ladies, darling,' his mother said. 'That will cheer you up. I will rescue your father and keep an eye on Sara.'

Ashe grinned at her and began to stroll along the edge of the ballroom. As an unaccompanied male he was unable to approach any lady to whom he had not been introduced, which was curiously restful. There had been few ladies on their ship and he had been re-called from Kalatwah with too much urgency to reac-quaint himself with European society in Calcutta, so he was finding the presence of so many highly sociable women strange.

Pleasantly strange, he thought, allowing his gaze to skim over white bosoms exposed by low-cut gowns, unveiled faces, unmarried girls talking uninhibitedly to men not of their own family. He'd be used to it soon enough, he thought, making eye contact with a strik-ing blonde who held his gaze for a daring second too long before lowering demure lashes over her blue eyes.

A flash of clear green, like leaves unfurling beside a waterhole, attracted his attention. The unmarried girls were all wearing white or pastel gowns, the matrons strong jewel colours for the most part. That green gown was unusual, delightful in its freshness. Ashe propped one shoulder against a pillar and watched as its owner stood and talked with another lady.

The backs of these gowns were almost as intriguing as their low-cut fronts, he was coming to think. With their wearers' hair piled high, the columns of white necks, the vulnerable napes, the tantalising loose curls or dangling earrings all had a subtle erotic charm.

It was definitely too long since he had lain with a woman. Ashe shifted against the pillar, but did not take his eyes off that particular neck even though it made the tension in his groin worse. The lady in the green gown had a mass of shiny brown hair caught up in a knot with a single ringlet left to fall on her shoulder. He imagined curling it around one finger, feeling its caress like raw silk. He would pull each pin from her hair and the whole mass would come down, spilling over his hands, veiling her breasts as he freed her from the verdant silk…

A tall young man joined the two ladies and Ashe saw a resemblance between him and the brown-haired charmer at once. High cheekbones, straight noses, that dark hair. She seemed to be introducing the man to her companion and after a moment they walked on to the floor together to join the next set that was forming. The brunette watched as the dance struck up and then strolled away.

Ashe narrowed his eyes as she wandered along the edge of the dance floor, stopping now and then to chat. Three years in an environment where women habitually covered their faces with their *dupattas*, long semi-transparent scarves, had left him able to identify individuals by their walk, by their posture, their gestures. And he had met that woman before somewhere.

But where? Intrigued, Ashe began to shadow her along the opposite edge of the ballroom. Despite her fashionably languid progress she had an air of suppressed energy about her, as though she would rather run than walk, as if there was not quite enough time in the day for all she wanted to do. He was becoming fanciful, but her quick, expressive gestures when she stopped to talk, the direct way she resumed her trajectory when she parted from each acquaintance, attracted him. He liked energy and purpose.

'Clere.'

He was so caught up in his pleasantly erotic pursuit it took him a moment to recall that was him. Ashe stopped and nodded to the man who had hailed him. They had been introduced earlier. A baron... Lord Hardinge, that was it. 'Hardinge.'

'Enjoying yourself?'

'Frantically remembering names, if the truth be told,' Ashe lied to cover his hesitation. He liked the look of the other man who seemed bright, alert, with a humorous glint in his eyes.

'Stuck with anyone in particular?'

'I was wondering,' Ashe said, 'who the brunette in the pale-green gown was. She looks familiar, but I can't place her.'

'Want an introduction?' The other man was already heading in her direction. 'She's Fransham's sister.'

And who was he? The tall man she had seen on to the dance floor, presumably.

'Miss Hurst?' Hardinge said as they reached her. She turned as Ashe was working that out. *Miss*, so her brother was of the rank of a viscount or lower. That didn't narrow the field much.

'Lord Hardinge.' Her smile was immediate and genuine. Ashe registered warm brown eyes, white teeth, attractive colour on her high cheekbones... And then she turned to smile at him and went pale, as though the blood had drained out of her.

'Miss Hurst? Are you quite well?' Hardinge put out one hand, but she flicked her fan open and plied it vigorously in front of her face.

'I am so sorry, just a moment's faintness. The heat.' Her voice was low and husky. Ashe found himself instantly attracted, even as his senses grappled to make sense of what he was seeing. The fan wafted the subtle, sweet odour of jasmine to him and only yesterday those brown eyes, now shielded by lowered lids and fluttering fan, had glared indignantly into his as he lifted his mouth from hers. *That mouth.*

'Allow me to assist you to a chair, Miss Hurst.' He had his hand under her arm, neatly removed the fan from her fingers and was waving it, even before the other man could step forwards. 'There we are.' In front of them a window embrasure was shielded by an array of potted palms. The casement had been opened several inches for ventilation and there was a bench seat just big enough for two. 'It is all right, Hardinge, I have her. Perhaps you could get hold of some lemonade?' That would get rid of him for a few minutes.

Miss Hurst did not resist as he guided her through the fronds to the padded seat. For a moment he thought she was, indeed, overcome, but as he sat beside her he saw from her expression that she wanted privacy just as much as he did.

'You!' she hissed with real indignation. 'What do you think you are doing?'

Ashe raised an eyebrow in deliberate provocation. The angrier she was, the more off guard she would be. 'What was I doing when we have met?' He began to count off points on his fingers. 'Disembarking from a ship, shopping with my sister, attending a ball with my family. All perfectly innocent activities, Miss Hurst, or whatever your real name is. What is your objection to them?'

'You are following me... No, you are not, are you? It is just horrible coincidence.' She sighed, all the fight going out of her, and leaned back against the heavy brocade swags of the curtains as if suddenly weary.

'I have been called many things, but never a horrible coincidence,' Ashe said. 'Ah, here is Hardinge with the lemonade. Thank you so much. Miss Hurst is feeling a little better, I believe. I'll just wait with her a while so no one disturbs her.' He smiled the frank smile that seemed to lull most people into believing him completely straightforward.

There was patently no space in the alcove. The other man handed over the glass with good grace. 'Clere, Miss Hurst.' He took himself off, leaving them alone in their leafy shelter.

'Thank you, Lord Clere.' Miss Hurst took the glass, drank and set it down on the cill. 'If it were not for you, I would not require reviving.'

Ashe was tempted to observe that all the girls said that, but one glance at her expression warned him that perhaps humour was best avoided. 'Hardinge never got the opportunity to introduce me. How do you know my name?' Had she been asking about him?

'I know your title, that is all, and he just called you Clere. I saw you come in with your family and Lady Malling deduced who you all were. I was attempting to avoid you,' she added bitterly, apparently with the intent of flattening any self-congratulation that she might be interested in him.

'My name is Ashe Herriard, Miss Hurst. Have you any other disguises I am likely to meet with?'

'No, you have viewed them all.' She regarded him, her head tipped a little to one side. He was reminded of Lucifer assessing a strange object for its potential as food or plaything. 'Ashe. Is that an Indian name? I know a trader down at the docks called Ashok. He has been here for years and has an extensive business, but he told me he came from Bombay.' She smiled. 'A bit of a rogue.'

'No, that element of my name is from my paternal grandmother's family. If you want the lot I am George Ashbourne Talish Herriard.'

'And Talish means?'

'Lord of the earth.'

'That seems...appropriate,' Miss Hurst observed astringently. She was still leaning back, gently fanning herself, but the tension was coming off her in waves.

'It is somewhat high-flown,' Ashe agreed. 'After my great-grandfather, the Raja of Kalatwah.' He might as well get that out of the way now.

'Truly?' Miss Hurst sat up straight, dark arched brows lifting. 'Does that make you a prince? Should I be curtsying?' That last, he could tell, was sarcasm.

'It made my grandmother a princess and it made my mother, who had an English father, confused,' he explained and surprised a laugh from her. 'I am merely a viscount with a courtesy title.'

'She is very beautiful, your mother.' He nodded. 'And your father is exceedingly handsome. I imagine most of the women in the room have fallen in love with him.'

'They will have to get past my mother first and she is not the demurely serene lady she appears.' He stretched out his long legs and made himself comfortable. On the other side of their jungle screen the ball was in full, noisy swing. Cool air flowed through the gap in the window, wafting sensual puffs of jasmine scent and warm woman to him. There were considerably worse places to be.

'Demure? She makes me think of a panther,' Miss Hurst observed.

'Appropriate,' he agreed. 'What is your first name? It seems hardly fair not to tell me when you know mine.'

She studied him, her brown eyes wary. 'Indian informality, Lord Clere?'

'Brazen curiosity, Miss Hurst.'

That produced another gurgle of laughter, instantly repressed, as though she regretted letting her guard down. 'Phyllida. It is somewhat of a burden to me, I have to confess.'

'It is a pretty name. And have I met Phyllida Hurst on a quayside, in a shop and in this ballroom? Or are there two other names you have not told me?'

'I will reveal no more, Lord Clere.'

'No?' He held her gaze for a long moment, then let his eyes roam over her, from the top of her elaborate coiffure, past the handsome cameos displayed on the pale, delicious, swell of her bosom, down over the curves of her figure in the fresh green silk to the kid slippers that showed below her hem. 'That is a pity.'

Chapter Four

Colour rose over Miss Hurst's bosom, up her throat to stain her cheeks. It was delicious, Ashe thought, like the flush of pomegranate juice over iced sherbet on a hot day. She was no wide-eyed innocent if she took the meaning of his glance and words so promptly. But then she was obviously no sheltered society miss.

How old was she? Twenty-five, twenty-six? Attractive, bright, stylish, but not married. *Why not?* he wondered. *Something to do with her secret lives, no doubt.*

'I would very much appreciate it if you did not mention that we had met before this evening, my lord.' She said it quite calmly, but Ashe suspected that it was a matter of far more importance than she was revealing and that she hated having to ask him.

'Members of the *ton* are not expected to be shopkeepers, I assume?'

'Precisely.'

'Hmm. Pity my maternal grandfather was a nabob, then.' He was unconcerned what people thought of his ancestry, but he was interested in how she reacted.

'If he was indecently rich, and is now dead, there is

absolutely nothing for the heir to a marquisate to worry about. Society is curiously accommodating in its prejudices.' Her expression was bleak. 'At least, so far as gentlemen are concerned. Ladies are another matter altogether.'

'So I could ruin you with this piece of gossip?'

'Yes, as you know perfectly well. Ladies are not shopkeepers, nor do they walk about anywhere, let alone the docks, unescorted. Did you spend much time as a boy pulling the wings off flies, Lord Clere?'

Ashe felt an unfamiliar stab of conscience. This was, quite obviously, deathly serious to Miss Hurst. But it was a mystery why a lady should be in business at all. Was she so short of pin money? 'I am sorry, I had no intention of torturing you. You have my word that I will not speak of this to anyone.'

The music stopped and dancers began to come off the floor. Another set had ended and he realised he should not be lurking behind the palms with Phyllida Hurst any longer. Someone might notice and assume they had an assignation. He could dent her reputation. 'Will you dance, Miss Hurst?'

He hoped to Heaven it was something he *could* dance. He was decidedly rusty and the waltz had not reached Calcutta by the time they left. He was going to have to join in Sara's lessons.

'I do not dance,' Miss Hurst said. 'Please, do not let me detain you.'

'I was going in any case. It would be more discreet. But you mean you *never* dance?'

'I do not enjoy it,' she said.

Liar. All the time they had been together on the window seat her foot had been tapping along with the music without her realising. She wanted to dance and for some reason would not. *Interesting.* Ashe stood up. 'Then I will wish you good evening, Miss Hurst. Perhaps we will meet window shopping in Jermyn Street one day.'

'I fear not. It is not a street where I can afford to pay the prices asked. Good evening, Lord Clere.'

He bowed and took himself off, well clear of her hiding place. He watched the couples whirling in the waltz, concluding that professional tuition was most definitely called for before he ventured on to the floor. After an interval Miss Hurst emerged and strolled off in the opposite direction.

Ashe wondered if there were any more unmarried ladies around with that combination of looks, style, spirit and wit. He had expected all the eligible young women to be cut from the same pattern: pretty, simpering, dull. Perhaps hunting for a wife would be more interesting than he had imagined. Miss Hurst had her scandalous secrets, and she was a little older than most of the unmarried girls. But she was certainly still well within her childbearing years and a shop was easy enough to dispose of.

He found his parents, who were watching Sara talk to a group of just the kind of girls he was thinking of so disparagingly. 'There you are.' His mother put her hand on his arm to detain him. 'Lady Malling, may I introduce my son, Viscount Clere. Ashe, this is the Dowager Countess of Malling.'

He shook hands and exchanged pleasantries. This was the lady who had been with Phyllida when they had arrived at the ball. As he thought it he saw her again, talking to the young man he had guessed was her brother.

'Perhaps you can tell me who that is, ma'am. The tall man with the dark brown hair just to the left of the arrangement of lilies.'

'Gregory Hurst, Earl of Fransham,' the dowager said promptly. 'A good-looking rogue.'

Had his study of the *Peerage* been so awry? 'I am a trifle confused. I thought the lady with him was his sister, but she was introduced to me as Miss Hurst and if he is an earl…'

'Ah.' Lady Malling lowered her voice. 'She *is* his full, elder, sister. However, I regret to say their parents neglected to marry until after her birth. Such a scandal at the time! It makes her, unfortunately, baseborn.'

'But she is received?'

'Oh, yes, in most places except court, of course. Or Almack's. Charming girl. But she won't make much of a marriage, if any. Even leaving aside the accident of birth, she has not a penny piece for a dowry—goodness knows how she manages to dress so well or where those cameos came from—and Fransham is wild to a fault and no catch as a son-in-law. Except for the title, of course. He may attach a rich cit's daughter with that.'

Hell and damnation. Eccentricity was one thing, but illegitimacy and no dowry on top of dubious commercial activities were all the complete opposites of what he had set out as essential qualities for a wife. Suddenly doing his duty seemed considerably less appealing.

Even as he thought it Phyllida turned and caught his eye. Her mouth curled in a slight smile and she put her hand on her brother's arm as though to draw attention to the Herriard party.

Still wrestling with that revelation, Ashe raised one brow, unsmiling, and inclined his head a fraction.

The smile vanished as she glanced from him to Lady Malling, then her chin came up and she turned away. Even at that distance he could see the flags of angry colour on her cheeks.

You clumsy fool. That had been ungentlemanly, even if it had been unintentional. He had been surprised and disappointed and… *No excuses. You were a bloody idiot*, he told himself. Now what? He could hardly go over and apologise, he had already dug himself into a deep enough hole and what could he say? *So sorry, I have just realised you are illegitimate and poor as a church mouse and absolutely no use to me as a wife, but I didn't mean to snub you.*

And then he stopped thinking about himself and looked at his mother, the offspring of an Indian princess and a John Company trader with an estranged English wife.

'Illegitimacy is not a barrier to being received, then,' she observed as though reading his mind.

One glance at Lady Malling told him she knew exactly what the marchioness's parentage was. 'Goodness, no,' the older woman said. 'It all depends on the parents and the deportment of the person concerned. And rank.'

'And money,' his mother observed coolly.

'Oh, indeed.' The dowager chuckled. Her eyes barely flickered in the direction of the suite of stunning Burmese sapphires his mother was wearing. 'Society can always make rules and bend them to suit itself. Do tell me, which are your days for receiving, Lady Eldonstone?'

'Tuesday, Wednesday and Friday,' *Mata* said. Only her family would know she had made that up on the spur of the moment. 'I do hope we will see you soon in Berkeley Square, Lady Malling.'

'Be sure I will call.'

Ashe looked back across the room. Phyllida Hurst had vanished.

The bigoted beast. Phyllida slipped through the crowd and into the ladies' retiring room before she betrayed her humiliation by marching straight over and slapping Ashe Herriard's beautiful face for him.

He had flirted—worse than flirted on the quayside— he had joked with her this evening, promised to keep her secret and then, the moment he discovered who she was, snubbed her with a cut direct.

She flung herself down on a stool in front of a mirror and glared at her own flushed expression. *Stupid to let myself dream for a moment that I was a débutante flirting with a man who might offer marriage. Stupid to dream of marriage at all.* What had come over her to forget the anguish of that struggle to resign herself when she had faced the fact that she would never marry? *I will not cry.*

'Is anything wrong?' She had not noticed it was Miss Millington on the next stool.

'Men,' Phyllida responded bitterly as she jabbed pins into her hair.

'Oh dear. One in particular or all of them? Only I liked your brother very much, Miss Hurst, he is such a good dancer and so amusing. He has not made you angry, surely?'

'Gregory? No, not at all.' Gregory was being a positive paragon this evening. 'No, just some tactless, top-lofty buck. I hope,' she added vengefully, 'that his too-tight silk breeches split.'

Miss Millington collapsed in giggles. 'Wouldn't that be wonderful? I believe the gentlemen wear nothing beneath them, they are made of such thin knitted silk. What a shocking revelation!'

Phyllida imagined a half-naked Lord Clere for a moment, visualised those long legs and taut buttocks, then caught Miss Millington's eye in the glass and succumbed to laughter, too. 'Oh dear. He is very good-looking and has a fine figure, but I suppose it is too much to hope for.'

The other young woman hesitated. 'I wonder if you might care to call on Mama, Miss Hurst. Perhaps it is forward of me, but I think we could be friends.'

Phyllida cast a hasty glance around the room, but they were alone at one end. 'United in our desire to study Classical statuary, or perhaps anatomy?' she asked wickedly. 'I would like that very much. Will you not call me Phyllida?'

'And I am Harriet.' Miss Millington fished in her reticule. 'Here is Mama's card. She receives on Tuesdays and Thursdays.'

'Thank you, I look forward to it.' Feeling considerably soothed, Phyllida dusted rice powder lightly over her flushed cheeks and went out to look for Gregory.

They found each other almost immediately, both, it seemed, ready to go home. 'I have done my duty by all six of the young ladies you listed for me,' he said as he helped her with her cloak in the lobby. 'If I stay any longer I will get confused between bankers' daughters, mill-owners' heiresses and the offspring of naval captains awash with prize money.'

'Did you like Miss Millington?' Phyllida asked as he handed her into a hackney.

'Miss Millington? She's the tall brunette with a nice laugh and good teeth. She has a certain style about her.'

'I have good news. She thinks you are a fine dancer, has invited me to call and we are now on first-name terms. I really like her, Gregory.'

'I did, too,' he admitted.

'Now all we have to do is to make sure she falls in love with you and that you do not fall into any scandals that will alarm her fond papa.'

'And we will do the difficult things after breakfast, will we?' he asked with a chuckle. 'I'll do my best to be a good lad, Phyll.'

Please, she thought. *And fall in love, for Harriet's sake.* And then she could retreat to the little dower house in the park and spend her time finding items for her shop, for which she would employ a manager. She would be independent, removed enough not to cause a newly respectable, and wealthy, Earl of Fransham any embarrassment and free from the deceits and dangers of her current situation.

It all seemed so simple. *Too simple? No, we can do it.*

Phyllida managed to maintain her mood of optimism through the short journey home, a cup of tea by her bedchamber fire and the rituals of undressing and hair brushing.

But when she blew out the candle, lay back and shut her eyes, the image against her closed lids was not of a happy bridal couple in a cloud of orange blossom, but Ashe Herriard's disdainful face as he watched her across the ballroom floor.

Bigoted, arrogant beast, she thought as she punched the pillow. *Your opinion isn't worth losing a wink of sleep over and so I shall tell you if I am ever unfortunate to meet you again.*

* * *

At five o'clock the next morning Phyllida was not certain how many winks of sleep she had lost, but it was far too many and lost not to constructive thoughts or pleasant half-dreams, but a miserable mixture of embarrassment and desire. She pushed herself up against the piled pillows to peer at the little bedside clock in the dim light. Quarter past five.

It was hopeless to try to get back to sleep. The best she might hope for was to toss restlessly, remembering the heat of Ashe Herriard's mouth on hers, his long-limbed elegance as he sat on the window seat. It was bad enough to have thoughts like that without entertaining them for a man who despised her for an accident of birth.

Phyllida threw back the covers and got out of bed to look through the gap in the curtains. It was going to be a nice day. If she could not sleep, at least she could get some fresh air and exercise. A walk in Green Park would relax her and put her in a positive frame of mind for the morning.

The water in the ewer was cold, of course, but that did not matter. She scrambled into a plain walking dress and half-boots, tucked her hair into a net, took her bonnet by its ribbons and threw a shawl around her shoulders.

Anna would be stirring soon, making herself breakfast down in the basement kitchen. Her maid liked to start the day well ahead of herself, as she put it. They could have breakfast together and then go out.

Anna was already halfway down the stairs. 'What are you doing up and about, Miss Phyllida?'

'Joining you for breakfast. Then I want to go for a walk.'

'Not by yourself, I'm hoping!' The maid went to the pump and filled the big kettle. She was in her forties, plain, down to earth and with a past she never spoke of.

'No, even at this hour someone might see me, I suppose, and that would be a black mark against my impeccable reputation.' Phyllida lifted half a loaf from the bread crock and looked for the knife.

'We wouldn't want to be risking that, now would we?' Anna enquired sardonically. She had been with Phyllida for six years now, knew about the shop and was not afraid to say what she thought about her mistress's life.

'No, we wouldn't,' Phyllida agreed, equally straight-faced. 'So I'll have a nice brisk walk and you can take a rug and a journal and sit on one of the benches beside the reservoir so the proprieties will be observed.'

It was just after six when they set out, weaving through the grid of streets that would take them into Green Park. Around them the St James's area was waking up. Maids swept front steps, others, yawning, set out with empty baskets to do the early marketing. Delivery carts were pulling up at the back entrances for the numerous clubs, hells and shops that served this antheap of aristocrats, rakehells, high-class mistresses and respectable households. The sprawl covered the gentle slopes down to the old brick Tudor palace of St James and, beyond it, St James's Park.

That would be too risky for an early-morning walk, Phyllida knew. Dolly mops and all their sisters of the night would be emerging from their places of business

in the shrubberies, along with the occasional guards-
man hurrying back to barracks having served a different kind of clientele altogether.

The early riders would make for the long tracks of
Hyde Park, leaving Green Park as a quiet backwater
until at least nine. 'You can sit and read while I go past
the lodge and the small pond down to Constitution Hill
and back,' Phyllida suggested as they turned up the
Queen's Walk towards Piccadilly. 'Unless you want to
come with me?'

'You look in the mood for walking out a snit,' Anna
observed. 'You'll do that better alone. Who upset you?'

'Oh, just some wretched lordling newly arrived in
town and shocked to the core to discover he's been flirting all unwittingly with a baseborn woman.'

'More fool he. You shouldn't let him upset you.'
There was nothing to say to that, but Anna seemed to
read plenty into Phyllida's silence. 'I suppose you were
liking him up to then.'

'Well enough.' She shrugged.

'Handsome, is he?'

'Oh, to die for and well he knows it.' And he had
seemed kind. He had a sense of humour, he loved his
sister, he was eminently eligible. If she had not been
who she was, then this morning she would have woken
hoping for a bouquet from him by luncheon. What
would it be like to be courted by a man like that, to
hope for a proposal of marriage, to look forward to a
future of happiness and children?

'A good brisk walk, then, and some stones to kick
instead of his foolish head.' Anna surveyed the benches.
'That one will do me, right in the sun.'

'Thank you, Anna.' The maid's brisk common sense

shook her out of her self-indulgent wonderings. 'If you get chilled, come and meet me.'

She waved and set off diagonally along the path towards the Queen's House on the far side of the Park. The early sunlight glinted off the white stone in the distance and the standard hung limp against the flagstaff in the still air. Phyllida breathed in the scents of green things breaking their winter sleep to thrust through the earth. That was better. When she was fully awake, feeling strong and resolved, then the weakening dreams could be shut safely away.

Rooks wheeled up from the high trees where they were building nests, jackdaws tumbled like acrobats through the air, courting or playing. Ahead of her the magpies had found something that had died during the night, a rat or a rabbit, she supposed, eyeing their squabbles with distaste as they fought for unsavoury scraps. She would have to detour off the path to avoid the mess.

As though a stone had been thrown into the midst of them the birds erupted up into the air, flapping and screeching at something that landed right next to their prize. For a second she thought it must be a bird of prey, then it turned its grey head and huge black beak in her direction, assessing her with intelligent eyes.

'Lucifer!' Surely the city had not been invaded by these grey-hooded crows? It stopped sidling up to the food and began to hop towards her. 'No, go away! I don't want you, you horrible bird. Shoo!'

As she spoke she heard the thud of hooves on turf coming up fast behind. The big bay horse thundered past, then circled and slowed as its rider reined it in and brought it back towards her at a walk. 'Lucifer, come here.' The crow flapped up to perch on the rider's shoulder, sending the horse skittering with nerves. The man on its back controlled it one-handed and lifted his hat to her with the other.

'Miss Hurst. I apologise for Lucifer, but he seems to like you.'

Of course, it had to be Lord Clere.

Chapter Five

Phyllida looked from bird to master. 'The liking is not mutual, I assure you.' Why couldn't Lord Clere ride in Hyde Park like everyone else? Why couldn't he ride with the fashionable crowd in the afternoon? Why couldn't he leave the country altogether?

'I imagine the dislike applies to me as well,' he said. 'May I walk with you?'

'I can hardly stop you. This is a public park.' It was ungracious and she did not much care. Phyllida started walking again, the crow flapped down to claim its prize on the grass and Ashe Herriard swung out of the saddle.

'Is it? Public, I mean? I assumed it was, but there are no other riders. I was beginning to wonder if I had broken some dire rule of etiquette.' He did not sound as though he cared a toss for such rules.

'The fashionable place to ride is Hyde Park,' she informed him. 'Even at this time of day those who wish for some solitude and a long gallop go there, leaving walkers in peace. I suggest you try it.' *Now.*

He did not take the hint, but strolled beside her at a perfectly respectable distance, whip tucked under one elbow, the horse's reins in the other hand. She could not have been more aware of him if he had taken her arm. What did he want? Probably, Phyllida thought, bracing herself, he was going to make some insulting suggestion now that he knew about her birth. He had kissed her by the river, flirted in the ballroom. What would the next thing be?

'Hyde Park was where I was going, but on the map this looked a more pleasant route than finding my way through the streets. I did not hope to see you.'

'Why should you?' Phyllida enquired with a touch of acid.

'To apologise.'

That brought her to a halt. 'Apologise?' It was the last thing she expected him to do. She stared up at him and he met her eyes straight on, his own green and shadowed by thick black lashes. Even in the conventional uniform of a gentleman—riding dress, severe neckcloth, smart beaver hat—he seemed faintly exotic and disturbing. But more disturbing was the expression on his face. He was not teasing her, or mocking her. She could have dealt with that, but he appeared quite serious.

'For my rudeness last night. I have no excuse. I had just discovered who your brother is, so I was confused by your lack of a title, then I was surprised when Lady Malling explained. Your smile caught me in the middle of those emotions with my thoughts…unsorted.'

'Do you have to sort your thoughts, my lord?' It was such a direct explanation with no attempt to excuse himself that Phyllida felt herself thawing a trifle. *Dangerous.* Little alarm bells were jangling along her nerves. *He cannot be anything to you and you do not want him to be, either.*

'My brain feels like a desk that has been ransacked by burglars,' he admitted and her mouth twitched despite everything. 'Or one where all the files have been overstuffed and have burst. I am still, even after three months at sea, having to remember to think in English all the time. There are all the rules of etiquette that are different enough to European society in Calcutta to be decidedly confusing and so removed from my great-uncle's court where I have spent the past few years that they might be from a different planet.

'Then there is all the family stuff to learn, the estate, the… But never mind that, it sounds as though I am excusing myself after all and that was not my intention.'

'You did not want to come back, did you?' Phyllida asked. It was not a lack of intellectual capacity to cope with all those things that she heard in his voice, but the irritation of a man who did not want to be bothered by them, yet was making himself care. How interesting. Most of London society assumed that there was no greater delight and privilege than to be part of it and absorbed in every petty detail.

'The only one for whom England is *back* is my father. For my mother and sister it is as strange as it is for me. But I offended you and I apologise.'

'You are forgiven.' And he was, she realised. It had not just been good manners that made her say it. *Why? Because you have beautiful green eyes? Because you have been honest with me? Because I am deluding myself?* 'So, what do you intend to do with yourself now, Lord Clere?'

'We will stay in London for the Season and see my sister launched. We all need to outfit ourselves, the town house must be resurrected from fifteen years of neglect. I must learn to be a viscount, the heir and an English gentleman. Dancing lessons,' he added grimly, surprising a laugh from her.

At some point they had veered from the path towards the Queen's House. Phyllida looked round and found they had reached the edge of the park close to the point where Constitution Hill met the Knightsbridge Road. 'You cross here to Hyde Park.' She pointed. 'That is the Knightsbridge Turnpike.'

'Then Tattersalls is near here. I was intending to find it after I had ridden.' He whistled. The big crow flapped up and perched on the fence, eyeing her bonnet trimmings with malevolent intent.

'That is not something a young lady knows about, my lord.' She attempted to look demure. 'But, yes, it is just around the corner behind St George's Hospital.'

'Thank you.' Ashe swung himself up into the saddle, all long legs, tight breeches, exquisite control. 'I hope we will meet again, Miss Hurst. Now we know each other better.'

The stuff of every maiden's dreams. Phyllida suppressed a wince at her choice of words and lifted a hand in farewell as he took the horse out into the traffic and across to the other park. Ashe had been surprised and taken aback at what he had discovered about her and confessed as much, she thought as she made her way back to Anna. It was honest of him to admit it so freely.

And yet, thinking about it without his distracting presence looming over her, she had the uneasy feeling there was more than that in the blank look he had sent her last night, if only she could put her finger on it. He had apologised with disarming frankness, but he had not told her the whole truth. It would be as well to be wary of Lord Clere, however decorative and amusing he might be. *Now we know each other better.*

That had been a stroke of luck. Ashe turned his hired hack's head towards what he guessed was the famous Rotten Row and pressed the horse into a canter. He had not wanted to enquire about the Hursts' address and risk drawing attention to his interest in Phyllida, nor had he wanted to disconcert her by turning up in her shop. This encounter had been ideal, without even a passer-by as witness if she had done what he deserved and cut him dead in her turn.

But she had not. She had been gracious, ladylike with an edge of acid humour that he enjoyed. She had poise, intelligence, looks and enough maturity not to be expecting hearts and flowers and hypocritical pro-testations of love. *Damn it, she is perfect.* He liked her, he was attracted to her and she bore not the slightest re-semblance to Reshmi, his dead love. In fact, he would have no objection to marrying her tomorrow and cut-ting short this tiresome search for a wife.

Except that Phyllida Hurst was baseborn and, as if that was not enough, had a secret life that would ruin her if it was exposed and a brother who was, apparently, no catch as a relative. That old harridan Lady Malling had made it quite clear how ineligible she was.

Phyllida would not be received at court and she was not the sister-in-law for a young lady making her come-out and who deserved to be launched into the highest echelons of society.

Ashe guided his mount on to a smaller track, away from a group of riders in the distance, and gave it its head. She was twenty-six, he had discovered last night.

Unmarried, ineligible, old enough to have forgotten girlish fantasies about love. Might she find the prospect of a liaison interesting? His body tightened at the thought and he knew it had been in the back of his mind, unacknowledged, since he had discovered the truth about her.

He explored the idea. For three years he had been in an environment where encounters with respectable women were formalised, distant and impersonal. The women one knew, in all senses of the word, were *not* respectable, they were courtesans like Reshmi. He had no model for a sexual relationship with a lady in this world. How did one manage a liaison in this chilly, alien, new society? He had no wish to ruin her in its eyes, but he could be very, very discreet and with her two secret identities she had already proved she could be, too.

He would think about it. But first, before anything, he had to get a decent horse because this slug was useless. Tattersalls, his objective this morning, might be open by now and there, at least, he could get what he wanted, simply by exercising good taste and expending money. Horses were much less trouble than women.

'I've been talking to that Indian chap.' Gregory strolled into the sitting room and collapsed on to the sofa with his usual indolence.

'Ashe...I mean, Lord Clere?' Phyllida dropped a handful of paste jewellery she had bought from a dealer in Seven Dials back into its box and hoped she was not blushing.

It seemed her brother did not possess the instincts of a natural chaperon. 'Oh, you know him, do you? Interesting fellow. Great eye for a horse and the money to back his judgement.'

'You haven't been betting again?' Her heart sank. Had Gregory's virtuous resolutions been too good to last after all?

'No!' He looked wounded. 'I was round at Tatts, just looking, blowing a cloud, chatting. You know. Clere bought two riding horses for himself, a pretty little mare for his sister and a carriage pair.'

'Good lord.' She pushed away the jewellery and tried some mental arithmetic. 'That is a huge amount of money, all in one go.'

'I know. And they were all good buys. No gulling him. They've got that pair of greys that Feldshore had to sell to meet his gaming debts, you remember them? Showy as they come. Clere just walked round them, had them trotted out and said, "Weak pasterns." What do you think of that?'

'Amazing,' Phyllida agreed, trying to recall what a pastern was. 'I hope he can pay for all this.' She could just see Ashe surveying the bloodstock down that straight nose of his, rejecting the inadequate with a word. It took no leap of imagination to see him as a raja in his palace, waving a dismissive hand as slave girls were paraded in front of him, or crooking a long finger in summons if one pleased him.

'Grandfather was a nabob. Father's a marquess, he's the only son. Must be rolling in it,' Gregory said with amiable envy.

'And his grandmother was an Indian princess,' Phyllida could not resist adding.

'You've really been talking to him by the sound of it.'

'Mmm.' Phyllida tried to focus on the clasp of a rather pretty necklace of polished Scottish pebbles.

'You'll be pleased that I've invited him for dinner, then.'

'*What?*' The necklace ran through her suddenly nerveless fingers and back into the box with a rattle.

'You're *not* pleased?' Gregory's normally cheerful expression became a scowl. 'Has he acted in some way you did not like? Or said something out of turn? Because if so…'

'No, nothing like that.' The last thing she wanted was her brother charging off issuing a challenge. 'He did not realise about our parents' marriage and then, when he did find out, he allowed his…surprise to show. That was all. He apologised.'

The scowl was still in place. 'You liked him, didn't you, Phyll?'

She managed a rueful smile and a shrug. 'He is intelligent and attractive. I found him amusing to talk to.'

'He'll be looking for a wife,' Gregory said cautiously.

'I know, that is only to be expected.' Her stomach took a sickening swoop. *That* was what he was skirting around when he apologised. He had mentally assigned her to the ranks of eligible young women—despite what he had seen of her business—and he was inclined to like her. And then he had discovered that she was completely unsuitable…

'And if he liked you he might have been interested and then he discovered—' Gregory ploughed on, in unwitting echo of her thoughts.

'That I am baseborn. Quite. Don't look so tragic, Gregory. Lord Clere and I had a conversation, that is all. It is not as though we had been meeting for weeks and formed an attraction and then he found out. He is no different from all the rest of the gentlemen we socialise with. I really do not regard it.'

But I do, she realised, even as she spoke. Everyone was perfectly civilised about her status, she was invited to many events, received by all but the highest sticklers. She would never get vouchers for Almack's, of course, never be presented at court. Her marriage prospects were non-existent, at least amongst the *ton*, who would object to her birth in an alliance with one of their sons, or amongst the rich middle class families who wanted impeccable bloodlines for their money.

It had never mattered so much before, Phyllida realised. She could not recall the time when she was ignorant of her status, of the oddity of her parents' marriage and what it meant for her. She had her own interests, her business, her friends and her ambitions for Gregory and that was enough. It had to be. There were daydreams, of course, moments of sadness. Of more than sadness when she had held friends' babies in her arms, but she had learned to control those foolish hopes.

But Ashe Herriard had shaken her. She liked him and she was attracted to him. It would always have been impossible, of course. The consequences of the choice she had made when she was seventeen meant marriage was out of the question anyway.

Yet somehow, with this man, it hurt. They had only just met and she might yet come to find she only felt mild attraction to him, or she might discover something to dislike in him. He could well have paid her no more attention after the ball. But it was as though someone had just told her for the very first time that she was unmarriageable: shock, a sense of loss, a dull pain some-where under her breastbone.

Foolishness, she scolded herself. *A kiss, a pair of green eyes, a sense of strength and virility, that is all it takes to fill you full of pointless yearnings.* It was use-less to repine and wish that things were different. They were not and that was that.

The thoughts had run through her mind in seconds and Gregory was still watching her with trouble in his brown eyes. 'I will tell him we've a crisis in the kitchen or something and take him to White's,' he offered.

'No, don't be silly.' Where the bright smile came from she had no idea. 'We will have a dinner party, it will be a pleasure. Now, who else can we invite? I think we must stick at eight of us, otherwise we will be un-comfortably cramped. Shall I see if Miss Millington's parents will allow her to come? If we invite a married couple, then I cannot see they will have any objection. Lucy and Cousin Peter would be ideal—I am sure Mrs Millington would find a baronet who is a Member of Parliament respectable company for her daughter.'

'That's six, including us. I'll invite the Hardinges as well, shall I?'

'Mrs Millington will be in a second heaven! An earl, a baronet, a viscount and a baron. I cannot believe she can refuse to allow Harriet to come. I will call tomor-row. What day did you tell Lord Clere?'

'I said I must check dates with you and would get back to him. He seemed pleased.' Gregory frowned again. 'He had better not be trifling with you, Phyll.'

'No, of course he is not. No one trifles with me. Now, shall we see if Wednesday will suit everyone?'

* * *

'A letter for you, my lord.' Herring proffered a silver salver.

Ashe ran his finger under the red-wax seal and scanned the single page. 'My first dinner invitation,' he remarked to his father who was seated in the chair opposite him, long legs outstretched as he studied the surveyor's account of the state of Eldonstone, the Hertfordshire country house.

'Bachelor affair?'

'Apparently not. It's from Fransham. I met him at Tattersalls today. He says he's invited Lord and Lady Hardinge—he was at the ball yesterday—and a Sir Peter Blackett who is an MP, with his wife, and a Miss Millington, whoever she is.'

'Your mother is threatening a dinner party.' Lord Eldonstone made a note against a column of figures and tossed the bundle on to a side table. 'I suspect we won't get away with only seven sitting down to eat.'

'Eight, if Fransham's sister is acting as hostess.'

Ashe could have sworn he kept his voice neutral, but his father arched an eyebrow. 'Miss Hurst? She looked an intelligent and refined young woman. Unfortunate for the poor girl to have had such a careless father.'

'Yes,' Ashe agreed. *And she is mysterious, and smells of jasmine and has an edge to her tongue. And I cannot get her out of my head.* 'Is that report making depressing reading?'

His father grimaced. 'About what I expected. You neglect a place that size for as long as my father did, and screw every penny out of the land while you are at it, and the results are never going to be good.'

'Sounds expensive. Should I have taken more care with the amount I have just spent on horseflesh?'

The marquess shook his head. 'We can cope easily enough with this, and when we get the estate turned around and the income recovers it will look after itself. I was thinking of going down there next week for a few days—do you want to come?'

They had agreed on board ship that Tompkins would organise the essential cleaning and restocking of the house, engage more servants and generally get it habitable before the family visited. Establishing themselves in society, launching Sara and holding endless meetings with lawyers and bankers had to take priority over the country estate.

'So soon?' Ashe acknowledged to himself that he was ambivalent about the Hertfordshire house. London was a city and he felt comfortable in cities. But rural England was a foreign country. Green and lush as though there was a monsoon every day of the year, foxes to hunt, not tigers. Tenants to get to know, not hundreds of subsistence peasants totally at their raja's beck and call. And part of him knew that it was the country estates that defined the English nobleman: the unknown house was his fate and his responsibility.

Ashe smiled grimly to himself. He had been trained to fight—this was simply another battlefield, a more subtle one that would require all his diplomatic skills.

'Just a flying visit. We'll leave your mother and sister here.'

'I'll come, with pleasure.' His father wanted his support, although he would never admit it, and the sooner they got this over with, the better. 'After all, there is no waltzing in the countryside.' *And no distracting Miss Hurst, either.*

Chapter Six

By the time Wednesday came around Ashe, like the rest of his family, had an array of gilt-edged cards to sift through and they were all keeping Edwards, the marquess's new secretary, busy with acceptances and the occasional regret.

But this dinner party would be a modest beginning to his London social life, he supposed, eyeing the narrow house in Great Ryder Street. When he mounted the steps and knocked, only to have the door answered by a maid, he realised just how modest. Male staff only above stairs in the afternoon and evening was the rule, Perrott had explained, although to find female staff anywhere but in the ladies' bedchambers was a novelty to Ashe.

Inside there was none of the oppressive splendour of the Herriard town house, for which he envied them. But it was elegantly, if simply, decorated and furnished and he suspected Phyllida's eye for style and her nose for a bargain had contributed to that.

'Clere! Glad you could come. Welcome.' Fransham came forwards with outstretched hand and began to introduce him. Hardinge greeted him as an old acquaintance and Ashe liked the direct friendliness of his wife. The Parliamentary baronet, Blackett, was thin and serious, but his wife made up for it with plump joviality and then there was a Miss Millington, who was introduced as 'My sister's friend.' From the shy glance she directed at Fransham, Ashe suspected there was something more to her presence than that.

Phyllida came in as he was agreeing with Miss Millington that the sunshine that morning had been very pleasant. 'Lord Clere will consider it the depths of winter, I imagine,' she said as she smiled in greeting. 'Good evening, Lord Clere. Confess, you do not consider our feeble spring sunshine worthy of the name.'

'I will admit to not having been warm since about Gibraltar,' he countered. 'But I have high hopes that the summer may reach the temperature of an Indian winter, Miss Hurst. Meanwhile, I am thawing in the kind welcome I have received in London.'

Hardinge chuckled. 'A diplomat, forsooth.'

'I was, after a fashion. I acted as an aide for several years to my great-uncle, the Raja of Kalatwah, and that involved some diplomacy.'

'In which languages?' Sir Peter enquired.

'Hindi and Persian. I speak some native dialects with rather less facility,' Ashe admitted.

'We shall have to enlist you to the Foreign Office.' How serious he was, Ashe could not tell.

'It would be most interesting, I am sure, but I will be much engaged with our estates for some time. My grandfather was not able to give them the attention they required.' Which was code for, *Spent all his time and money drinking, gaming and wenching while the place crumbled about him.* By the look of it the other men understood exactly. They had probably known the old devil, Ashe thought.

'Dinner is served, ma'am.'

The maid must be their only upstairs servant, Ashe concluded as the party paired up to go through. He was the highest-ranking male guest so Phyllida took his arm and showed him to the seat at her right hand. He was flanked by Lady Hardinge, but with such a small party it was easy to talk to everyone and no one seemed to have any inhibitions about conversing across the dining table.

'You are in town for the Season, Lord Clere?' Lady Hardinge enquired.

'My mother wished my sister to come out this year and, arriving from India as we have, there is much to arrange as you may imagine. Staying in London for the Season seemed sensible. But I am merely an appendage to the ladies of the household, I can hardly be said to be doing the Season.'

'I think you will find you are, whatever your intentions,' Lady Blackett said with a chuckle. 'What a fortunate thing that with the sea voyage and so forth you are out of mourning. I imagine that you too will have matrimonial ambitions, Lord Clere. From what I hear, the gossip is all about the dashing new bachelor who has joined the Marriage Mart.'

'I have certainly not done that, ma'am. It sounds quite alarming.' He must find himself a wife, true, but he had no intention of making himself a target.

'Terrifying,' Hardinge agreed in a stage whisper, causing general laughter. 'Avoid Almack's like the plague, is my advice,' he added.

'But have you not read *Pride and Prejudice*, Lord Clere?' Phyllida enquired. When he shook his head she quoted, '*"It is a truth universally acknowledged, that a single man in possession of a good fortune must be in want of a wife."* All the matchmaking mamas will have you in their sights already, I fear.'

'That sounds decidedly dangerous and I will have to take evasive action,' he said. 'I have been stalked by tigers before now, so hopefully my skills will enable me to escape.'

'You will have to succumb sooner or later, Clere,' Fransham observed with a grin. 'I used to be just as skittish myself, but now I am beginning to see the benefits of matrimony.' He did not glance at Miss Millington as he spoke, but she coloured faintly.

'I expect I shall, too,' Ashe agreed. 'But I prefer to make my own choices and not to be hunted down by terrifying matrons in search of a son-in-law with a title and all his own teeth.'

'We must stop teasing poor Lord Clere,' Phyllida said amid the general laughter. 'He has come to London expecting stately banquets and refined conversation and finds himself at a small dinner party with frivolous friends.'

'But charming frivolous friends,' Ashe corrected her. He caught her eye as he spoke and smiled, thinking how warm her brown eyes were and how delightful she looked when she was happy.

She became serious as he looked at her. Her eyes widened and he had a sudden fantasy of her lying beneath him, looking up with fathomless eyes and parted lips. *Oh, yes. Spread on a coverlet of green silk, gasping her pleasure as I lick every inch of those pale curves.*

The thought of her skin against his, ivory against gold, was an erotic provocation all of its own. Why had he been undecided for a moment about his intentions towards her?

His thoughts must have heated his gaze, for Phyllida blushed and turned to the maid. 'That will be all for the moment, Jane. I will ring when I need you.'

She spoke to Lord Hardinge on her left about an opera he had missed the previous week and conversation turned to the theatre and the arts. Ashe joined in the ebb and flow of talk, but mainly listened, absorbing information with the same focus he had employed when on a mission for his great-uncle.

Anything about this new world was useful, but he found himself listening more and more to Phyllida as the meal progressed. She was an excellent hostess, keeping conversation flowing and drawing everyone in with the skill of an accomplished matron. Her own contributions revealed an interest in cultural matters that seemed far reaching and well informed. One would not be bored after the lovemaking. She would not be a mistress from whose bed one hurried.

There, he had thought the word. *Mistress.* A long-term relationship, not the brief liaisons he had been making do with since Reshmi died. And this time he was forewarned not to become emotionally involved, nor to let his partner in passion become so, either. Reshmi had been his first, his only, love and that had hit him hard. Now he was more experienced, was on his guard against that kind of devastation to his heart, and it would not happen again.

'They say there is a consignment of remarkable Chinese porcelain just arrived,' Sir Peter said, cutting into his musings. 'But whether that is rumour or fact I cannot establish. Perhaps it will be offered at auction, but as far as I can tell none of the big houses are handling it.'

'It does exist and is very fine, but the shippers are intending to sell direct to dealers from the warehouse,' Phyllida said. Everyone looked at her with polite astonishment. 'That is…I heard someone discussing it at the Trenshaws' musicale the other day and complaining that by the time the public sees the items they will have increased in price considerably.'

'Just for a moment I had visions of you inspecting the goods in some ghastly warehouse down at the docks, Phyllida dear,' Lady Blackett said with a chuckle. 'I know how much you like fine porcelain, but wouldn't that be a scandal!' She laughed and everyone joined in. Ashe thought Phyllida's amusement was forced and her brother's smile was tight, but no one else seemed to notice.

'And dangerous,' Ashe said. 'From what little I saw of the docks area, it is no place for a lady.'

This time the look Phyllida directed at him aroused no fantasies of lovemaking. She looked as if she wished she had a hatpin to apply to his anatomy. 'Some unfortunate women must carry on their business in that area, Lord Clere. If it is dangerous for them, it is because they are at the mercy of the men who lurk there and who try to take advantage of them.'

'Yes, but *working* women,' Sir Peter said. 'Many of them no better than…' He seemed to recollect that he was in mixed company and not making a speech in the House. 'Not refined ladies, is what I meant. What a scandal it would be, to find a gentlewoman in such an area.'

There was a general murmur of agreement before, to Ashe's surprise, Miss Millington said, 'I believe many ladies support charities in the East End of London and go there themselves to give succour, even to the unfortunate women to whom Sir Peter referred.'

That turned the conversation to a discussion of charities and the best way to support the deserving poor. Ashe aroused considerable interest by describing the *sadhus* who, clad only in a sacred thread and a thick smearing of ashes, lived on the offerings of passers-by.

'Naked? But surely ladies cannot avoid encountering such men? Is it not a public outrage?' Lady Hardinge asked.

'In India nudity may be considered shocking, erotic, aesthetic, practical or religious, depending entirely on context,' Ashe explained. 'My mother or sister would think nothing of dropping a few coins into the begging bowl of a naked *sadhu*, but they would be shocked to find a member of the household walking about without a shirt, for example.' They still looked dubious. 'Have the ladies here never viewed naked Classical statuary and admired it for its aesthetic qualities?'

That made them laugh in rueful acknowledgement that he had scored a point. 'But cold white marble is quite another thing from real live flesh,' Phyllida objected. 'If I came upon the figures from Lord Elgin's marbles walking in Green Park, coloured as in life, as I believe they once were, I would be shocked.' Ashe caught her glance at Miss Millington who was obviously suppressing a smile at some secret joke they shared.

The unmarried ladies were not as uncurious about men as they were supposed to be, he concluded. Ashe

imagined Phyllida viewing the erotic carvings that decorated some of the rooms in the palace at Kalatwah. She
would be shy, perhaps, but also intrigued and aroused.
He found the thought more than arousing himself, his
intent hardening along with his body.

There was that amused, appreciative look in Lord
Clere's eyes that made her want to blush. Phyllida felt
as though he could read her mind and see her memory
of telling Harriet Millington that she wished his tight
evening breeches would split. Provoking man, he was
able to flirt without a word spoken.

She caught the attention of her female guests.
'Ladies, shall we?'

When they reached the drawing room the door was
hardly closed behind them when Lucy Blackett exclaimed, 'What an attractive man! So exotic with those
golden good looks. You are a dark horse, Cousin Phyllida, keeping him a secret.'

'Not at all,' she protested. 'He is Gregory's friend.
He met him at Tattersalls the other day and invited him.
I feel sorry for the whole family, don't you? It must be
so strange finding themselves in England for the first
time with such a vast, neglected inheritance and everything so strange.'

The other women looked disappointed that she was
not admitting to an ulterior motive in inviting Ashe, but
Phyllida turned the conversation and they were discussing Harriet's plans to visit the Lake District with her
parents in the summer when the men rejoined them.

The rest of the evening passed pleasantly. At length
Jane came in to announce that the carriages had arrived

and there was a general move to depart before the three equipages completely jammed the narrow street.

Harriet's maid came up from the kitchen and Gregory offered to escort Miss Millington home. 'I can get a hackney back,' he explained, running down the steps, hat and gloves in hand.

'Am I right in assuming your brother wishes to fix his interest with Miss Millington?'

Phyllida turned to find Ashe right behind her in the hallway. 'I hope so,' she admitted. Jane was holding his hat, cane and gloves, but he made no move to take them. 'I like her very much.'

'I wonder if I could have a word with you before I go, Miss Hurst?'

Phyllida realised she was alone in the house except for the servants. She should ask Jane to sit in the corner of the room, or ring for Anna, but it seemed priggish to insist on the proprieties and no one was there to wag a disapproving finger at her.

She went back into the drawing room and noticed that he left the door open behind him which was, she supposed, a relief. Ashe Herriard seemed to take all the air out of the room. Or perhaps it was just that there was none left in her lungs. She sat down and gestured to a chair, but he remained standing.

'You are going to that warehouse by yourself to buy some of the porcelain, aren't you?' he asked without preamble.

She was, of course. If it was half as good as they were saying, she would buy all she could afford and turn a healthy profit on it. But she had no intention of revealing her plans to anyone, let alone autocratic gentlemen. 'I have not decided, Lord Clere.'

'Oh, yes, you have, I saw it in your face. But you must not go, it is not safe in that area.'

Phyllida got to her feet in a swirl of rose-pink muslin. 'Lord Clere, you have no right to dictate my actions.'

'A gentleman is duty-bound to protect a lady.'

'I have a brother, sir.'

'He seems either unwilling, or unable, to control your activities.' Ashe leaned against a chair, apparently unshaken by either her tone or her frowns.

'As we are alone, my lord, allow me to remind you that I have a business to run. I am twenty-six years old and I do not need *controlling*. But I do need stock of the highest quality and this porcelain promises to be just that.'

'I will buy it on your behalf.'

She sat down again with an undignified thump. 'You? What do you know of porcelain?'

'At least as much as you, I would wager.' Now she was sitting again he dropped into the chair he had been leaning against with considerably more elegance than she had just displayed. 'I was brought up in one of the great trading cities of the East with a grandfather high in the East India Company and I have spent the last three years in the court of an immensely wealthy prince with a taste for collecting.'

'I need to make my own judgement. I know what will sell in my shop, what my limits on price are.'

'Then I will come with you.' He was pleasant, he smiled, he might as well have been made of granite.

'And buy the best pieces from under my nose?'

'Now I know about the collection it will not take me long to discover where it is. I do not need to accompany you, I could cream off the best items tomorrow.'

'Oh…!' Phyllida was not used to being thwarted in her own world. She was limited by her birth, her secrets and the need, endlessly, to make money, but within those constraints, she was in control. This infuriating man who just sat there patiently waiting for her to finish fulminating and give in to him was completely outside her experience.

'You, sir, are no gentleman,' she said with an icy determination to put him in his place.

'Oh, yes, I am.' Ashe Herriard got to his feet, making her clench her teeth because she could not help but note the ease with which he stood. Some wretched feminine instinct was clamouring at her to look at him, to admire him, to exert herself to make him like her.

He came over and held out his hands to her. Puzzled, she put her own in his. Was this some way of admitting defeat in Indian society? Even as she thought it he pulled, bringing her to her feet. 'It is just that I am not an *English* gentleman,' he said and drew her close, as close as a waltz hold, as close as a kiss…

If he tries, I will slap him, she resolved. And yet the resolution did not make her twist her fingers free of his hold. Phyllida looked up into the deep-green eyes that always seemed a little amused, at the firm mouth and the chin that hinted at determination, and swallowed.

'I have been brought up to understand the jungle and its dangers. Your East End is a jungle without tigers or cobras, but a jungle none the less. I do not allow women to wander unprotected into such a place. That is not negotiable. But we can negotiate a truce,' Ashe said. 'You will promise me that you will not visit the warehouse without my escort. I promise you that I will not attempt to buy any item until you have made your selection.'

'We cannot go in some smart carriage with a crest on the door.' Phyllida knew she had admitted defeat. 'We must take a hackney.'

'Of course. It would not do to arrive flaunting wealth,' he agreed. 'You know this is sensible and you are a sensible woman, so why are you still unhappy about it?'

Of all the flattering things he might have said to her, *sensible* was not one of them. Phyllida tried to accept it as Ashe doubtless meant it. His fingers were still wrapped warmly around hers, he was so close she would smell sandalwood and linen and man if she was so foolish as to inhale deeply. Her *sensible* brain appeared to have taken a holiday somewhere. 'Because it means going with you,' she blurted out.

Ashe did not appear offended, although his dark brows arched up. 'You dislike me so much?'

'You know I do not. But I do not know what you want from me, why you persist in pursuing our acquaintance. You seek a wife and I am totally ineligible, as we both know. An acquaintance of my brother, a gentleman who dines with us, has no reason to be escorting me in this way. What does that leave?'

'Friendship?' he suggested after just the merest pause. Why did she suspect he had almost said something else?

Phyllida stared at him. 'Men and women are not *friends* in English society. Not unless they are of mature years or closely related.'

'It is the same in European society in India. And as for Indian society—a man risks death for the slightest intimacy with a woman. But why shouldn't we be un-conventional? I enjoy novel experiences.'

There did not seem to be anything she could say. The truth—that she found him far too disturbing to be around—was hardly something she could admit. 'Very well. Can you call for me tomorrow at about ten? And please wear something inconspicuous.'

'Ten it is. And I promise not to look like a rich and over-eager English collector with more money than judgement.'

'Until tomorrow then, my lord.' She gave her hands, that had rested in his for a quite scandalous length of time, a little tug.

'*Ashe*, Phyllida. Friends, remember?' And he bowed his head as he lifted his hands, bringing his lips to her knuckles. The shock, even though she was wearing thin kid evening gloves, shot up her arm as she felt the heat. Her lips parted as though he had kissed them instead of the unyielding ridge of her knuckles. 'Goodnight,' he said, releasing her. 'Thank you for a delightful dinner party. I can see myself out.'

My friend Ashe. Phyllida sat as the front door closed behind him and wondered what on earth she had let herself in for. She looked down at her hands, clasped in her lap, then slowly raised the one he had kissed to her lips.

Friends sounded safe. *Do I want to be safe? Or have I just agreed to be friends with a tiger?*

Chapter Seven

It was 'Mrs Drummond' who was waiting for Ashe when he arrived promptly at ten. She wore a brown wool gown, darker-brown pelisse with braid trim that had rather obviously been re-used from another garment, a plain straw bonnet retrimmed with a bunch of artificial flowers, darned gloves and sturdy shoes. Under the gloves, if one looked hard enough, was the shape of a thin wedding band.

'Good God.' Ashe stopped dead and stared at her. 'That's worse than the outfit you were wearing when we first met.'

'Never mind me,' Phyllida retorted. 'What on earth are you doing looking like that?'

He was wearing a high-necked coat of dull black brocade, tailored in at the waist with skirts to the knee all round. Beneath were tight, dark-red trousers tucked into boots of soft black leather and a sash of the same dark red circled his waist. He had not shaved and his morning beard, darker than his hair, made his skin seem darker, too. And the final touch of exoticism was his hair, freed from its tie and touching his shoulders. As he moved his head she caught the glint of a gold ear stud in his right lobe.

'Don't you like it?' One eyebrow rose. Phyllida could have sworn he had done something to make his lashes even sootier. She wished she dared ask what, it looked a useful trick.

'You look magnificent and you know it,' she snapped. Over her dead body was she going to let him see that he was the personification of every daydream of the exotic Orient. 'Do not fish for compliments, Lord Clere. That is hardly the outfit for where we are going.'

'But I look like a dealer from the East. Someone who knows about Chinese ceramics.'

'We will see who gets the better deals,' Phyllida said. 'Are we acquainted with one another?'

'I do not think so. I will get the driver to drop me off around the corner and I will go in first.'

'Why?' Phyllida picked up her reticule and dropped in the front-door key.

'In case there is any danger, of course.' Ashe followed her out and pulled the door to. Phyllida told the driver where to go and they climbed into the hackney.

'You will deal with that by throttling assailants with your sash?'

'You are more exhausting than my sister,' Ashe complained. 'No, I will stab them with one of the three knives I have about my person.' He settled back against the battered squabs and crossed long legs.

Knives? Gentlemen did not stroll around London armed to the teeth with knives, not these days. He was teasing her, he had to be. Phyllida resisted the temptation to look for betraying bulges in case he thought she was studying his body.

'Who is Miss Millington?' he asked in a rapid change of subject. 'I couldn't find her in either the *Peerage* or the *Landed Gentry*.'

'You can't have her!' Phyllida sat bolt upright and gripped her reticule. 'She is for Gregory.'

'I didn't say I wanted her, I was simply trying to place her.'

'Her father is a prominent banker.'

'Ah, I see. She will come with a substantial dowry and your brother comes with land and title.'

'Exactly. And they like each other, so I have every hope they will make a match of it.'

'Your doing, I suspect.'

'Certainly. It is no secret that our father left Gregory the earldom, a crumbling house, a great deal of entailed land in poor heart and a mountain of debt. We sold off everything that we could and cleared the debts, but that left virtually nothing to live off and certainly no resources to restore the Court and the estate.'

'So you support the pair of you with your dealing and the shop. What happens to you when Fransham marries? You appear to be a notable matchmaker—can you not turn your talents to your own benefit?'

'I will not marry.' Phyllida began to fiddle with a darn on her right glove. 'In my position...'

'Nonsense. Someone will fall in love with you—a professional man, a younger son.'

And then she would have to confess the truth about her past. 'I will not marry,' Phyllida repeated stubbornly. 'I have no wish to.' And even if she could find the right man, and even if he did not care about her birth or her past or the shop, could she bring herself to be a wife to him?

She shivered. Just because she found one man attractive and still dreamt about his kiss and the pressure of his fingers on hers did not mean that if things went beyond kisses that she could bear it. Her body's instinctive reactions, female to male, were one thing, her mind's capacity to overcome horror and memory was quite another. Better never to risk it. It felt as though Ashe was tugging her closer and closer to a cliff edge and she had no strength to resist him.

'We are close.' She pulled the check string. 'If you get out here and walk around the corner to the left, you'll see the warehouse. Tell the driver to take me to the entrance in a few minutes.'

When she entered the warehouse with a nod to the guard on the door and the scurrying clerks, she found men she recognised inside. Taciturn, shabby figures with notebooks, they made secretive jottings as they passed amongst the packing cases and racks. Her fellow dealers spared her curt greetings and assessing looks, their faces as blank as those of card players in the midst of a high-stakes game.

It was not hard to locate Ashe. He was strolling along the crowded aisles, a faint sneer curving his lips, Joe Bertram, the warehouse manager, at his heels. She watched as he stopped and shook his head over a display of just the sort of small items she was interested in.

'Who the blazes is that?' One of the dealers stopped next to Phyllida and jerked his head at Ashe, who was rolling his eyes at a large vase.

'I have no idea,' she said, hardly able to recognise the supercilious Indian gentleman they were looking at. 'But he looks as though he knows what he is talking about.'

'He's putting the wind up old Bertram. Might lower the prices for all of us,' the man said with a chuckle and moved on.

Ashe approached her, paused and produced a slight inclination of the head. His face was expressionless, an aristocrat showing courtesy to a lesser being. Phyllida ignored him and made a pretence of studying some vast urns before going to the small items. Her heart was racing as she picked up the first delicate tea bowl. There was high-quality *famille rose*, some exquisite blue-and-white incense burners, charming unglazed terracotta miniature figures, plates... She would have to consider very carefully and bargain hard.

On the edge of her concentration she could hear Ashe, his voice strongly accented as he condescended to take an interest in a suite of vases. She put the pieces she wanted to one side, added some more as sacrifices once the bargaining began, and looked around for Bertram or one of his assistants. At the doorway there was jostling, laughter, a string of swear words, then Harry Buck and his bullies swaggered in. All around her the dealers faded into the background, like terriers yielding to a bulldog at the bear pit.

Only Ashe, inspecting the base of a bowl, the nervous Mr Bertram and herself were left exposed to the stare of Buck's muddy brown eyes. They flickered over Ashe, visibly dismissed him as a foreigner, over Bertram, who hurried to Buck's side at the jerk of his head, and then fixed on her. Phyllida could feel the stare like the touch of greasy fingers on her skin. Her nightmares began and ended with Buck, his coarse laughter, his thick fingers, the smell of onions on his breath. Why was he here? She was trapped.

She kept her eyes fixed on the bowl she was holding, its sides so thin she could see the ghosts of her fingers through the white porcelain. If it had a mark, it was blurred. Phyllida put it down before it fell from her fingers and pretended to make a note.

'Wot we got 'ere, then?' Buck sauntered over. 'Some dolly mop looking for a nice teapot, eh? Bit pricey for you, darlin', best look down the market. Or I can put you in the way of earning some dosh. Take the weight off your feet.'

Perhaps he wouldn't recognise her. He never had in all the times he had glimpsed her in the East End after that first time and she had taken great care that they were only glimpses. She fought to reassure herself. Why should he recognise in the drably dressed woman in her mid-twenties one terrified seventeen-year-old virgin? How many other desperate girls who needed to earn some *dosh*, bargaining with the only thing of value they possessed, had passed through those dirty hands since then?

But Buck had never been so close, so focused on her alone before. She had always managed to slip away, vanish around corners, merge behind something more interesting when she had inadvertently strayed across his path.

She could smell him now: tobacco, sweat, onions, a cheap cologne. Phyllida gripped the edge of the table and fought the primitive instinct to run.

'I know you, don't I? Where do you deal?' Buck demanded. His shrewd eyes were narrowed on her face.

Phyllida fought for self-possession. If she showed fear, it would only intrigue him more.

He raised one hand as if to take her by the chin and hold her while he studied her face. 'Wot's your name?'

'I do not think the lady wishes to talk. You are distracting her from studying the goods.' The calm accented voice came from her right, then she felt the brush of his coat hem against her skirts as Ashe moved to stand between her and Buck.

'You're not from round 'ere, are you?' Buck said. 'Perhaps you don't know how things go. I was talking to this piece.'

'Things go the same around the world,' Ashe said calmly. 'A gentleman does not trouble a lady.'

'Yeah? Well, I'm no gent and she's no lady.' Buck slammed down a hand on the trestle table beside Phyllida's hip. She flinched away and found one of the bullies had moved round behind her. 'So you take yourself off, pretty boy, before you gets hurt.'

There was a sudden movement, a flash, and a thin knife was quivering in the wood between Buck's thumb and forefinger. The porcelain shivered and clattered together with the force.

'My hand slipped,' Ashe said into the thick silence. 'I find that happens when I am crowded. What a pity if anyone was to fall and break your valuable consignment, sir.'

'Mine?' Buck did not move his hand. His attention had shifted from Phyllida like an actual weight lifting from her chest.

'I think you are the money behind this, are you not? I really do suggest you ask your men to move away. If I were to faint from terror I think I would probably fall against that stand of Song Dynasty wares, which would be a tragedy, considering how valuable they are and the fact that I was prepared to spend a significant sum on that set of vases.'

'You were, were you?' Buck eased his hand away, his eyes fixed on Ashe's face. He was a lout and a bully, Phyllida thought as she fought to get her breathing under control, but he was not stupid enough to lose money to make a point, not if he could save face. No one else could see the knife. And then it vanished as fast as it had appeared, point first into Ashe's left sleeve.

'I was. If we can agree on price. And, if you do not frighten the lady away, I imagine she was about to enquire about the cost of the articles she has set to one side.'

She looked up at Ashe looming large and dangerous next to her. He seemed completely relaxed, but then she was probably tense enough for both of them. He held Buck's stare with his own and the man's wavered.

'Show us your money first.'

'No. We agree a price first. Then I send for the money, then we make an exchange,' Ashe said as pleasantly as if they were chatting over afternoon tea.

'Done,' Buck said with a grunt and moved away, his men pushing past Ashe and Phyllida to follow him.

'Oh, my God.' She unclenched her fingers from the trestle table and painfully massaged life back into them. 'Are we going to get out of here alive?'

'If I spend enough money,' Ashe said with a suppressed laugh. 'Have you chosen?'

'Yes.' Phyllida knew she could not just bolt from the warehouse, which was what every instinct was screaming at her to do. It would draw attention back to her and

Ashe would be curious. She righted a little figure that had been knocked over with the force of the knife blow.

Ashe gestured to Bertram and stood back as she haggled. Her voice shook at first, but the familiar cut and thrust of bargaining soothed her a little and they agreed a price that gave her almost everything that she wanted. 'I'll take them now,' she said, paid, then stood aside while a porter packed the pieces and Ashe negotiated the price of the vases.

'They are Northern Song,' Bertram declared. 'Very rare.'

'No, they are southern celadon ware. Thirteenth century, quite late for Song,' Ashe countered.

He knows what he is talking about. It was easy to watch and listen to Ashe, to the rhythm of that lovely, lilting accent, to the fluent movement of his hands as he gestured. He had become less European, more Indian, just by the way he pitched his voice, the way he stood. He did not nod, but swayed his head from side to side in the sinuous Indian gesture of agreement.

Fascinated, she watched, saw Bertram's nervous glances to the back of the warehouse, guessed he was under orders from Buck about the price. Ashe was going to pay in money for coming to her rescue.

'I'll help this lady out with her purchases,' he said when the deal was concluded. 'And I will send for my man with the money. Do not pack them until I get back, we wouldn't want anything to get chipped, would we?'

Or substituted, Phyllida thought. But what man with the money?

Ashe summoned the waiting hackney, helped her in and put her purchases on the seat. 'Go around the corner and wait,' he said to the driver. 'I'll be about half an hour. If anyone else approaches, drive off and circle round, I do not want the lady bothered.'

No one approached, but after a few moments Buck strolled out and leaned against the door frame, his eyes fixed on the hackney. He made no effort to approach, but it felt as though his speculative gaze could penetrate the walls and see her, huddled in the furthest corner like a rabbit in a trap.

Twenty minutes later Ashe wedged the box containing his vases on the seat next to Phyllida's porcelain and swung into the hackney. 'All right? I had to make a pretence of going for the cash. If they'd had any idea how much I was carrying…'

'Yes.'

Ashe studied her face and the way she gripped the strap far too tightly, even allowing for the carriage's lurching progress over the uneven cobbles. 'That was Buck again, wasn't it? The man from the quayside.'

'Yes.' After a moment she seemed to force herself to add to the stark monosyllable. 'You might say he's the local lord of crime. He owns the b-brothels, runs the gaming dens, takes protection money from all the shopkeepers.' Her voice was as tight as her fingers on the leather loop.

'You are scared of him.'

'Everyone with any sense is scared of Buck. Except you, apparently.'

'Perhaps I have no sense. Why do you come into this area and risk meeting him?'

'Because this is how I earn my living.' The look she shot him said clearly that he did not understand. 'I have to buy cheap and sell high, so I scour the pawnshops, talk to the sailors, buy from warehouses like this one. But if I had known Buck owned it, I wouldn't have come,' she admitted. 'And thank you. I should have said that immediately. You were... You knew exactly how to treat him. I just freeze, he makes my skin crawl.'

'He's a bully. He won't risk being hurt—in his body or his wallet. A man prepared to stand up to him, someone he doesn't know, armed and unpredictable—he would back down. There is nothing you, or any woman, could have done with him in those circumstances.'

'Yes,' Phyllida agreed, her knuckles almost splitting the thin leather of her gloves. She was still desperately upset by the threat of violence, Ashe realised. All this calm acceptance of what he said was simply a cover.

'Phyllida, it is all right to have been frightened, you can stop being brave about it.'

She shook her head and muttered something he did not catch, beyond one word, *feeble*.

'That is nonsense,' he said sharply and could have kicked himself when her lower lip trembled for a second before she caught it viciously between her teeth. 'Come here.' He turned and, before she could protest, lifted her on to his knees. He untied her dreadful bonnet and threw it on to the seat opposite. There was a tussle over her grip on the strap, then she let it go and turned her face into his shoulder. 'You can cry if you want to, I don't mind.'

Phyllida took a deep breath, but there were no sobs. Ashe put his arms around her to hold her steady from the jolting and waited. 'Thank you,' she muttered.

'Don't mention it. I mean it, you may cry,' he added after a moment. 'I'm a brother, don't forget, I have training for this.'

That provoked a muffled snort of laughter from the region of his shirt front. She was not weeping, he realised, although she seemed to find the embrace comforting.

Sara always used to hurl herself into his arms and sob noisily over the frustrations of life, the little tragedies, the general unfairness of parents. But it was a long time since his sister had cried on his shoulder. As Phyllida relaxed, her body becoming soft and yielding against his, the memory of a sisterly hug faded.

The last time he had held a woman like this it had been Reshmi in his embrace and she had been weeping in bitter, betrayed grief because he had told her he would not take her back with him as his mistress when he came to England. And they had both known that he could not marry a courtesan from his great-uncle's court.

Phyllida stirred, settled against him, taking comfort, he supposed, from his warmth and the strength of the man who had just intervened to protect her. His reflexes, sharpened by the aggression at the warehouse, brought the scent of her, the feel of her, vividly to him. Subtle jasmine, the heat of her body sharpened by fear, the rustle of petticoats beneath the plain woollen fabric of her skirts, soft, feminine curves made to fit his hard angles and flat planes.

His body reacted predictably, hardening, the weight low in his belly, the thrill of anticipation, of the hunt. He would protect her against everything and everybody. Except himself. He wanted her and he would have her.

Chapter Eight

It would be bliss to stay here, wrapped in Ashe's arms, sinking into the sweet illusion that everything was all right, that she was loved and cared for by this strong man who would sweep her away from all her troubles. *I love you, Phyllida,* he would murmur. *I do not care about your birth or any secrets you keep from me. I will marry you.*

Such a sweet fantasy. Just a minute more. *Or perhaps not.* Phyllida became aware that however gallantly Ashe had protected her at the warehouse, and however brotherly this embrace might have been at the beginning, he was not thinking brotherly thoughts now.

He was aroused. As she snuggled into his lap there was no mistaking the matter, the crude physical reality of male desire. His hands might be still, but his breathing had changed. His body was tense, as though he was holding himself in check. It would not take very much encouragement, she sensed, to shatter that control. She was not the usual unmarried lady, fenced about with rules and assumptions that a gentleman was expected to observe, and she had given him every reason to believe her unconventional and reckless.

The temptation to twist around in Ashe's arms, to seek his mouth, to savour his heat and passion and strength, fled like mist in the sun. He would, she sensed, be a generous, careful lover, but even if she could subdue her fears about making love with him, she could not hide what had happened to her from a man with experience.

And afterwards? Had she really been thinking of risking that hard-won acceptance in society, her good name, simply for the dream of an hour in this man's arms? Besides, Ashe might well reject her encouragement, she told herself. Just because his body reacted to a woman on his lap it did not mean that he wanted *her*.

The shock of the confrontation with Buck, the heart-stopping threat of violence, had disordered her emotions and her judgement.

'Oh, good Heavens, look, we are nearly at Great Ryder Street,' Phyllida said with a brightness that sounded entirely false to her own ears. 'What on earth has happened to my bonnet?' She regained her seat with as much dignity as she could muster and found the hat lying on the dusty floor of the cab. 'Thank you, I am so sorry I allowed my nerves to be so overset.' She swiped at the dust with enough violence to crumple the bunch of artificial violets tucked under the ribbon.

'Where do you want the porcelain taken? Here or the shop?' Ashe asked, as though they had not been entangled in an embrace in a public vehicle, with no window blinds, for the past ten minutes.

'Here, please.' She would not be flustered or allow him to guess how she had so nearly allowed her feelings to overcome her good sense just now. The cab drew up at the kerb, Ashe helped her down and took the key to open the door for her before lifting down her package and carrying it into the hallway.

'You will not go back there.' He seemed to tower over her in the narrow space and she could feel her resolution not to reach for him weakening again.

'The warehouse? No.' She could promise that with heart-felt sincerity.

'Too much to hope that you will not go into that part of London again, I suppose.' Ashe touched her cheek with the back of his hand. 'I have been able to distract Buck twice, I might not be there the third time.'

'I will be careful.' Her own hand was over his, although she had no recollection of lifting it.

'Here, guv'nor! You want to go on, or wot?'

'My coachman awaits,' Ashe said. He stopped at the foot of the steps and looked back. *'Au'voir.'*

'Au'voir,' she echoed as she pushed the door closed. The box sat in the middle of the hall, something immediate to do. Something real. Phyllida took a deep breath. 'Gregory! Are you home? I need some help.'

'This is from Lady Arnold.' Anusha Herriard looked up from a letter in her hand. 'She invites us for a few days at the end of the week to their estate near Windsor. I had been speaking to her about Almack's and the importance of vouchers for Sara and she tells me that two of the patronesses will be there, which is thoughtful of her.'

'Ashe and I were going down to Eldonstone,' the marquess said. 'Are these vouchers so important?'

'Essential, Papa.' Sara shook her head at him in mock reproof. 'You have not been paying attention. If you want to marry me off well, then Almack's is the main Marriage Mart.'

'Ghastly expression.' Ashe put down his own afternoon post and shuddered. 'Someone asked me if I was taking part, as though it is a sporting event.' He supposed it might be, if he saw himself as the waterbuck pursued by the hounds.

'There is no hurry for you,' his mother said, passing the letter to her husband. 'Do not look so harassed, Ashe.'

'There is no denying that a daughter-in-law who knows the ropes would be a help for you,' Ashe pointed out. It was one of the reasons for marriage that he kept reminding himself about and his mother's rueful smile only reinforced the point.

'It sounds as though you would have plenty of choice if you come to this house party,' his father remarked as he scanned the sheet in his hand. 'And several of the peers I want to talk to will be there by the look of it. Sooner or later I must sort out my political affiliations and a relaxed country gathering is probably a good a place as any to make a start.'

'So you want to postpone our trip to Eldonstone?' Ashe asked him.

'I would say, yes, but then there is this letter from Perrott.' He handed it across the luncheon table. 'It seems my father had no patience with the ornaments and collections of his forebears and the place is stuffed with crates and boxes filled at random with every kind of stuff. Perrott frankly confesses himself at a loss as to know how to begin to sort it out and what is of value and needs special care and what is not.'

'Poor devil,' Ashe said with a grin. 'He sounds thoroughly exasperated. I'll go by myself, if you like. At least I can sort out Oriental porcelain and ivories for him and have a stab at any gemstones.' His father was expressionless and Ashe tried to assess how many bad old memories the thought of the family home was stirring up. 'Of course, if you want to be the first one to return there…'

'No.' The marquess shook his head. 'I only ever saw the place once. My father and grandfather were at odds, as you know. By the time I came along my father was not received. I went there in the hope the old man would stop my father packing me off to India. I got as far as his study and no further.'

'I'll go, then,' Ashe offered. 'I can manage to postpone my plunge into the Marriage Mart for a few days.' The feeling of reprieve was a surprise. He had not expected to actually enjoy the experience of finding a wife, but neither, he thought, had he been dreading it. Not that Eldonstone, haunted by his ancestors and heavy with the burden of unwanted responsibility, was likely to be much of a holiday.

'We'll have to hire an expert, I suppose,' his father said. 'Get it sorted, cleaned up, catalogued and evaluated.'

There was a murmur of agreement from his mother. No one, it seemed, was eager to tackle the chaos of the big house. The gloom of the town residence was bad enough. 'I have made some progress here,' she said. 'Most of the clutter has been stripped out of the main salon and I had that cream silk I brought with us made up into curtains. Come and see what you think.'

They followed her through into the largest reception

room, full of admiration for the transformation. 'This is just the right setting for a present I have for you, *Mata*.'

Ashe fetched the celadon vases from their packing case and set them on the grey marble of the mantelshelf. The subtle green seemed to glow in the light the cream curtains allowed into the room.

'Now those are perfect. Thank you, darling. Where did you find them?'

'A warehouse in the East End,' Ashe said. 'Miss Hurst mentioned it at dinner the other evening and I escorted her to look around.'

'Miss Hurst?' Sara said. 'Lord Fransham's sister? Why was she interested?'

The plan seemed to present itself fully formed in Ashe's head. 'Because she is an amateur expert in *objets d'art*,' he said. 'Rather more than an amateur, but you won't mention that to anyone, I'm sure. They are somewhat short of funds and she buys items that appeal to her and then sells them discreetly. Auctions and so forth.' He was not going to mention the shop and her other personas. He had promised, and this was quite enough to explain what he was about to suggest. 'You might have noticed that fine suite of cameos she was wearing at the Richmonds' ball. If we were to offer her a fee…'

As he expected, none of his family seemed shocked. 'How clever,' Sara approved. 'I know they are not well off—I was warned not to set my sights on her brother— but that must be a great help. No wonder she always dresses with such style. I was wondering about that shopkeeper in Jermyn Street, where we bought my moonstone, but Miss Hurst would be much better.'

'Certainly,' Ashe agreed, straight-faced. 'We wouldn't want a Frenchwoman.'

His mother was frowning. 'Miss Hurst can hardly go off with you unchaperoned, Ashe.'

'There is Great-Aunt Charlotte in the Dower House. She could stay with her,' Ashe pointed out. 'Or Aunt Charlotte might prefer to come to the house. If I hired a chaise for Miss Hurst and she had her maid with her, I cannot imagine that would be a problem.'

'All I know of my aunt is that she cordially disliked my father,' the marquess said. 'But I can write, see if she's willing to assist us in this, if your Miss Hurst is prepared to oblige us.'

My Miss Hurst. Now there was a concept that appealed to him. Ashe kept his face neutral. 'I will sound her out in principle. If Great-Aunt is not willing to have a guest or move to the main house, then we will just have to think again.'

Great-aunt or not, he was going to offer Phyllida a fee that would keep her from the necessity of going into the East End for months. Months while he persuaded her into his bed, months while he enjoyed her as his mistress.

'You want me to come with you, alone, to your family home?' Phyllida sorted through a jumble of emotions. Surprise, a surge of wicked excitement, rapidly suppressed, outrage if this was deliberate plotting, delight that she might earn a fee so easily and in such surroundings.

'I am asking you to accept my escort, with your maid. My great-aunt Charlotte has condescended to move into the main house for the duration—largely out of curiosity, I suspect, but she will make an unexceptionable chaperon should anyone discover your presence.'

'But—'

'I am suggesting a generous fee by the day, as we have no idea of the extent of the problem, and you have the first opportunity to negotiate on items we wish to sell.' Ashe Herriard sat back in the chair, crossed long legs in elegant relaxation and waited. 'Naturally we will not be making it known that we have employed an expert, let alone who it is,' he added.

'I suppose I could develop exhaustion from all the gadding about I have been doing and need to visit a friend in the country for a few days' rest,' Phyllida pondered aloud. A generous fee and time alone in Ashe's company. It was very tempting. But could she trust him? Or, rather more to the point, could she trust herself?

'You would not have to venture anywhere near Buck's territory for months,' Ashe remarked.

Cowardice? Or the perfect excuse to yield to Ashe's persuasions? Whichever it was, that was a powerful argument. 'I will be glad to do it,' she agreed before she could talk herself out of it. 'Gregory is going to the same house party as your family, and so is Miss Millington. Lady Arnold has promised to exert her best endeavours to secure her vouchers for Almack's because she is Gregory's godmother and thinks Harriet will be good for him.'

'And you are not invited?'

'Best not to remind the patronesses about our parents' casual approach to marriage,' she said with a lightness she was finding hard to maintain lately.

'May I ask what happened? I do not mean to pry if it is not something you choose to speak of.'

There was a faint snort from Anna, sitting in the corner with a basket of mending to keep up the appearance of propriety. Phyllida shrugged. 'It is no secret. They were madly in love—or, at least, Mama was—eloped and then Papa just kept vaguely failing to get round to marrying her.

'He made every excuse you might imagine. His father would forgive them in time and then they could have a proper society wedding, he'd run out of funds for Mama's bride clothes, he had to come back to London from Tunbridge Wells where she was in lodgings in order to make money for the rent by gambling. One pretext after another.

'And once Mama was expecting me she was hardly the slender girl who had attracted him in the first place, so she saw even less of him. Finally a frantic letter brought him back to marry her. But, of course, he stopped off for a prize fight on the way, got drunk and surfaced a day later. A day too late, as it turned out, for I had been born the night before.'

'That,' Ashe said austerely, 'is outrageous.'

'Mama put it rather more strongly, apparently. But she loved him, at least enough for Gregory to be conceived. After that we hardly saw him. Money would arrive erratically.'

And then Mama had become ill and so, with no family alive on her mother's side, Phyllida had set out for London to find Papa. But that had cost more than she had imagined. He was not to be located, not immediately, so she had to pay for lodgings and food and gradually she had become more and more desperate until there had been only one stark choice. Sell the last thing of value she had, or starve and fail her mother and brother.

'Miss Hurst?'

She started, looked up and found Ashe watching her, his faint frown at odds with the relaxed pose he still held. 'Sorry. I was just remembering. It was not a happy time. But that is all in the past now. Anna, we must pack and prepare for a trip of— How long, Lord Clere?'

'Five days? We can do the journey in a day, easily, I understand, so that would give you three to assess the situation. I hoped to leave the day after tomorrow at nine.'

'Very well. I will be waiting.'

Phyllida found herself staring rather blankly at Ashe's broad shoulders as he made his way out in Anna's wake. Had she just made a terrible mistake in trusting his discretion? The consequences of this getting out were serious. Not for her reputation, as such, for if Ashe said his great-aunt was to be there as chaperon, she was certain she would be. But she was risking being exposed as a dealer, as not just dabbling in trade, but being deeply immersed in it.

It was, she thought with a sigh, thoroughly unfair. If Gregory pulled off the successful wooing of a mercantile heiress he would be warmly congratulated by everyone and his wife accepted everywhere.

'Penny for them?' Her brother was lounging in the doorway, an amused smile on his face at her abstraction.

'I was just thinking about you. Have you seen Harriet today?'

'Barely ten minutes ago. I took her walking in Hyde Park under the eye of her mama. The approving eye, I flatter myself.' He came and sat down where Ashe had been, another long-legged, attractive aristocrat to grace the little room.

Phyllida's conscience gave a twinge. 'You do like Harriet, don't you, Gregory? Really feel some affection for her, I mean? I like her very much and I would hate to think she was going to end up the loser in a transaction between her parents and you.'

He raised an eyebrow. 'Are you asking if I will be faithful to her?'

'Well, yes, I suppose I am. And kind to her, a proper companion. She is too intelligent and sensitive to be fobbed off while you gallivant about town spending her money.'

'Ouch.' To her surprise he neither laughed it off or became angry. 'You are right, of course. If she was one of those empty-headed little geese who only wants a title it wouldn't matter, but I do like her and I think we could make a go of it.' He grimaced. 'If she'll have me.'

'Are you going to speak to her father?'

'They've asked me to their box at the theatre on Monday. I was going to see how Millington seems towards me then. If he looks amiable, I'll go and talk to him on Tuesday. If he's starchy, I'll expose them all to my many charms and talents for a few more days before I put it to the test.'

'Would you mind if I left town for a while?'

'No, of course not. Where are you going? Amanda Lewis in Essex?'

It was harder to explain than she thought it would be. Phyllida found herself scrabbling round for the right way to word it, almost as though she had a guilty conscience. *This is business*, she told herself. 'Lord Clere has asked me, on behalf of his father, to assess some items at their country seat in Hertfordshire. I would need to leave the day after tomorrow. It should take about five days in all.'

'That's good,' Gregory said. 'I should imagine you'll get on well with the marchioness and Lady Sara. Finding the pace in town a bit hectic and needing a rest, are they?'

'Actually...' *Oh Lord, how to put this?* 'They aren't going. Nor the marquess. Lord Clere is arranging a chaise for me and Anna.'

Gregory, it seemed, was not quite as relaxed as he looked. 'What?' He sat bolt upright. 'Are you telling me you are going off with that rake?'

'He is not a rake! Is he?' she asked, suddenly dubious. 'How do you know?'

'It takes one to know one,' her brother said darkly.

'Oh, really, Gregory! Either come up with some evidence—ruined maidens, drunken orgies or three-day gambling sessions—or stop slandering the poor man. I thought you liked him and, besides, he is not coming in the chaise and his great-aunt will move from the Dower House, so I will be perfectly adequately chaperoned.' *I hope.*

'I ought to go and talk to him about this.' But her brother sat back again, apparently mollified.

'Certainly,' Phyllida said, hoping she did not sound uncharacteristically meek. *Please don't!* 'I really appreciate you doing something so potentially embarrassing for me,' she added with sisterly cunning.

He rolled his eyes. 'I suppose it would be a bit awkward, asking him his intentions like that. Might be open to misunderstanding.'

'Whatever you think best, Gregory,' Phyllida said. 'But the real danger is that anyone discovers why I am away. So, if you're asked, just say that I've gone into the country to stay with friends for five days for a rest. Will you do that?'

He nodded and got to his feet. 'Got to get changed. I'll see you at dinner, Phyll.'

Left alone, she tried to decide whether she was happy that she had persuaded Gregory of the wisdom of this expedition or not. Five days with Ashe Herriard. Was that going to be Heaven—or hell?

Chapter Nine

'Good morning, Miss Hurst.' Lord Clere stood on her top step, looking indecently awake and perfectly groomed, just like the rather handsome bay gelding that was tethered by its reins to the area railings. Also sleek, male and alert was Lucifer, perched on the pommel.

Phyllida, on the other hand, was feeling harassed, wan, decidedly out of sorts and in no mood to be amused by evil-minded crows. It was one thing to agree to hazard one's reputation in the safety of one's own drawing room, but two nights in which to fret over it—in the intervals between fantasising most unwisely about the person of Ashe Herriard—was two nights too long.

'Lord Clere. We are ready, as you see. Come along, Anna, don't keep his lordship waiting.' The street, mercifully, was empty. It had only just occurred to her that to be seen getting into a hired chaise in the company of a man not her brother was more than enough to cause scandal, regardless of her motives for doing so.

'Are you comfortable, Miss Hurst?' he enquired when she was seated and wishing she had thought to add a veil to her bonnet.

'Perfectly, thank you. Anna, pull the blind down on your side. If we can depart as soon as possible, my lord, I would appreciate it. I have no wish to be seen, under the circumstances.'

'Of course.' He closed the carriage door and the vehicle jerked into motion.

Eleven words. I can hardly convict him of attempting to seduce me with his charm this morning, she thought as she huddled back against the seat and hoped that no one could see through the glass at the front of the chaise between her and the bobbing backs of the postillions. *But then, all the thoughts about seduction are in your head, your fantasies. Probably.*

Then a rider on a raking bay gelding passed the team and she found herself smiling. Why not have fantasies? The man looked magnificent on a horse and she was not made of stone. Fantasies were safe, much safer than yielding to impulses. In her daydreams passion was safe, romantic, pleasurable. Unreal.

'This will make a nice change,' she said to Anna. 'It is a while since we've driven out to the country. I wonder what Lord Clere's great-aunt is like.'

'An old dragon, I expect,' the maid said with a sniff. 'At least, I hope she is. If she exists at all,' she added.

'Are you suggesting that Lord Clere invented her and that there will be no one to chaperon me?' Phyllida demanded.

'Could be.' Anna pursed her lips. 'Or perhaps that's what you're hoping for, Miss Phyllida. He's the gent you were talking about in the park, isn't he? Handsome as sin, that one.'

'Nonsense. At least, anyone who isn't as blind as a

bat must agree Lord Clere is good-looking. But he is on the hunt for an eligible wife, so—'

'It isn't marriage I'm talking about, Miss Phyllida, and you know it. What's his lordship going to say if you come home ruined?'

I am *ruined*. Phyllida bit her tongue more painfully than she had intended as the carriage bounced over a rut. 'I'm not a green girl, Anna. If Lord Clere has any intentions towards me other than the friendship he professes, I am quite well aware that they would be dishonourable ones and I have no intention of ruining all my plans for the sake of a risky dalliance.'

'I'm glad to hear it, Miss Phyllida.' To Phyllida's relief Anna settled back in her corner and turned her attention to the passing landscape, leaving her to her own, not very comfortable, musings.

What if Ashe did make a move, of any kind? Was she strong enough to resist the temptation? He was attractive, attractive enough to break through all her fears and qualms about a physical relationship, at least at first, she thought with a shiver. Kisses and caresses, so long as she remained in control, would be wonderful. But he was a full-bloodied man, passionate, strong. She had no hope of controlling him and then… Phyllida shuddered. She liked him as well, too much for her own peace of mind.

Her sensible self told her firmly that to become involved with Ashe Herriard risked all her plans, all her practical, prudent schemes for her future. But at the back of her mind a small, seductive voice murmured that if she was never going to marry she ought to experience what she was missing. That as an independent woman she had the right to make her own decisions about her life.

And what would the Millingtons say if there was a scandal? common sense demanded. *And I'm probably quite wrong and Ashe has merely been flirting and has no interest in me at all, that way,* she added firmly. *I am perfectly safe and the only danger is my overactive imagination. Probably.*

Lady Charlotte Herriard proved to be a Roman-nosed spinster of formidable assurance and considerable age who had no qualms about saying exactly what was passing through her mind at any moment. Ashe and Phyllida were shown into her drawing room amidst half a dozen lapdogs that skirmished about their ankles.

'Lord Clere, Miss Hurst, my lady,' the butler announced. 'I will have the tea tray brought up immediately.'

'Plenty of cake, mind, Sparrow.' She set down the book she had been reading and crooked an imperious finger at Ashe. 'So, you're Nicholas's son by his Indian wife, are you? You've got the air of your great-grandfather about you. Come here, Miss Hurst, and let me have a look at you. Who are you, eh?'

'The sister of Lord Fransham, ma'am.'

'Ah!' She raised a lorgnette and studied Phyllida with all the arrogance of age and rank. '*Those* Hursts. Your father always was a fool, even as a child. So you're a woman of business, are you? Causes a scandal, eh?'

'No, ma'am. I am very discreet.' Phyllida kept a bridle on her temper and thought about the significant fee she was going to earn.

'You'll need to be, because don't think I'm going to

drag myself over to the house just to act the chaperon all day long! I'll come to play propriety, but you set out to be independent, my girl, and you'd better be able to look after yourself.' She smiled thinly. 'I certainly did.'

Phyllida was digesting that statement and wondering what Lady Charlotte had got up to in her youth as she was waved to a chair, apparently dismissed as a source of interest.

'Clere, bring those side tables over for the tea and then sit here so I can look at you.' Ashe did as he was bid and sat down opposite his great-aunt. 'You going to behave yourself with this young lady or have I got to set a maid to keep an eye on her?'

'I can assure you, Great Aunt, that I would do nothing that Miss Hurst would not wish.' Phyllida knew him well enough by now to tell he was amused by the old dragon, but not well enough to tell whether that was a double-edged reply or not.

Lady Charlotte seemed to have no doubts. She raised one thin grey brow. 'Oh, yes, you do indeed remind me of my father.'

'Not his son, my grandfather?' Ashe asked, apparently at ease under the scrutiny.

The tea tray was brought in before Lady Charlotte could answer him. 'Be so good as to pour, Miss Hurst. And eat some cake and then I can do so and keep you company. My doctor forbids it, old fool.' She fixed her gaze on Ashe again. 'No, you do not have the look of your grandsire, for which you may be thankful. Every family mints a bad penny now and again and he was certainly one. Go and have a look at the Long Gallery and the family portraits and you'll see.'

* * *

Ashe rode on from the Dower House after an ago-
nising hour of interrogation, leaving Phyllida's chaise
and his aunt's travelling chariot to follow him. He told
himself that the faint feeling of nausea in the pit of his
stomach was partly the acerbic questioning of Lady
Charlotte and part the consumption of an unwise quantity of excellent lemon cake. It was nothing to do with
apprehension over what was waiting for him at the end
of the carriage drive as it wound through the shrubberies to the front of Eldonstone House.

He had fought in battles in the heat of the Indian sun,
he had dealt with palace plots, he had foiled an assassination attempt on his great-uncle and he could out-
wit a French diplomat. What was there to set his nerves
on edge here other than a house that held no memories
for him and a straightforward duty to be undertaken?

Lucifer gave a harsh *caw* and flew down to his shoulder as though seeking reassurance and then the house
came into view.

It was an imposing, alien-looking pile of grey stone
and red brick, begun, he had learned from his ship-
board studies, under Charles II, but owing most of its
character from the reign of the first George. Used to
small windows, carved grilles and screens and all the
details of inward-looking palaces, the expanses of un-
shielded glass in numerous windows made the house
seem almost indecently exposed. Almost as exposed
as the English ladies in a ballroom with their revealing
gowns, he thought.

The front doors opened as he approached and
liveried servants emerged with Perrott in their midst,

his red head a familiar sight. 'My lord! Welcome to Eldonstone.'

Grooms ran to take his horse, the staff lined up to be introduced by Stanbridge the butler and Ashe found himself inside his ancestral home.

He turned a full circle in the hallway, swearing softly under his breath in Persian as he took in the smoke-stained hangings on the walls, the lack of ornament or signs of care, the stack of packing cases pushed partly under the arc of the handsome flight of stairs.

Stanbridge cleared his throat. 'His late lordship professed himself uncaring about the state of the house, my lord. He refused to waste money, as he put it, on upkeep or even thorough cleaning and, with a skeleton staff, I regret…'

'I understand. But he lived here?'

'Most of the time, my lord. This is where he mainly, er, entertained.' The butler's face was so expressionless that he might as well have shouted his disapproval.

'Entertained? In this?' Ashe opened a door into what must once have been an elegant salon.

'His lordship's company was more concerned with drinking, hunting and the young female persons who were hired than with the amenities of the house, my lord.'

'So I see. Well, there is no way that my mother and sister are going to come and live in this.' The picture over the mantel was enough to make even Ashe, inured to erotic carving, raise his eyebrows.

'Quite so, my lord,' Perrott agreed. 'However, even the more objectionable items appear to be of some value and I could not undertake to dispose of them on my own initiative. I understand you have brought an expert to assess things?'

'Miss Hurst, who is coming on from the Dower House with Lady Charlotte. We will start work in the morning. Have bedchambers prepared for the ladies, Stanbridge.'

'Certainly, my lord. One of the footmen will attend you in the Garden Suite, the traditional rooms for the heir.' He regarded Lucifer through narrowed lids. 'I will have a large bird cage sent up, my lord. Dinner will be ready in an hour, if that is acceptable?'

Ashe climbed to the first floor, wondering if the best thing would be to set a match to the entire edifice. And yet... He paused on the landing and looked down the sweep of stairs, the proportions of the hallway. This was an elegant, well-made house that had been ravished and neglected. It could be saved, it could become a home if the ghosts that haunted it could be exorcised.

'I am glad I came and not my father,' Ashe said as Phyllida stood beside him in the hall the next morning and stared about her. 'He will have some concept of it as it should be.'

'It needs a platoon of scrubbing women, a good clear-out and a family living in it again and then it will be a lovely house,' she said stoutly, trying not to feel daunted by the gloom, the neglect and the clutter. 'Where shall we start?'

'Here and the drawing room, I thought—then it will at least appear more welcoming. Then the master suite and rooms for my sister. I should warn you, some of the artwork is of an indecent nature.'

'I will avert my gaze,' Phyllida said and Ashe smiled

for the first time that morning. 'You will trust my judgement?' Three days to start to bring some order to this was a significant challenge. 'May I direct the staff to clean and move things?'

'I leave it entirely to you,' he assured her. 'Stanbridge, place everyone at Miss Hurst's disposal and hire additional cleaning women as she directs. She will doubtless need footmen to help her move things. I will go and inspect the stables.'

Three hours after breakfast the next morning Phyllida felt she was beginning to make progress. She had commandeered a long chamber as a sorting room, had directed the footmen to set up trestle tables and was dividing up items from the hall and drawing room into things which just required cleaning and which could then go back, things that seemed beyond repair, items of poor quality and, forming a dauntingly large section, items of some value, but in dubious taste or of an indecent nature.

The tapestries in the hall were fine Flemish work and were being lowered and rolled to go off for cleaning, maids were scouring the marble floors and washing down the walls and she had found some unexceptional pictures to hang.

Phyllida pushed up the sleeves of her cambric morning gown and rummaged in one of the chests brought in from the hallway. It was a good thing, she decided, swiping dust from her nose with the back of one hand, that she had not come here hoping to seduce Ashe Herriard. Not only had she hardly seen him since yesterday, but she must look a complete fright with her hair wrapped up in a linen towel, a copious apron borrowed from Cook and dust everywhere.

A wrapped object proved to be a charming porcelain figure of a lady, caught in the middle of executing a dance step, her hand raised as though to take her partner's hand. 'And where are you, young man?' Phyllida muttered, delving again. 'There you are!' She emerged triumphant and unwrapped the male dancer, tipped him up and studied the base. 'Meissen. Lovely.'

She set them carefully on the table of items to keep and caught her own skirts up with one hand as she raised her other arm in imitation of the lady. 'Exquisite.'

'Indeed.' Fingers interlaced with hers and she found herself turned to face Ashe. 'Shall we dance?'

He was teasing her, of course. There was no need for her heart to pound or her cheeks to colour and no excuse at all for letting her fingers curl into his as he kept their hands raised in the graceful hold. 'A minuet? Sadly dated, I fear, my lord.'

'You forget, I am lamentably behind the times, Miss Hurst. It might be just the dance for me. Shall we try?' He turned her under his arm and she found herself toe to toe with him. A little panicky tug and her hand was free, only to find that allowed him to put both arms around her, drawing her close. 'There are other dances we could enjoy together,' Ashe suggested, his voice husky.

She could not breathe. There was no mistaking his intent. But was he asking her to be his mistress or simply to indulge in a liaison here for a few days? Either of those possibilities should have sent her fleeing from the room and yet, in the fleeting seconds before he bent his dark head and captured her lips, she could not feel outrage or fear or anything she should have experienced. Only desire. Desire mercifully untainted by fear or apprehension.

Phyllida closed her eyes as Ashe drew her close against him. It was not from modesty, but simply for the sheer pleasure of his hard body against hers, the strength of him, the male heat and scent, the deliciously contradictory sensations of safety and danger. Ashe's kiss on the quayside had fuelled arousing dreams, but that had been the merest caress, she realised as her lips parted under his and he took possession of her mouth. Then his attention had been half on the man who had made her so afraid, now he was focusing every iota of his formidable expertise on reducing her to quivering surrender.

Did he expect her to respond? She had no idea how to answer this onslaught, although her hands had curled instinctively around his neck, her lips had parted and her tongue seemed to be doing daringly wicked things without her conscious direction. *He believes me to be a virgin, to be innocent*, she reassured herself as she wondered dizzily if she was about to faint from lack of air, or simple lust.

Ashe seemed to sense her weakness even as her legs began to give way. He broke the kiss and she opened her eyes to find herself still held in his arms. His heavy-lidded gaze studied her face. 'I thought I was not wrong,' he murmured.

Arrogant man. The thought flashed into her head as a deep indrawn breath steadied her. What had she been thinking of? This was madness. Delicious, exciting, infinitely tempting, but completely wrong. Besides, it could come to nothing. She liked Ashe, he took the trouble to kiss with finesse and consideration for her pleasure, but she could not pretend to herself that the delight would last were matters to go any further.

'You thought me a lightskirt?' she flashed at him. She would *not* back away. Phyllida stiffened her spine and her quaking knees and did her best to ignore the clamouring instinct to throw herself back into Ashe Herriard's embrace and find out if he could, after all, work magic and banish her memories and her nightmares.

'No. I thought you a passionate woman it would be a pleasure to kiss and I judged you would respond if I did.' He was watching her like a man confronted by an unpredictable danger, calm but poised to evade both a slap on the cheek or a lashing from her tongue.

'And now what?' Phyllida demanded.

'We could do it again?' That wicked mouth was serious, but his eyes were filled with laughter.

'That is not what I meant! Am I to expect kisses whenever you find me alone—or do you have the intention of taking me to your bed, my lord?'

'*My lord,*' he echoed. 'Am I so in disgrace? Would you come to my bed if I asked you? It is what I hope.'

Chapter Ten

Phyllida hesitated a betraying second too long. 'No! Of course I will not come to your bed!' Her hands were knotted in her apron and she made herself release it, smooth out the creases.

Ashe half-turned and moved to examine the Meissen figures as though to soothe her by putting a little distance between them. 'A pity. I am very attracted to you.'

His long fingers caressed down the bare arm of the dancing lady and Phyllida shivered as though they touched her own naked flesh.

'You told me you wanted to be friends,' she accused.

'I have always been friends with my lovers,' he countered.

'How pleasant for you! I am very conveniently here, am I not?' *And I am a weak-willed woman who has been dreaming of the touch of your lips, the pressure of your hands, the hardness of your body and I am not sophisticated enough in these matters to hide that.* 'And there are no other distractions to entertain you.'

'There are plenty of distractions, Phyllida. Not that any of them are very entertaining,' Ashe said wryly.

'But are you telling me that you feel nothing for me? That I am so far adrift in my reading of you?'

She moved round the packing case, glad of its bulk between them, and reached in for another wrapped object. 'I am a respectable woman, my lord.' *Liar.* 'I cannot afford to allow my feelings to dictate my actions.' The wrappings fell away to reveal a pot-pourri bowl. She set it down on the table too hard and the fragile pierced lid rattled like her nerves.

'Then you do have feelings for me?'

'Only the realisation that you kiss very well.' She wiped her hands on her apron and dug into the chest again. If she fled from the room, she would never have the nerve to return and the work steadied her hands. 'I expect you have had a great deal of practice. Or perhaps it is simply that I have had very little and you are actually quite mediocre at it.'

That surprised a chuckle of laughter from him. 'Should I be suffering from any excess of masculine conceit, you, Phyllida, are a most certain cure for it.'

She removed the paper from around a stack of delicate Worcester fruit plates, lips tight on a thoroughly unladylike retort. After an interval when he said nothing, made no move to touch her, she asked, 'You expect feelings in your liaisons, do you?' His face went very still. 'You charm your mistresses with talk of love, perhaps?' She had meant to be sarcastic, to show her scorn for his talk of feelings when all he wanted was to bed her, but the expressionless face was suddenly vulnerable. For a second she thought he flinched.

'Ashe? What did I say?' Phyllida realised she had blundered into something she did not understand.

'I no longer make that mistake,' he said tightly.

'You loved one of your mistresses? What happened to her?' As she asked it she guessed. There was loss, bleak and cold, in those green eyes. 'She is dead.'

'Yes.' Ashe turned away as though to study the porcelain she was setting out. 'All this is European. Is it any good?'

'It is excellent.' If he thought to divert her by changing the subject she would not oblige him. 'And valuable. And that is not important. Tell me about her, the mistress you loved.'

'She was the only mistress I ever had, I suppose,' he said, his attention apparently fixed on the piece of Meissen in his hands. 'Before her there were…encounters. After her, liaisons. I learned my lesson with Reshmi.'

'She was Indian?' Phyllida took the statuette from his unresisting hands. 'Tell me.'

'Her name means *The Silken One*. She was a courtesan at my great-uncle's court. Beautiful, very sweet, gentle. Exquisite.' Phyllida saw with a pang that his eyes were closed, the thick, dark lashes shutting her out. 'I let myself fall in love with her and, far worse, I let her fall in love with me. The mistress of the women's *mahal* spoke to the raja and he showed me that I was simply being unkind to her and that it must stop.'

'But why? If you loved each other—'

Ashe opened his eyes and smiled, the twist of his lips bitter. 'My great-uncle pointed out to me that I was the heir to a marquess's title, that I would be leaving India for England very soon. Did I expect to drag an uneducated Indian girl halfway across the world to be my mistress for as long as I remained besotted with her? I protested that this was love, that I would marry her. He told me not to be a fool and to go away and think about it.'

Phyllida watched him as he wandered across the room to end up with one foot on the hearth stone, his hands braced on the mantelshelf, his back to her. 'So I thought about it. My mother is half-Indian, an educated daughter of a princely house, trained to run a great household, confident and used to European society and yet I knew she dreaded coming here, however well she tried to hide it. How could I uproot the daughter of a peasant from everything she knew—and how could I create such a scandal for my parents with such a marriage?'

'How did she take it?' Phyllida asked, dreading his answer.

'She sobbed and pleaded and then, when I was adamant, cruel because it was hurting me so much, too, she controlled herself, bowed her head, murmured that it should be as her lord commanded. She walked away into the gardens at the foot of the walls and I let her go, thinking she needed to be alone to compose herself.'

'Ashe, she didn't kill herself?'

'No. I tell myself not. She trod on a *krait*, a small, very deadly snake, and died in agony.'

Oh, God. Phyllida struggled to find the right thing to say, if the words even existed.

Ashe pushed himself away from the fireplace and came back to stand beside her. 'And when I had stopped wallowing in my self-indulgent grief I understood two things. That I would marry as befitted a future marquess, someone who would be a support to my parents, not a source of embarrassment to make their lives harder, and I would put juvenile fancies of love to one side before I hurt anyone else, let alone myself.'

'Ashe, love is not a juvenile fancy, it is real and strong. It exists.' She took his hand as though she could somehow infect him with that belief. 'Don't your parents love each other?'

'Passionately, without reservation. That sort of love is like a lightning strike, rare beyond belief.' The emotion, the pain, had gone from his eyes as he pulled his hand free. 'Enough of this.'

He would not confide further, not now. She had caught him off balance and he was regretting exposing that emotion and that weakness.

'If you wish to be useful, you could help me unpack these chests,' Phyllida said briskly, as though she had not wanted to weep for him and for that poor girl. *And for yourself. All you can ever be to him is a lover.*

'The tartness of your tongue is a constant delight to me,' Ashe observed, his change of tone startling her so much she almost dropped the set of fire irons she had found packed at the bottom of the chest.

'Then you must give me leave to observe that you are attracted to the strangest things in a woman.' He appeared to have recovered, which she found worrying. All that had happened, she was certain, was that he had buried the pain behind a formidable barrier of charm.

'And whoever packed these things away had the oddest ideas of what could be safely placed with what,' she added, beginning to drag the empty box towards the door.

'Let me.' Ashe strode across the room and lifted it, dumped it outside and took the chisel she was using to pry off the lid of the next one. 'Why are the footmen not assisting you?'

'I have them moving furniture so the drawing room can be cleaned.'

'Then sit down here,' he ordered, placing a chair next to a clear length of table, shrugging out of his coat and rolling up his shirtsleeves. 'And I will lift things out for you to check.'

'Very well,' Phyllida agreed meekly. Her legs were a little tired, to be sure, but it was also a pleasure to watch Ashe working, however unladylike it was to appreciate the play of muscles in his back and shoulders and the way his breeches pulled tight over an admirably trim backside when he bent over. He seemed to find some relief for his feelings in physical work.

The desire to see him naked, to touch him, to run her fingers over those muscles, those tight buttocks, warred with the need to hold him and comfort him. The former he would agree to without hesitation, the latter was impossible.

'To revert to your observation just now,' he continued as he lifted a bronze figure out, grimaced at it and took it straight to the rejects table, 'I have spent a lot of time in a place where I could not converse at all with respectable ladies and then three months on board ship with only my mother and sister for feminine company. It is a pleasure to talk to an intelligent woman who is neither a relative, a servant nor—'

'A concubine?' she murmured and could have bitten her tongue out.

'Exactly.' Ashe dumped the rest of the contents of his box on to the table and pushed a stack of badly chipped delftware towards her.

She pushed it back. 'This is in too bad a state.'

'That's the last of the boxes from the hall. Come and help me explore some of the rest of the house for half an hour.'

If he could act as though nothing had happened, so could she. Phyllida pulled the towel-turban from her head and tried to pat her dishevelled curls back into some kind of order. 'Where is Lady Charlotte?'

'Interrogating Cook. She tells me we need a new closed stove, whatever that is.'

'Expensive.' Phyllida removed her apron and went out into the hall. 'Where shall we go?'

'I thought the Long Gallery so I can inspect my host of ancestors.' Confront them, was a more accurate word, from the set of his shoulders and the tight line of his mouth, unless those were the outward manifestation of her refusal to be his lover or the painful story of Reshmi.

'Do you know much about them?' Phyllida asked as they trod up the staircase side by side. She ought to be feeling apprehensive, going off alone into the depths of a strange house with a man who had just professed his desire to make her his mistress, but instinct told her that Ashe would not force her. The fact that he seemed to have no qualms about offering near-impossible temptation was a truth that she pushed to the back of her mind.

Ashe pushed open the door into the Long Gallery. His body thrummed with unsatisfied desire. He was certain now that he wanted to make Phyllida his mistress and certain too that she could be persuaded. It had been agony to speak of Reshmi, but, strangely, a relief, too. And Phyllida would understand him better now.

He needed her, he realised, for more than the physical release of lovemaking. He liked her and trusted her and he could not let this drop now. But it was a fine balance between leading her into something she truly wanted and forcing her hand. He would take no unwilling woman.

His mood changed from a mixture of arousal and sadness into dark oppression almost as soon as he began to walk along the Gallery. It was uncanny. If he had believed in ghosts, he would think the place haunted by some spectre blowing cold misery over his soul.

Ashe stopped halfway along the long, narrow room and strove for some sort of equilibrium as he studied the life-sized portrait of a man in puffed breeches, ruff and bejewelled doublet. There were so many ancestors, all with his nose, most with the same green eyes that looked back at him from the mirror in the morning. All utterly confident that they belonged here and that he did not. No doubt they were correct.

The Jacobean marquess stared back, daring Ashe to walk on past him towards the most recent portraits at the far end of the gallery

'They are all exceedingly blond,' Phyllida remarked. 'Your portrait will be a pleasant change. Is your father here, do you think?'

'I doubt it.' He could not decide whether she had noticed his withdrawal or was simply ignoring his mood. Ashe walked on slowly, past Cavaliers with ringlets, Carolingian beauties with too much bosom on display and roving, protuberant eyes and into the last century. The house and park began to appear as the background in some pictures.

His pace slowed as he approached the picture almost

at the end. Phyllida peered at the gilded frame. 'I think this is your great-grandfather with your uncle who died and your grandfather.' She pointed at a tight-faced lad leaning sulkily against a tree while his father held a fine bay horse, his elder brother played with a spaniel and a small child held a ball. 'Is that Lady Charlotte?'

'Probably.' He tried to feel some connection with the two men who were so close to him in blood, but he could only feel dislike. The younger had sent his own son off thousands of miles away to almost die on a voyage into the unknown, simply because he resented the boy's likeness to his dead mother and the way he defied him over his treatment of her. The elder had stood by and done nothing to check his wastrel son or protect his grandson.

It would give his father some satisfaction to hang a new family group next to this one, an affirmation that despite everything he had survived, a far better man than either of his forebears had been.

'Do you feel a connection?' Phyllida asked, startling him. He had been so deep in his own brooding thoughts that he had forgotten he was not alone.

'No.' What he felt was oppression, the weight of hundreds of years of expectation on his shoulders. The expectation that he would carry on this line, this name, that he would devote himself to a cause that had not been his and a duty that he would never have chosen.

'Think what it must be like for a royal prince,' Phyllida said, chiming uncannily with his thoughts. 'Not just a name and a great estate, but a whole country to care for and all that on your shoulders because of an accident of birth.'

'How does your brother feel about inheriting a title

and an estate? Or does he simply take it for granted, being the only son?'

She went still, all the energy seeming to ebb out of her. Her memories, he was coming to realise, were not good. Finally she shrugged. 'When Gregory inherited things were in such a bad state that he almost gave up caring, I think. He was too young for the responsibility and he ran away from it to be with his friends. I was angry with him at first, until I understood that it was a form of self-protection, pretending not to care.'

'But *you* cared?'

Phyllida turned her back on the ranks of portraits and crossed to look out of one of the windows that formed the opposite wall. 'I am older than Gregory and I think women are better suited to cope with seemingly hopeless situations. Gregory would have fought if it had been a battle, climbed a mountain if that was what it took, but he could not deal with the daily dragging misery of having no money, a load of debt and no training for what he was facing.'

'It sounds as though your father and my grandfather were well matched.'

'I believe they knew each other.' Phyllida's mouth twisted in a fastidious moue.

'So it fell to you to find a way out of the situation.' Her face was still bleak. He saw how she would look as an old woman, all the colour stripped away, her fine bones and the delicate arch of her eye sockets still holding a elegant beauty. Ashe wondered just how bad things had been, how much strength it had taken to keep fighting until her reputation was established, their finances were under control and her brother finally matured into his responsibilities.

'It fell to me to scheme and nag, yes. You joke about my sharp tongue, my lord—it has been honed on my brother's skin. I just clung to the hope that one day he would grow up, see for himself that if he exerted himself there was a way out.'

'And now he has?'

'I think so. I hope so! And I suspect Harriet will be the making of him. Gregory is not very used to examining his own feelings, but I believe he may be falling in love with her.' She glanced up at him. 'Do not smile so mockingly, I will not accept your assertion that love is so rare, so unlikely.'

'Was I mocking you? But it seems to me that to hold out for romantic love is almost always to doom oneself to disappointment or disillusion.' He went back to the beginning of the gallery to look at the Tudor portraits once again.

'Your parents give the lie to that—one only has to look at them.' Phyllida followed him, refusing to let go of the subject as he had hoped.

'Their story is almost a fairy tale—the hero rescues the princess from a fortress under siege, they escape across a hostile land, fight dacoits, elude pursuing maharajahs. How could they fail to fall in love? The whole thing must have been conjured up by some djinn. My mother jokes that if we ever fall upon hard times she will turn novelist and write tales of dramatic romance and make our fortune again.'

'And you fear you will never find anything as wonderful as they have.' He shrugged. 'And so you will not hope, you will not seek it, because that way you will not be disappointed,' Phyllida observed.

That was too near the knuckle. Ashe glared at a

wooden-faced couple almost obscured by heavy varnish. He would not delude himself that affection, desire or liking were love and he would not risk hurting himself, or another woman, as he had so carelessly with Reshmi.

'I must choose with my head, not with my heart,' he said when he had bitten back the angry retort. 'I cannot afford to drift around, hoping my fancy will fall upon a woman of the right breeding and temperament and connections.'

'Instead you will approach the matter of marriage as you would buying a horse?' Phyllida snapped, suddenly and inexplicably irritable. 'You left out inspecting her teeth and checking for child-bearing hips.'

The hold on his own temper broke. 'And just what have you been doing to marry off your brother that is so different? Making lists of wealth, temperament, looks—and parents who want to buy a title.'

'That is different! Gregory will be ruined if he does not make a good match. Everything that I have done will have been for nothing.' She was sheet-white and there were tears in her eyes.

'And my family have given up everything that was dear and familiar to come here and take up this responsibility. I do not give a damn about this lot.' He swept an arm round to encompass the entire pantheon of ancestors. 'But I will find someone to support my mother socially, help with Sara's come-out, bring my father connections in politics and at court. I cannot play around living some romantic daydream.' *Damn it, I will not feel responsible for upsetting her! She started this.*

'I am going to ride out around the estate,' Ashe said. If he didn't walk away he was going to find himself with a sobbing female in his arms. 'Get one of the footmen to help you and don't lift anything heavy.'

Phyllida watched the tall figure stride out of the Long Gallery. 'I am not going to cry,' she said out loud as the door closed behind him with a thud. 'You don't have to run away.'

It would be pointless to weep just because Ashe had held up a mirror to all the things she had done since their father left them: all the work and the sacrifices and the bitter decisions. What he saw reflected back was a managing, nagging sister pushing her reluctant brother into marriage for convention's sake.

That wasn't true, was it? She found she was curled up on one of the broad window seats overlooking the gardens at the back of the house without any clear memory of how she had got there. If she hadn't been strong, hadn't bullied and cajoled and schemed, Gregory could have ended up like their father.

Movement pulled her out of her introspection. A rider was galloping at full stretch across the parkland beyond the ha-ha. Ashe, of course, riding as though all the devils in hell were after him, Lucifer soaring above him like a dark familiar spirit.

That outburst had not just been the irritation of a man being forced to turn his mind to marriage, she realised as the horse and rider vanished behind a copse of trees. She had touched a raw wound. Love... Ashe did not believe he could ever find it again and his spirit revolted at making a suitable, emotionless, match. Did he realise that was what was wrong? She doubted it. In her experience men would sooner poke out their eyes with red-hot needles than contemplate their own emotional state. His confidences about Reshmi had ended with him putting up the shutters again with a vengeance.

Phyllida put her feet up on the seat, wrapped her arms around her legs and rested her chin on her knees. No wonder Ashe was so straightforward about proposing she should come to his bed. He had decided to put sex and marriage and affection into separate boxes and that way no unpleasant, risky, messy emotions could interfere.

No risk of loving a wife and being hurt by her lack of response. No danger of it with a mistress, someone paid to respond to his body's needs, not his mind.

She ached for his hurt, ached for the walls he had built around his heart. And she feared for herself. It would be too easy, perilously easy, to let liking and desire for Ashe Herriard slip over into something dangerously like love.

Chapter Eleven

Green, peaceful… Ashe wondered if this was typically English. He reined in and began to look around him at the expanse of parkland that surrounded the house. His anger had evaporated in the clear air, leaving him light-headed, as though he had been ill with a fever and was recovering.

Time enough to worry about that flash and spark of emotion between him and Phyllida just now in the Long Gallery. He knew he had overreacted and he was not certain why, for he could have sworn he had his emotions under control again after his weakness in blurting out the story of Reshmi. Nor could he fathom what he had said to distress Phyllida so deeply. She was not a woman who used tears as a weapon—that anguish had been genuine.

Ashe shook his head to clear it and made himself study the land around him. It was beautiful. The ground rose before him with a mass of curving woodland that clad the upper slopes in soft curves like the bosom of some generous earth goddess. There was a glint of water ahead, and coppices of slender trees of fresh green, un-like the heavy woodlands beyond.

But surely the parkland should be grazed? The grass was almost high enough to conceal large game. And there was dead wood in the coppices, bricks had fallen from the ha-ha and as he approached the lake he saw that it was muddy and overgrown with weeds.

There was money to make this right and surely there were men who would want the work? Had his grand-father really hated the place so much? Ashe rode on, found a hedge and a gate with farmland beyond. That was better. The methods of farming and the crops were strange, but this was well tended, in good heart.

'Can I help you, sir?' A man reined in a stolid cob.

A countryman, Ashe decided, looking at the sturdy, self-possessed figure in corduroy breeches and work-ing boots. 'I am Clere.'

The man doffed his hat, but showed no other sign of deference. 'Then welcome to Eldonstone, my lord. I am William Garfield from the Home Farm. We look forward to having the family back at the house.'

'There's work to be done before then, I fear.' The other man grunted. No doubt he knew what the house was like. 'I know little or nothing about farming in this country, but your acres look in good heart.'

'I've farmed this land for twenty years, my lord, and my father rented it from the marquess before me. I hope my elder son may carry on in his turn. But your small tenants are not in such good shape—the ones who rely on you for repairs to their dwellings and investment in the land.'

Ashe liked the direct look, the honest criticism. 'Have you time today to show me?'

'There's your land agent, Mr Pomfret...' Garfield began.

'Who has connived in the neglect. I would prefer to see for myself before I tackle him.' When the other man gave a brisk nod he reined back to allow him to open the gate.

'We'll begin with the smallholdings then, my lord.'

Ashe followed as he cantered away across the park. This was not what he had come here for, he had never had the slightest interest in agriculture, but something was pulling him to investigate.

'What have you been doing with yourself all day, Clere?' Lady Charlotte demanded from her place at the foot of the dining table. Phyllida, who had been dying to ask the same question, kept her eyes on the cruet in front of her and congratulated herself on having asked for four sections of the dining table to be removed.

'Miss Hurst has been making admirable progress, I have to say,' Lady Charlotte added. 'I am sure she would have welcomed some assistance—or was vanishing into the blue your idea of discreet behaviour?'

Phyllida flinched inwardly. The older woman had no regard for the footmen ranged around the room, no doubt absorbing every word. 'Lord Clere was very helpful,' she said hastily. 'But, really, I get on well by myself.' She risked a glance at Ashe, immaculately attired in evening dress that had, at least, won the approval of his aunt. There was a magnificent emerald in the centre of his neckcloth.

He was smiling, apparently without strain. She reminded herself that he had been a diplomat. 'I have been exploring the estate in the company of Mr Gar-

field, our tenant at the Home Farm. I found it unexpect-
edly interesting.'

'I imagine you know very little about agriculture,
my lord,' Phyllida ventured.

'Which may be why I find it intriguing. But even I
can see that there has been a scandalous neglect of the
land and the properties,' he said with a complete absence of his usual faintly amused tone. 'The tenants are
living in poor conditions and the land is in bad heart,
which reduces their yields and our rents.'

'Pomfret was your grandfather's creature,' Lady
Charlotte observed. 'Idle devil. I wouldn't put it past
him to have been lining his pockets.'

'I intend to dismiss him tomorrow,' Ashe said. He
glanced around the room at the footmen. 'That goes
no further, do you understand?' He ignored the chorus
of muttered, *Yes, m'lord*, and added, 'I have employed
Garfield's second son in his place.'

'High at hand!' his aunt exclaimed. 'Without con-
sulting Eldonstone?'

'I found I did not want to have this continue a day
longer. My father will agree.' He glanced at Phyllida
and caught her watching him. 'I have discovered, to
my surprise, that although I do not care one jot about
my ancestors, I do care about the land and the people.'

His great-aunt snorted. 'You give me cause to doubt
that you are a Herriard! Every one of them of recent
generations has cared more for the name and the standing than for the estate, provided it kept on bringing in
money.'

'The land and the people are all that matters,' Ashe
said. To Phyllida's ears he sounded even more surprised
at himself than his great-aunt had been.

'You can fall in love so easily?' she asked in jest, with some instinct to cut the intensity that seemed to thrum in the air, and then bit her lip. She should not joke about love to Ashe.

'It seems I can,' he said slowly, his eyes shadowed as he met hers across the table. 'With an idea, that is. I felt the connection, the history, the link back for hundreds of years, more closely riding around the estate this afternoon than I ever did reading about my ancestors or seeing their portraits in the Long Gallery.'

'If that means you are going to apply yourself to dragging this estate out of the slough it has fallen into, then it doesn't matter what high-flown sentiments you express about it,' Lady Charlotte said tartly.

'My father always intended to do that, and I to help him. I have no idea what his feelings might be when he comes here. If he dislikes the place, then I suppose he will leave it to me to deal with.'

'You had best find yourself a wife to help you sooner rather than later if that is the case,' Lady Charlotte observed. 'Have you any idea of the duties the lady of the house has towards the estate?'

'No, but I expect you will tell me,' he said with a smile that Phyllida thought a trifle forced.

'I do not need to. Marry the right girl and she'll have been trained to it and she'll need all that experience. This is not just a large house, but one that will need dragging into the nineteenth century. I wonder if there are any of the local misses who would do,' she mused.

'That would save you the tedium of Almack's, my lord,' Phyllida said sweetly to cover a little jolt of discomfort at the image of a flock of local eligibles fluttering around Ashe. Each would bear some valuable piece of adjacent land as her dowry, no doubt.

'I have a strong suspicion that my father is going to desert the field and leave me to squire my mother and sister to that place,' Ashe said darkly. 'I doubt I can escape it. I return to town the day after tomorrow.'

The ladies retired to bed after the tea tray was brought in. Ashe kicked off his shoes and swung his feet up on to the sofa as the sound of Lady Charlotte bemoaning the poor quality of the Bohea tea faded into the distance.

It was some kind of miracle the connection he felt to this place now, as though a key had turned in a lock in his brain, a door had opened and he had recognised the rightness of this estate for him. Home. He was, by some miracle, genuinely a Herriard of Eldonstone and so, he hoped, would his sons be.

Which brought him back neatly to the inescapable fact that he needed a wife. What were the duties of the lady of a great holding like this? His mother was going to have to discover them, fast, and a daughter-in-law raised on just such an estate would be invaluable to her.

If he could only conjure up some image of the woman he wanted. He closed his eyes and tried. He knew what her qualities must be, her breeding, but what would she look like, what would her character be?

The trouble was, the image he found himself painting on the inside of his eyelids was of medium height, had wide brown eyes, a dimple in her chin and was all too inclined to laugh at him, argue with him...kiss him.

Hell's teeth, I need a mistress. I need Phyllida. Then he could concentrate on finding a wife. Ashe stood up, found his discarded shoes and took himself off to the library in search of something dull enough to send him to sleep.

By the third evening at Eldonstone Phyllida felt weary with the pleasant tiredness that comes with hard work and a successful outcome. Lady Charlotte had toured the finished rooms, declaring herself delighted with the hall, the drawing room, Lady Sara's chamber and the master suite. Ashe had been nowhere to be found—inspecting leaking roofs and fields in need of drainage, the two women agreed.

'At least now my nephew and his wife and daughter may sleep here without having nightmares,' the old lady pronounced at dinner. 'The sooner Miss Hurst works her magic on the rest of the bedchambers, the better. I declare I have hardly had a good night's sleep while I have been here. There is a stuffed bear in my chamber and my maid has had to turn most of the pictures to the wall!'

'There is a series of prints in mine that I have not inspected too closely, but which I fear may be hideous Chinese tortures and executions,' Phyllida said with a shudder.

'I deal with my bedchamber by the simple expedient of only using one candle and confining most of my activities to the dressing room,' Ashe contributed. He had come in just before dinner looking windblown and energised.

They exchanged horror stories about the house all through the meal. Her companions spoke as though it was an established fact that she would come back and work on more rooms, but Phyllida was doubtful. She would help the family dispose of any items they wished to sell, of course, but she found herself shying away from the idea of continued close contact with Ashe as he pursued a wife with increased motivation.

He had said nothing more about a liaison between them and had not so much as touched her hand. It seemed she was safe now, but she was too attracted to him, she acknowledged as she ate syllabub abstractedly, her gaze fixed on the quite hideous urn on the sideboard. And if she was not careful that attraction could grow and become more. It would be very easy to become exceedingly attached to Ashe Herriard.

'Miss Hurst?' Lady Charlotte said impatiently. 'You are woolgathering! What are you thinking about?'

Phyllida jumped and almost dropped her spoon. 'Lo—' *No, don't even think the word!* 'I am sorry! I was just envisaging lovely expanses of clear walls and polished surfaces, all ready for Lady Eldonstone to decorate as she pleases.'

Ashe, speaking to the footman about the dessert wine, did not seem to notice her stumble. Lady Charlotte gave her a considering look, but made no comment beyond saying, 'If you are ready, Miss Hurst, we will leave Clere to his port.'

Phyllida followed her out of the room, braced for a lecture on either daydreaming at table or, if Lady Charlotte was as perceptive as she feared, committing the heinous crime of falling for the heir when utterly ineligible herself.

But the old lady chatted about local gossip—all of it impenetrable to Phyllida—complained about the new curate's sermons, asked her opinions on roses, then disagreed with everything she said and finally rang for her maid. 'I am for my bed.' She creaked to her feet, waving aside offers of assistance. 'That boy is turning out better than anyone might have hoped,' she remarked just as Phyllida was resuming her own seat and offering up thanks that she could now relax.

'You mean Lord Clere, ma'am? Hardly a boy!'

'No, he is not, is he?' The faded hazel eyes rested on Phyllida's face for an unnervingly long time before Lady Charlotte turned and walked to the door. 'I just hope he knows what he's about, that is all. Goodnight to you.'

'Goodnight, ma'am.' *What on earth does the old dragon mean?* She could make no sense of it and her own thoughts were too uneasy to add speculation to them. If Ashe wanted tea, he would have to consume it alone, she decided, she could not face being alone with him just now. Besides, they had a journey ahead of them in the morning and she should try to get some sleep.

Ashe trod softly up the sweep of stairs. He had no desire to wake anyone up at this hour. As if to emphasise the point the long case clock in the hall struck two.

He was strangely unsettled. He knew he was unwilling to leave Eldonstone and uncomfortable with the prospect of wife hunting, but those sources of discomfort did not seem enough to account for this mood. He would be coming back here as soon as he could and he had accepted that the search for a bride was a priority. There was nothing new there.

His nagging state of physical frustration was not new, either. He could deal with that himself, he supposed, while he brooded on tactics for the seduction of Phyllida Hurst. *No, persuasion,* he corrected himself.

He could live with persuading her to do something she already wanted to, he was not such a rake that he would seduce her against her better judgement.

He padded past the first of the bedchamber doors. His, the vast and gloomy Heir's Suite as Stanbridge insisted on calling it, was inconveniently placed right at the back of the house.

'Let him go!'

Ashe stopped dead in his tracks, the shadows created by his candle swooping wildly across the walls. The silence that had followed that demand was almost more alarming than its suddenness had been. He was outside Phyllida's room, he realised. Just a nightmare? Or could there possibly be something wrong—an intruder, illness?

The knob turned under his hand and the unlocked door swung open silently. The candlelight flickered over the bed and he saw that Phyllida was sitting bolt upright, her face turned towards him, her eyes open

'Phyllida?' She made no reply, so he entered. The door clicked shut behind him, the small noise like a gunshot to his straining ears. Ashe held his breath and listened. They were alone—he could hear her breathing, feel his own heartbeat—but nothing else stirred.

When he reached the bed she did not move and her wide eyes were unfocused. A nightmare after all. Ashe wondered whether to leave her, but as he watched she stirred, put her hand to the top of the covers as though to push them back. No, he would have to wake her, he could not risk her sleepwalking around the house.

Setting the chamberstick down loudly on her bedside table did not rouse her. 'Phyllida! Wake up.'

She gave a little gasp and wriggled back in the bed,

her eyes still staring past him. 'No,' she whispered and raised her hands as though to fend off someone. Some *thing*.

Ashe sat on the edge of the bed and took her firmly by the shoulders. 'Wake up, Phyllida, you are quite safe. I am here.'

Between his palms her shoulders felt thin, fragile, although he had seen her lifting heavy ornaments with ease. It was as though this night-terror had sapped her strength. She blinked and he saw focus and consciousness return like wine being poured into a glass. 'Ashe?'

'You were having a nightmare and I thought it best to wake you.' He kept his voice low and matter of fact. 'Do you sleepwalk?'

'Not for years.' In the warm candle-glow she seemed to lose colour.

'It was a bad dream, I heard you call out. What was it about?' Perhaps if she spoke of it the thing would become less terrifying.

'You,' she whispered.

'*Me?* You were having bad dreams about me?' The shock made him pull back, his hands still cupping her shoulders, jerking her towards him.

'You were trapped under all those portraits of your ancestors, as though they had fallen off the walls and somehow thrown themselves at you. They were talking, gibbering.' She shuddered and he brought her close against his chest for comfort. 'I could see your left hand and you were wearing your father's signet ring. Then you threw them all off and got to your feet, but they were reaching out of the frames for you, all those white hands with the same ring, all reaching, scrabbling.'

Ashe encircled her with his arms and she burrowed

in, her cheek against his shirtfront, her hands sliding under his coat to hold him. At that moment Ashe was as glad of the human contact as she seemed to be. He could well do without that image to come back and haunt his own dreams. As soon as she was settled he was going up to the Long Gallery to face down the spectres himself.

But now the cold finger of superstition was being thawed out by the pleasure of holding an armful of warm, soft woman. 'Thank you for having my nightmare for me,' he murmured in her ear. Strange that she had been so perceptive, so in tune with his mood, despite his reserve and ill temper.

Phyllida gave a small laugh, her sense of humour apparently resurfacing as the dream faded. 'I do not think it works like that, but perhaps I was a lightning rod for it. Thank you for waking me.'

'I was passing.' His hand, of its own volition it seemed, stroked down the supple curve of her back, warm through the thin lawn of her nightgown. His thumb ran down her spine, traced each vertebra, and she arched against his palm like a cat being stroked.

'Ashe.' She wriggled a little and looked up, her head tipped back because she was so close.

He had no idea what she was going to say, nor any conscious intent to kiss her, but he dipped his head and found her mouth with his, and was lost.

Chapter Twelve

Phyllida was all soft, warm, scented femininity against him, every inhibition seemingly lost in the haze of waking from her nightmare. Her arms were around his torso, her breast heavy and rounded in his hand as he palmed it, the nipple hard beneath the thin veil of lawn.

Urgent for her touch on his naked skin, he fought his way out of his coat, ripped off his neckcloth, pulled his shirt over his head, all the time with one hand touching her, caressing her. He caught her up and felt her gasp as her hands pressed against his back, heard the soft whimper of arousal as he bent his head to bite gently along the white slope of her shoulder, into the angle of her neck, up to the alluring soft skin below her ear.

'Ashe.' It was a whisper.

He lifted his head and read the trouble in the darkness of her eyes, the tremble of her lip, smooth and plump, ripe for his kisses. He only had to close his eyes against hers, only had to take her in his arms and use all the expertise he had to overcome her fears and scruples and the thing was done.

Damn it. He couldn't do it. *Persuasion, not seduc-*

tion. As though it was physically painful he forced his body further away from her. His hands slid down to rest on her forearms, her fingers turned up to clasp his wrists.

All his mistresses before now had been Indian and he had loved the contrast of his pale golden skin on theirs. Now the whiteness of Phyllida's long fingers on his arms was like cream over honey and he bent to run his tongue-tip along one of them.

'Ashe, no. I cannot. I cannot be your mistress.' She pulled her hands back until their fingers meshed as they had in that impromptu minuet days before.

'Why not?' he asked, trying not to make it a demand, calming his breathing as if he was about to take aim with a bow and arrow and must be utterly still. 'When we kiss—'

'I want you. I am not such a hypocrite to pretend otherwise. We spoke of this, Ashe. I have not changed my mind and I thought you had understood that.'

'I had. I do.' Was that a lie? No, he understood her decision, but he was determined to change it. 'When I came into this room I had no intentions other than to make certain you were safe. When I took you in my arms it was to offer comfort and then—' he met her eyes squarely '—then my intentions changed. I have no excuses.'

She should make a fuss, be indignant, make him feel guilt and shame and then he would never tempt her again. 'Yes, there are excuses. Real ones,' Phyllida found herself saying. 'I reacted as though I would welcome your caresses.' She forced herself to as much honesty as she dared. 'I *did* welcome them. I wanted to touch you, to kiss you. Most men would not have stopped, would have argued that I led them on.' *Stop pretending* you *don't want it, you need a real man to show you...* Somehow she repressed the shudder lest he think it was for him.

So close to his naked torso, her hands still on him, she wondered again what would it be like to lie with Ashe. Would his kisses sweep her away so the fear was lost, submerged by a roaring wave of passion, or would he coax her out of her fears, softly, gently, replacing nightmare with pleasure?

Or would she panic when those caresses moved beyond kisses? She closed her eyes, imagining her own screams, her nails ripping down his cheek. And he would know her deepest, darkest secret, that she had given herself, her innocence, to another man, not out of love but for money. Like a whore. *Not* like, the inner voice of her conscience chided her. *You* were *a whore.*

'No, you did not lead me on,' he said as he freed her hands and stood up. 'I take responsibility for what I do and I may want you too much for my own peace of mind, but I am not some rutting beast whose lusts must drive him. Are you all right now? Perhaps you should ring for your maid, send her for some hot milk or chocolate to soothe you.'

'It would take more than chocolate to soothe me after that kiss,' she said wryly. 'And why should the poor woman lose her own sleep because I am restless?' She watched him pull on his shirt and tuck it into his evening breeches, deliberately heaping coals on the smouldering fires he had kindled. The feel of that smoothly muscled back, the memory of the trail of dark hair from his chest down past his navel, the easy breadth of his shoulders—those were going to haunt her dreams for nights to come.

'Goodnight, Phyllida.' He caught up his neckcloth from the back of a chair and draped it around his neck. 'Dream of rare porcelain and precious gems. Sleep well.'

Phyllida slept and, if she dreamed, did not recall it when she woke, wincing, to the clatter of curtain rings.

'Good morning, Miss Phyllida.' Anna sounded indecently bright and cheerful. 'Rise and shine! We're away after breakfast and his lordship has ordered it for eight o'clock.' She came to the bedside and looked down, her smile fading. 'Are you well, Miss Phyllida? You're as white as a sheet.'

'I feel it.' Phyllida struggled up against the pillows and took stock of herself. 'I have a horrible suspicion that I'm going to be sick, Anna.'

The maid whisked the basin off the washstand and dumped it on her knees. 'It's that whiting from last night. We had the leftovers for dinner in the servants' hall and William the footman swore it was off.'

'It tasted all right. Oh!' Phyllida doubled up over the basin with a groan. When the worst was over she lay back, a wet cloth in her hand, and thought back. 'I do hope Lady Charlotte didn't eat any. At her age sickness could be dangerous.'

'Most of it came back down to the kitchen,' Anna said, frowning in recollection. 'That's why there was enough for the staff. But no one fancied it much because the stew was so good. William didn't finish his and Cook got the hump because of him saying it wasn't right, so she took it off the table. I'll go and get you some hot water and I'll let his lordship know you can't be travelling today.'

'No!' She had to get home, safely away from Ashe and all the temptation he offered. 'Lord Clere has to return and I cannot expect Lady Charlotte to spend any more time away from her own home. I'll be fine now. Just bring me my breakfast up here. Some toast, perhaps.'

Phyllida managed to keep down a slice of dry toast and a cup of weak tea, wash and get dressed, although her stomach was cramping and she felt ridiculously weak. Lady Charlotte was in perfect health and unbent as far as to offer her cheek to be kissed before she was helped into her travelling coach for the short ride home.

'In we get.' Phyllida urged Anna towards the chaise the moment the postilions brought it round. She had no intention of standing in the bright sunlight for Ashe to observe her pale, green-tinged complexion. He would probably put it down to a broken night spent fretting over him and simple vanity stopped her admitting to something as prosaic as an upset stomach.

By the time he had waved his great-aunt off and come to the chaise, she was sitting well back in a shadowed corner.

'What an admirably prompt woman you are,' Ashe said. 'The day looks set to stay fair and we'll be back to London in good time.'

'Wonderful!' Her cheerful response must have convinced him all was well for he closed the door, mounted his horse and they set off down the drive.

After ten minutes Phyllida was recalling all too vividly why post chaises were nicknamed Yellow Bounders. This one seemed to have extra-firm springs to make sure that every pothole, rut and stone contributed to the eccentric motion of the vehicle.

She doggedly chewed on the spearmint leaves that Anna had found in the kitchen garden and focused on Ashe's tall figure. But after a while the even cadences of the cantering horse on what must be a smooth verge only emphasised the swaying and jolting of the chaise. 'I've never felt sick in one of these before,' Phyllida lamented.

'Well, you hadn't eaten stale fish before, had you, Miss Phyllida?' Anna pointed out. 'We'll be stopping to change the horses in an hour.'

An hour! Phyllida bit down grimly on another mint leaf and tried to think of anything but her stomach and her swimming head. The only possible benefit of feeling so queasy, she had decided by the time the chaise reached King's Langley, was that it was a most effective antidote to amorous thoughts of Ashe.

'We're stopping, Miss Phyllida.'

'Thank goodness for that, because I do not think my breakfast is going to stay down any longer.' Phyllida clamped a handkerchief over her mouth. As the chaise clattered to a halt in the inn yard she opened the door and stumbled down, clutching the high wheel for support.

'What is wrong?' She had not even seen Ashe, but he was there at her side, his hands supporting her.

'Bad fish,' Anna said. 'She's going to be sick any moment, my lord.'

'Hang on.' Ashe bent and scooped her up in his arms, strode into the inn and snapped, 'A room, hot water, a basin.'

'Please…I can manage…' She glanced around as

best she could over the lace of her handkerchief. This was a large, smart inn, obviously one catering to the carriage trade, not some shabby little place where she could be ill in dingy privacy.

'In here, sir. Oh poor dear. Increasing, is she?' A woman's voice…a stranger. She was settled in a chair, hands—Ashe's—pressed a bowl onto her lap. Somehow her bonnet had gone and so had her pelisse.

Phyllida retched miserably, someone held her shoulders, a damp cloth smelling of lavender was put into her hand as the bowl was removed. She leaned into the supporting arm and smelled sandalwood beneath the lavender.

'Here's a little peppermint cordial. That'll settle you nicely, my lady.'

Hazily Phyllida realised that Ashe must have made his title known to secure prompt service and the woman attending her though she was his wife. And pregnant.

She sipped the cordial and swayed as the room lurched around her. This was ridiculous. She would *not* faint, she was made of sterner stuff than that.

'She is going to faint.' Ashe's voice came from a long way away. 'I had better put her on the bed.'

If she did lose consciousness it could only have been for a moment. Phyllida found herself propped up against pillows and lying on a vast patchwork quilt. 'I am sorry,' she managed.

'Don't you worry, my lady,' the other woman's comforting voice said from the doorway. 'I'll just pop down and get you a hot brick.'

'Where's Anna?' Phyllida asked, scrabbling ineffectually at her bodice. Her stays were like a vice, stopping her breathing.

'She's gone to find an apothecary for what she swears is an infallible potion to stop the nausea. What is the matter? Stays?' Ashe enquired. 'I can't say I've much experience with the things, Indian women have more sense than to wear them, but let's see what I can do.'

With a gasp Phyllida found herself tipped forwards against Ashe's broad shoulder while his fingers dealt efficiently with the buttons at the back of her gown and then the laces of her corset. 'Oh! Ashe, really you cannot—'

'I can,' he said. 'Thought I might have to cut them, but it was a nice easy bow. Now then, how are we going to do this?' He slid her dress off one shoulder, still holding her up from the pillows. 'Then this one...' The corset came away and she took a deep breath. 'There, is that better?'

'Lord Clere and his *wife*, you say? And the poor lady is sick? I must see what aid I can give. In here where the door is open?' A penetrating female voice, a rustle of skirts and Phyllida opened her eyes to see Lady Castlebridge, an earl's wife with the longest tongue in society, standing just inside the door, her expression avid with curiosity. 'Miss Hurst!'

Phyllida laid her forehead on Ashe's shoulder with a faint moan and the impossible hope that she could conceal just how much of her bosom and arms were laid bare. This was utter disaster and she could not think of a thing to do to rescue the situation unless the earth opened and swallowed her up.

'Madam?' Ashe laid her unresisting against the pillows and flipped the counterpane over her. 'I do not believe we have been introduced or you would know I am not married.'

'Well, everyone knows who you are, Lord Clere!' The delight of discovering a scandal right in front of her nose was all too apparent. 'And we had heard nothing of a wife, which is why it is such a surprise to find Miss Hurst with you and *enceinte*, poor dear.' The skirts rustled in to the room and the door clicked shut. 'I am Lady Castlebridge. Naturally, you may rely on my total discretion.'

'Far from being in an interesting condition, Miss Hurst is suffering from food poisoning and was taken ill on the road. We are the merest acquaintances, but naturally I could not leave the lady in distress when she fainted at my feet.' Ashe sounded aloof and faintly puzzled, as though he could not quite believe the intrusion. 'You are a close family friend, it seems. Perhaps you could hold the bowl for Miss Hurst when she vomits again while I go and find out what has happened to her maid?'

Despite everything Phyllida felt a faint flicker of amusement at the sounds of her ladyship's hasty retreat.

'Not that good a friend. I am certain Miss Hurst will want her maid to attend her. Er...perhaps I could find her.'

'Excuse me, madam.' Blessedly, Anna's voice, so polite it verged on insolence. 'Thank you, my lord, I can manage now.'

The door closed. After a moment Anna said, 'They've both gone, Miss Phyllida. He looked fit to strangle the nosy old besom, his lordship did. How are you feeling?'

'Dreadful.' She sat up and opened her eyes. Her stays were draped over the footboard of the bed, presumably

GET FREE BOOKS and FREE GIFTS WHEN YOU PLAY THE...

Lucky 7

Just scratch off the silver box with a coin. Then check below to see the gifts you get!

SLOT MACHINE GAME!

YES!

I have scratched off the silver box. Please send me the 2 free Harlequin® Historical books and 2 free gifts for which I qualify. I understand I am under no obligation to purchase any books, as explained on the back of this card.

246/349 HDL FV69

FIRST NAME

LAST NAME

ADDRESS

APT.#

CITY

STATE/PROV.

ZIP/POSTAL CODE

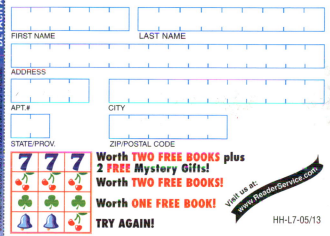

7 7 7 Worth **TWO FREE BOOKS** plus 2 **FREE** Mystery Gifts!

Worth **TWO FREE BOOKS!**

Worth **ONE FREE BOOK!**

TRY AGAIN!

Visit us at: www.ReaderService.com

HH-L7-05/13

Offer limited to one per household and not applicable to series that subscriber is currently receiving.

Your Privacy—The Harlequin® Reader Service is committed to protecting your privacy. Our Privacy Policy is available online at www.ReaderService.com or upon request from the Harlequin Reader Service. We make a portion of our mailing list available to reputable third parties that offer products we believe may interest you. If you prefer that we not exchange your name with third parties, or if you wish to clarify or modify your communication preferences, please visit us at www.ReaderService.com/consumerschoice or write to us at Harlequin Reader Service Preference Service, P.O. Box 9062, Buffalo, NY 14269. Include your complete name and address.

DETACH AND MAIL CARD TODAY!

© 2012 HARLEQUIN ENTERPRISES LIMITED
Printed in the U.S.A. ® and ™ are trademarks owned and used by the trademark owner and/or its licensee.

HH-L7-05/13

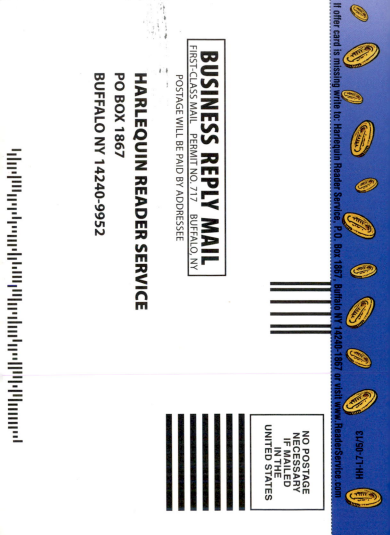

HARLEQUIN® READER SERVICE—Here's How It Works:

Accepting your 2 free books and 2 free gifts (gifts valued at approximately $10.00) places you under no obligation to buy anything. You may keep the books and gifts and return the shipping statement marked "cancel". If you do not cancel, about a month later we'll send you 6 additional books and bill you just $5.44 each in the U.S. or $5.74 each in Canada. That's a savings of at least 16% off the cover price. It's quite a bargain! Shipping and handling is just 50¢ per book in the U.S. and 75¢ per book in Canada.* You may cancel at any time, but if you choose to continue, every month we'll send you 6 more books, which you may either purchase at the discount price or return to us and cancel your subscription.

*Terms and prices subject to change without notice. Prices do not include applicable taxes. Sales tax applicable in N.Y. Canadian residents will be charged applicable taxes. Offer not valid in Quebec. All orders subject to credit approval. Credit or debit balances in a customer's account(s) may be offset by any other outstanding balance owed by or to the customer. Please allow 4 to 6 weeks for delivery. Offer available while quantities last.

BUSINESS REPLY MAIL
FIRST-CLASS MAIL   PERMIT NO. 717   BUFFALO, NY

POSTAGE WILL BE PAID BY ADDRESSEE

HARLEQUIN READER SERVICE

PO BOX 1867

BUFFALO NY 14240-9952

NO POSTAGE
NECESSARY
IF MAILED
IN THE
UNITED STATES

where Ashe had tossed them. Her gown was round her waist and only her chemise gave any vestige of decency.

'Who took your stays off?'

'His lordship.'

'Oh, lumme.'

'Exactly.'

'And old sharpnose saw? Here, drink this, Miss Phyllida. I ran down the street to the apothecary.'

'She not only saw me on the bed, in Lord Clere's arms in my shift, she also heard the landlady's opinion that I am suffering from morning sickness.' Phyllida sipped the hot brew and felt it settle soothingly in her abused stomach. 'I rather think I am ruined, Anna.'

'Surely not? You'll be out and about in town tomorrow quite obviously not with child,' the maid protested.

'That is not the point. I am supposed to be staying with friends in Essex. How am I going to account for being in bed in a Hertfordshire inn on such terms with Lord Clere that he removes my underwear in a crisis? I will wager fifty guineas she has already discovered that we arrived together, even if he was not in the chaise.' She threw back the cover and got up. 'The smoke is all it takes, Anna. There doesn't have to be any fire, not when one's position is as ambivalent as mine is.'

This is a complete disaster, she thought as Anna did up her gown, bundled the corset under her own cloak and found Phyllida's bonnet and pelisse. Then another thought hit her: Gregory. 'Oh, my Lord.' She sat down on the edge of the bed. 'What is Mr Millington going to say when he hears? He'll never allow Harriet to marry my brother after this. We must get back to London as soon as possible. I must speak to Gregory, find some way of persuading Mr Millington that this will not come to reflect on his daughter.'

'Miss Phyllida!' Anna followed her down the stairs. 'You need to rest.'

'I can rest in the post chaise.' She gathered all her strength and swept into the hallway, praying that her shaky legs would continue to hold her up. 'Good morning, Lord Clere.' She stopped and bobbed a curtsy. 'Thank you for your assistance, but as you see, I am able to resume my journey. Lady Castlebridge! It is quite all right, there is no need to stand back in the shadows, I am not suffering from anything contagious, merely the effects of some bad fish last night. I will see you at the Fosters' musicale, I am sure.'

She made it to the sanctuary of the chaise before either could say a word. Anna called to the postilions to make a start and they rattled out of the yard and turned towards London and disgrace.

Chapter Thirteen

Ashe found his father and Edwards, his secretary, in the study dealing with a pile of correspondence.

'You have made good time.' The marquess's smile faded as he took in Ashe's expression.

'Sir. Excuse the intrusion, but I need Mr Edwards's advice. What are the laws concerning marriage in England?'

His father went very still, then set down the pen he was holding. The secretary pushed his spectacles firmly on to his nose and cleared his throat, his face entirely blank of expression. 'Banns of marriage must be called in the parishes of both bride and groom over three weeks. This may be avoided, and often is by the Quality, by the provision of a common licence from a bishop. For marriages at very short notice a special licence from the archbishop is required, which in London will involve a personal visit to Doctors' Commons and a not inconsiderable fee.' He glanced at the clock. 'If one is needed, I fear it must now wait until the morrow.'

'Thank you, Mr Edwards, that is very clear. I was not contemplating matrimony within the week.' Ashe moved to the empty fireplace and rested one foot on the fender. 'Would you excuse us for a moment?'

When they were alone he said, without preamble, 'I have compromised Miss Hurst and therefore I regret that I must marry her.'

'Regret?' His father's brows rose.

'She is not an eligible bride. She is illegitimate, she is not received at court or accepted at Almack's and therefore she cannot assist my mother or Sara.' Ashe made himself continue dispassionately down the list. He was not going to fudge what a disaster this was. 'Her brother has no political influence, his lands are a significant distance from ours and will bring no benefit to you or to the estate. She has no dowry. She owns a shop and buys and sells for it herself—in other words, she is a trader and if word of that ever gets out it will mean she is received in even fewer places.'

'Your mother is illegitimate and her father was a trader,' his father said in the quiet tone that Ashe knew disguised tightly reined emotion.

'Yes,' he agreed. 'But she is the daughter of a princess, he was a nabob. You are a marquess. The case is very different in the eyes of society.'

'How is she compromised? Is she with child?'

'No!' Ashe caught up the unravelling ends of his temper. *Guilty conscience*, he told himself. 'No, it was all very innocent and damnably unfortunate. She was taken ill as we returned and fainted in the inn. I was loosening her stays in a bedchamber when Lady Castlebridge, who appears to be a voracious scandalmonger, walked in on us.'

The marquess gave a bark of laughter that sounded as though it was wrenched unwillingly from his throat.

'It is not funny,' Ashe said mildly. He was inclined to kick something. Someone. Probably himself.

'It has all the elements of a farce,' his father countered. 'But there is nothing to be done about it. You are quite right, you must marry the girl and we'll make the best of it.' He narrowed his eyes at Ashe. 'Do you like her?'

'Yes.' Ashe shrugged. 'As far as that goes it would be no hardship to be married to her.' And making love to Phyllida would be a perfect pleasure.

'A special licence would appear to be the best method under the circumstances.'

'No. I have been thinking about this.' All the way back from Hertfordshire. 'I believe less damage will be done if I very publically court Miss Hurst and marry her after a couple of months. There will be no question of her being with child then, which should confound the gossip and retrieve her name somewhat.'

'There is a question of pregnancy?'

'She was casting up her accounts after eating bad fish. The innkeeper's wife assumed she was increasing and said so loudly for all to hear.'

The marquess sat back in his chair and ran both hands through his hair. 'God! And to think I had assumed we could descend on England and sink quietly into society with hardly a ripple.' He gave a huff of laughter that sounded more like genuine amusement. 'We had better go and tell your mother that she is about to acquire a new daughter.'

His father was taking this well. Ashe suspected that his mother, always unconventional, would forgive him, too, and Sara, the romantic chit, would think him in love and happily ignore any snubs that came her way as a result. He would rather they all abused him roundly for allowing this to happen.

And he would be rewarded for not closing a door and impetuously not waiting for a maid by having to marry the woman he desired as his mistress. *No*, his inconvenient conscience reminded him. *If you had not been as intimate with Phyllida as you were, then it would never have occurred to you to stay in the room, let alone loosen her gown and remove her stays, and you know it.*

He had always assumed duty and honour went hand in hand. It seemed that in this case his honour demanded that he default on his duty. *You reap what you sow*, he thought bitterly as he went to find his mother. He would do the honourable thing by Phyllida Hurst—now he had to find a way to do his duty by his family.

As for Miss Hurst, she would be delighted at a marriage beyond her wildest dreams and it should not be too much trouble to put an end to all those hidden elements of her life that proved such a risk. The shop must go, the stock be sold—she could have no objection.

'Gregory! Oh, you are home, thank goodness!'

He appeared in the doorway of the back parlour in his shirtsleeves, a pen in his hand, his hair on end as though he had been raking his fingers through it. 'Welcome home, Phyll. I have good news for you.' She stepped into the light from the open drawing-room door and he saw her face clearly. 'You are ill! Anna, what is wrong with Miss Phyllida?' He strode forwards, dropped the pen and took her arm.

'Anna, please go and ask for tea to be sent up. It is just bad fish, Gregory. I have been sick in the stomach, that is all. Come into the drawing room, we must talk.'

She let him guide her in, seat her on the *chaise* with her feet up, wrap a shawl over her legs. 'Give me that bonnet. Can you manage the pelisse? You should be in bed.'

Don't fuss, she wanted to shout. *Don't make me feel any worse than I already do.* 'Thank you. Gregory, what is your good news?'

'Harriet has accepted me!' Despite everything she felt a glow of pleasure at the genuine warmth and happiness on his face. He *did* care for Harriet.

'Thank goodness! How wonderful, Gregory.'

'And Millington has been all that is generous and welcoming. Very straightforward about settlements and what he expects and none of it unreasonable. I was just working through the papers when you got home. He wants certain guarantees for Harriet's future and trusts for the children and so forth.'

'He sees your true character, Gregory,' Phyllida said warmly, feeling the guilt like a knife in the stomach. 'But I am sorry, I have done something so imprudent that I fear Mr Millington may withdraw his consent to the match.'

'*What?*' He stared at her. 'What on earth could you have done? Is it Clere? I knew I should never have allowed you to go off with him!'

'Gregory, sit down, please. It was the most awful combination of circumstances and not Lord Clere's fault at all.' She explained what had happened at the inn while he paced up and down the room, swearing under his breath. 'I must go and speak to Mr and Mrs Millington before they hear of this in any other way.'

'Lord, yes.' Her brother sank into a chair and rubbed his hands over his face. 'I'll come with you, of course, they must see I support you completely. But where is Clere? He should be here with a special licence in his hand, telling me how he intends to safeguard your honour.'

'I have no idea where Lord Clere might be.' Phyllida closed her eyes, overcome with weariness. 'I escaped from the inn before we could speak of it. I do not wish to marry him.'

But she did need his help to calm the scandal and safeguard Gregory's betrothal. She had expected him to overtake them, stop the chaise, demand that they discuss it there and then. Now she wondered with a shiver whether Ashe simply intended to ignore the whole thing and brazen it out. She was on the knife-edge of respectability as it was, a completely unsuitable wife for him, but surely there was something he could do to help?

'Be damned to that!' her brother exploded. 'You must marry him. I am going round there right now and if he is not prepared to do the right thing he can name his seconds.'

'Gregory—' The knock on the door cut her short. *Ashe*.

'A letter for you, Miss Phyllida.' Jane had remembered to put it on the silver slaver and presented it with a flourish, all crisp expensive paper and heavy red seal.

Phyllida knew that seal. She broke it, spread open the single sheet with hands that shook and read out loud,

> *'Miss Hurst,*
> *I trust you will have recovered sufficiently from*
> *your indisposition to attend Mrs Lawrence's party*
> *this evening. I am reliably informed that Lady*
> *Castlebridge will attend, as will the Millington*

family. I intend to silence the lady and reassure
those whom you hope will be your future in-
laws in a manner that I trust will meet with your
approval.
I remain your obedient servant,
Clere.'

'He is going to propose and announce it there and
then,' Gregory said, mopping his brow with his handkerchief. 'Thank heavens for that.'

'I do not wish to marry him and there is absolutely
no reason why I should,' Phyllida protested. 'If I just
explain to the Millingtons, and then carry on as though
nothing has happened, it will quickly become apparent that the cause of my sickness is exactly what I say.'

'You cannot refuse an offer of marriage to the heir
to a marquisate,' Gregory protested. 'Besides, the mud
will stick.'

'I most certainly can refuse him. It would seem as
though I had schemed to entrap him! My only concern
is your marriage to Harriet and if we can convince the
Millingtons that there is no truth in this, then all should
be well.'

Gregory looked ready to argue the matter all day and
night if necessary. 'I am going to rest until this evening,'
she said wearily and cast the shawl aside. 'I cannot talk
about this any more now.'

'Miss Hurst, I am very pleased to see you again.'
Mrs Millington shook hands with a beaming smile. The
gossip had not reached her yet then. 'Lord Fransham
will have told you the happy news, I have no doubt,' she

added in lowered tones as Phyllida joined her and her husband in a quiet corner of the reception.

'Indeed, yes. I understand there is to be no announcement until Miss Millington's twentieth birthday next month, but I am very happy for both of them. She will make Gregory a wonderful wife and I know him to be deeply attached to her.' She plied her fan and tried to see if there was any sign of either Lady Castlebridge or Ashe in the chattering crowd that filled Mrs Lawrence's large salon.

'Are you quite well, Miss Hurst?'

She snatched the opportunity. 'To be frank, Mrs Millington, I am feeling somewhat fragile. An internal upset caused by bad fish,' she added in a whisper. 'Do you mind if we sit down?'

'Of course not. Mr Millington, do find a waiter with a glass of wine for Miss Hurst, she is not feeling quite the thing.'

She waited until he came back with a glass and when he would have moved out of earshot put one hand on his arm to detain him. 'Please stay, sir. I must confess I had a most unpleasant encounter this morning and it has quite shaken me. I was taken ill at an inn where we had stopped to change horses. I fainted and was observed by Lady Castlebridge being assisted by Lord Clere, who also happened to be there.' She did not have to act to produce the quaver in her voice. 'She leapt to the most appalling conclusions when she found him supporting me in a bedchamber and I fear so much that any scandal will reflect most unfairly upon my brother.'

'That woman,' Mrs Millington uttered in tones of loathing. 'She lives for gossip and has the most unpleasant, snubbing manner. Why, I would not believe a word she says, my dear Miss Hurst, if she swore the sky was blue.'

Her husband, Phyllida saw, was less certain. 'There is bound to be talk.'

Mrs Millington frowned, the import of the story obviously beginning to sink in. 'That is true. There was nothing more that might have made things worse, I trust?'

Phyllida could feel the blush mounting in her cheeks. 'Lord Clere was loosening my clothing and the landlady assumed I was *enceinte*.'

'What? Oh my heavens, the scandal! What is Clere doing about it?'

'I have no idea,' Phyllida said. 'He is an acquaintance of Gregory's, but—'

'Here he comes,' Mrs Millington said, sounding not a little flustered. 'And there is Lady Castlebridge.'

As a lady should, Phyllida showed no sign of having seen the approaching viscount, but continued to exchange meaningless pleasantries with the Millingtons. To her relief, they were continuing to talk to her. *So far.*

'Miss Hurst.' Did she remember his voice as being as deep, as carrying? Heads turned. The little group around Lady Castlebridge watched, agog. 'I am so relieved to see you here. Are you quite well now, ma'am?'

'Well?' What was he doing? Why on earth was he speaking in such carrying tones? The entire reception would hear.

'After your collapse this morning at the inn.' An expression of dismay that she knew perfectly well was feigned crossed his face. 'My apologies, ma'am, I should have realised that no lady would wish it bruited abroad that she had been taken ill.' His voice was hardly any less carrying. 'But it appears you were correct and the effects of the bad fish have worn off.'

'Lord Clere.'

He turned to Mrs Millington and bowed. Phyllida introduced them hastily.

'Ma'am?'

'You were able to assist Miss Hurst this morning?'

'Ineptly,' he said with a laugh. Phyllida realised that all eyes were on them and that Lady Castlebridge was frowning in apparent confusion. 'I should have done better to have laid Miss Hurst down on a settle until her maid came back from the apothecary. But what must I do, but catch her up in my arms—a fine sight for Lady Castlebridge to come across, indeed.'

So that was how he was going to try to play this! All she could do was to join him in brazening it out. 'Mrs Millington, I cannot tell you how embarrassing it was,' Phyllida said brightly. 'There was the landlady, giving her opinion as to why I was ill, for anyone to hear, the gallant Lord Clere with an armful of fainting lady *en déshabillé* and dear Lady Castlebridge not knowing what to do for the best.'

She turned and appealed, smiling, to the bridling countess, 'Confess, ma'am—was it not the most complete farce? If I had not been in the middle of it all and feeling so unwell, I would have been in ripples of laughter.'

'It had all the appearance of a most irregular situation,' her ladyship snapped. All around people were joining in with Phyllida's laughter and her lovely scandal was turning on its head.

'Exactly.' Phyllida forced a chuckle. 'Oh dear, I should not laugh, I know, for there is poor Lord Clere, who has hardly set foot in London, suspected of elopement or worse.'

'Miss Hurst,' Ashe said with considerable warmth. 'Any gentleman of sense would surely wish to carry you off.'

Phyllida found herself in the midst of a crowd. Ladies enquired sympathetically about her health, shooting dagger-glances at Lady Castlebridge who, it seemed, had made one bitchy remark too many to win friends. The men slapped Ashe on the back and told him what a slow-top he was not to have carried off Miss Hurst while he had the chance.

'That,' Mrs Millington remarked close to Phyllida's ear, 'was a masterly piece of strategy on Lord Clere's part. I can only hope it was enough.'

'Indeed,' her husband muttered. 'If this does not die down, I must reconsider Harriet's position.'

'Of course,' Phyllida whispered back, her stomach cramping with nerves. 'I do understand, but I am certain… If you will excuse me,' she added, more loudly, 'I think I should sit down. Perhaps I was a little ambitious in coming out this evening after all.'

'I hope I may take you driving in Hyde Park tomorrow,' Ashe said. Several young ladies pouted in chagrin at not being asked. 'Eleven o'clock?'

'Thank you, the fresh air would be delightful.' He bowed and strolled off, leaving Phyllida to wave her fan to and fro and try to congratulate herself on a lucky escape. Because, of course, she could not marry Ashe Herriard, she did not *want* to marry him and to feel at all disappointed that she was not now compelled to was positively perverse.

She cast a glance up at Mr Millington's stony countenance and tried to convince herself this was going to be all right. It must be, for Gregory's sake.

Chapter Fourteen

'I should wait and have a word with Clere.'

Phyllida adjusted her bonnet before the drawing-room mirror and wondered if her brother had reformed rather too far. 'There is absolutely no need. We discussed it last night and you heard yourself how cleverly he turned the gossip on Lady Castlebridge.' Gregory was still hovering. 'Go and take Harriet out for a walk as you promised. It is a lovely day.'

'Clere should marry you,' he said stubbornly. 'For your sake and…'

'Why? You making a good marriage is one thing, but it simply isn't an option for me. And I do not need to— the Millingtons are being understanding, are they not?'

Gregory shifted uncomfortably and then unfolded the letter he was holding in his hand. 'This came from Harriet first thing. She says her father was difficult at breakfast time. Apparently he mentioned our own parents' scandal and then made some remark about Clere's family, the fact that his mother was not born in wedlock and is half-Indian. He seems to think that makes Clere likely to be a bit lax about propriety.'

'He will withdraw his consent?' Phyllida dropped her gloves in agitation.

'He hasn't gone that far. I think if you stay in London and scotch the rumours of pregnancy and Clere continues to pay court to you in a respectable manner, that might set his mind at rest.' Gregory's normally cheerful countenance was set in an unfamiliar expression of resolve. 'If he does forbid it, then Harriet and I will elope.'

'*What?* Gregory, no! Her father will cut her off, you'd be penniless.'

'I'd manage and Harriet is willing, she says so in this note. We love each other.'

'Gregory, no, you must not do anything so rash. I will lay this scandal to rest, I swear. Now promise me you will do nothing irregular.'

He shrugged. 'Not unless I have to.'

To Phyllida's relief Ashe was prompt, although she was too agitated to admire the handsome curricle he was driving.

'We must talk,' he said as he drove up the hill of St James's Street towards Piccadilly.

'We *are* talking.' Her stomach dipped in apprehension.

'I do not mean social chit-chat. Where can we avoid the crowds?'

'Cross the Serpentine. I will point out the less-frequented routes where we will still be visible. And I agree, we need to talk. Urgently.'

He did not reply and she glanced sideways at his profile, very aware of the groom perched up behind them.

'Harris, you may get down here and wait.' Ashe drew up just inside the gate, waited for the man to descend from his perch and then urged the pair into a smart trot. 'Now then, how are you feeling?'

'Confused,' Phyllida said with a snap. 'Anxious.'

'I mean in the aftermath of the fish.'

'Perfectly fine, thank you. And my nerves have just about recovered from that outrageous play-acting at Mrs Lawrence's party. I have persuaded my brother not to call you out, but I am worried—his future in-laws are taking this very seriously. Mr Millington has dredged up the scandal with our parents and, forgive me, has even referred to your own family's unconventional background.'

'Hell.' She glanced sideways and saw his mouth was a thin line. Then he smiled at her. 'I am delighted that Lord Fransham is prepared to stay his hand. One hardly wishes to meet one's future brother-in-law in a cold field at the crack of dawn.'

'What?' Phyllida almost dropped her furled parasol. 'We need to behave like indifferent acquaintances until people believe there is nothing between us and I must stay very visible until it is obvious that there is no question of my being with child, but there is absolutely no need for you to marry me.'

'Smile,' Ashe said, reining the pair back to a walk. 'Someone you know is approaching, I think.'

'Lady Hoskins.' Phyllida produced an amiable expression and kept it steady under the stares of Lady Hoskins, her son and daughter. 'What a lovely day, is it not?' Once they were out of earshot she said, 'This is so embarrassing.'

'They will all get used to me courting you,' Ashe said calmly, looping his reins as they turned to cross the bridge.

'My lord… Ashe, stop this.' He reined in and turned to her, one eyebrow raised.

'I do not mean the carriage! I mean this nonsense about marriage. You know perfectly well that I am a completely unsuitable wife for you.'

'I compromised you. You know it, I know it and Lady Castlebridge knows it.'

'And the fact that I do not wish to marry you, you do not wish to marry me and your father must be tearing his hair out at the thought of me as a daughter-in-law means nothing to you?'

'It is a matter of honour. My family is in absolute agreement with me. And nothing would calm the Millingtons' nerves more than the assurance their daughter will be related by marriage to a marquess.' He sounded quite calm about the whole thing.

Phyllida wondered distractedly if this was actually a nightmare, one of those frustration dreams where the dreamer is thwarted at every turn and with the added torment of wanting to do exactly what he said and knowing she should not.

'Arguing with you is like trying to reason with a cat,' she said in exasperation. 'You just sit there, calm as you please, licking your whiskers and purring to yourself and not attending to a word I say.'

'Licking my whiskers?' At least he sounded taken aback.

'You know what I mean. And if you are so determined to marry me, why did you not appear on the doorstep with a special licence in hand?'

'And confirm the scandal? Have everyone watching your figure for months in expectation of a seven-month baby? With a leisurely courtship honour is satisfied, your reputation is unharmed and society will simply conclude that the incident at the inn brought us together and roused my interest in you.'

'Your honour may be satisfied, Ashe Herriard, but what about mine? Do you think a woman enjoys knowing she has entrapped a man, however unwittingly?'

'Nonsense. You were so far from entrapping me that you refused all my persuasions to become my lover.'

'Really?' Perhaps insult would convince him how insane this scheme was. She could hardly tell him why she could never marry any man. 'I hardly felt over-persuaded—you had not even begun on the inducements. Where were the offers of jewels and gowns and a luxurious apartment that I gather are a standard part of the negotiations? Or did you think that we could meet in the rooms over the shop and save money?'

Ashe flicked a rein and the pair began to walk on. 'If I had thought you were a woman who could be swayed by mercenary considerations, I would have raised the subject immediately.'

'So you thought your kisses were enough, did you?'

'I had hopes that you did not find me entirely repellent,' he admitted. 'I cannot imagine what gave me that impression,' he said mournfully.

Wretch. 'I do not, and you know it, so you may stop play-acting,' she said, smiling despite everything. 'Why I like you I cannot imagine. You order me about, organise my life, attempt to seduce me—'

'No,' Ashe interrupted. 'Never that. I tried to persuade you. Seduction involves bedazzling someone until they do something against their better judgement.'

'So, you would not seduce me into becoming your

mistress, but you will compel me to become your wife? It is a fine distinction I do not understand.'

He reined in again and this time shifted on the seat so he was three-quarters turned to her. His eyes were hooded and intense as he studied her face. 'What will compel you is your understanding of what society requires and your need to protect your brother's engagement to Miss Millington from scandal.'

'And what of the many reasons against you marrying me?' Phyllida half-expected him to deny that her birth, her unconventional way of earning her living, her lack of influence or wealth mattered. She would not believe him, of course, but it would be soothing to her pride and that was very much in need of something to heal it.

'I put them in the balance against what honour demands and the scale tips most definitely to marriage,' Ashe said with flattening honesty. That was one thing she could never hold against him, he had always been truthful with her.

Honesty or deceit. There was one way out of this, a way that would safeguard Gregory until his marriage was concluded *and* save her reputation. She could lie to Ashe, pretend that she agreed, allow the courtship to progress and then jilt him. Society would doubtless agree that it would be a lucky escape for him.

'I see,' Phyllida said slowly as she turned the idea over in her mind, trying to see beyond her instinctive feeling that this was a dishonourable thing to do. But if it saved Ashe from an unsuitable marriage, freed him to make a match that was everything his duty to his family demanded, then where was the dishonour in that? And she was hardly living a life of open, honest virtue now—she deceived the *ton* every day of the week.

'Very well,' she said with a show of reluctant capitulation. 'How do you propose we carry out this courtship?'

'As publically as possible.' He did not sound rapturous over her surrender, but then, what did she expect?

'In that case, in the interests of openness, I suggest you drive back towards the more populated parts of the park. How long do you suggest we should wait before you are overcome with a passionate, if unwise, desire to marry me?'

'Four weeks?'

'Four weeks it is.' The Millingtons, she knew, had been happy to have Harriet marry Gregory fairly shortly after their betrothal was announced. She had four weeks of simulating a growing love. Then there would be a few weeks after she 'accepted' Ashe, during which time Gregory would be married and then she could develop cold feet, or a nervous collapse or some other excuse for quietly breaking it all off.

Four weeks in the company of a man she was perilously close to wanting to make her own, a few weeks of pretending to be a happily engaged bride-to-be. She could not bring herself to look beyond that.

Phyllida was not happy and he did not trust her capitulation. Ashe turned the curricle and tooled it back over the bridge and along the now-crowded Rotten Row.

He was getting the same prickling between the shoulder blades that he had come to recognise as a diplomat when someone was lying to him with skill and conviction and yet he knew, deep inside, that it was a front.

She had accepted him and she was planning something. Probably to jilt him as soon as she felt safe to do so, Ashe thought with a grim twist of his lips. That would solve the problem of her unsuitability, but his pride rebelled at such a reprieve. Or was it simply pride and would it be so much of a reprieve? He glanced across at Phyllida's profile. She was smiling slightly, her eyes darting from side to side, her hand lifting every now and again to greet acquaintances, acknowledge other waves.

Why had he not noticed before that her nose was very slightly upturned at the end or that her lashes were really ridiculously long? Probably because he had been focusing on her mouth with the intent of kissing it, he acknowledged.

'What are you staring at?' she asked. 'Have I a dirty spot on my face or is my hair escaping?'

'I was admiring your eyelashes,' Ashe admitted. She turned and laughed and something inside twisted with a kind of pleasurable discomfort. Ridiculous, to be so captivated by a laugh, especially when he strongly suspected Phyllida was laughing *at* him. Yes, it would hurt more than his pride if he allowed her to escape his net, he realised. 'They are very long.'

'So are yours.' She studied him openly for a moment before turning back to watching the crowd. 'But yours are darker than mine, which is unfair. Ashe, when you were dressed as an Indian at the warehouse, had you put something on them?'

'Kohl,' he admitted. 'You can have it if you like, I doubt I'll need it again in this country. When I was at my great-uncle's court I found it handy on the occasions I wanted to pass unnoticed as an Indian on diplomatic missions.'

'Was it dangerous, that work?'

'Sometimes.' He had the thin knife scar over his ribs and the nick out of his collarbone to prove it.

'Will you be going back to Eldonstone Hall soon?' Phyllida asked after a moment, as though that was a logical continuation to his answer. He supposed it was, if she was wondering how he intended to fill his time now without the stimulus of intrigue and danger.

'Perhaps, for the odd day or so. But I will need to be here, courting you, don't forget.'

'What about the unsorted objects? I do not think I had better go there again, not until our betrothal is announced.' Then she answered herself before he could reply. 'Have Perrott pack up all the items we weeded out and any more of the indecent objects and paintings that he discovers and send them to London. I can assign them to the right dealers and auction houses for you in my guise as Madame Deaucourt. That will at least save your mother and sister the worst of it when they visit.'

Thinking about her work had meant she had relaxed in his company again, Ashe realised. 'Thank you, I will do that.'

He watched as she greeted some more acquaintances. Ambivalent as her position might be, Phyllida knew everyone who was anyone in society and knew, too, how to navigate its shoals and rapids. It made him think of the less pleasant social obligations. 'I have been taking dancing lessons,' he admitted. 'It was rather worse than learning Persian, but I think I have the waltz under control now, as well as the others, so will you dance with me?'

'That was very fast,' she exclaimed. 'Or did you dance in India? Of course you will have done, English society in Calcutta must have had regular dances.'

'I usually managed to avoid them, although I could stumble through a cotillion and the country dances if I had to,' Ashe admitted. 'But I learned to dance at court in Kalatwah.'

'Will you show me?' Her eyes were wide, her lower lip caught between her teeth as she turned to him, full of interest.

'In India men dance with men and not for a female audience.'

'Oh.' She sent him a sliding, sideways look full of speculation. 'You must not demonstrate for me, then? It would be improper?'

'Very improper. So, not until we are married.' She had not answered his question. 'Will you waltz with me?'

'I have not been approved by the patronesses,' Phyllida said and the laughter vanished from her eyes.

'You aren't approved by them for *anything*,' Ashe countered. 'Why should you care about this? If they won't let you into their stuffy club, one more infraction will not make any difference.'

'True.' Her lips curved into a reluctant smile. 'But everyone knows I do not dance.'

'Dance with me and they will see you have changed your mind. You know you want to—you enjoy it, don't you?'

'You could tell? Oh, yes, so much. But then gentlemen started getting warned off by their mothers in case they forgot my situation. So I stopped.'

He imagined the subtle snubs, the gradual realisation that this was happening. Or perhaps it had been sharp, like a slap in the face. Now if anyone tried to wound Phyllida in his presence, he would call them to account for it. His conscience jabbed at him. So he was the only one to be allowed to hurt her then, forcing her to do what she did not want?

'There is Lady Castlebridge,' Phyllida said, her voice tight.

'Excellent.' Ashe began to rein in, ignoring Phyllida's hand closing hard on his left forearm.

'I don't want to talk to her,' she hissed.

'Oh, but I do.' The curricle came to a halt beside the open carriage Lady Castlebridge was occupying with three other ladies of a similar age. 'Lady Castlebridge, good day to you. Ladies.' He gave them the look that Sara described, amidst giggles, as his *seducer's smoulder* and they fluttered their plumage a little and smiled back.

'Miss Hurst, fancy seeing you with his lordship. Are you quite well now?' Lady Castlebridge asked, her eyes narrowed on Phyllida's face.

'I believe Miss Hurst feels better for the fresh air,' Ashe said before Phyllida could reply. 'I was just congratulating myself on the very mischance that led us to meet,' he added. 'It is probably most ungentlemanly of me to be grateful that a lady was indisposed, but I suspect that she would not have agreed to accompany me to try out my new curricle if had not been for that chance encounter at the inn.'

Four sets of feminine eyebrows arched upwards. Phyllida's unobtrusive grip on his arm developed claws. 'I certainly realised you were a safe pair of hands, my lord,' she said demurely.

Ashe bit the inside of his cheek hard to stop himself laughing. 'Good day, ladies.' He raised his whip in salute and drove on. 'For goodness' sake, Phyllida, you almost had me losing my countenance then. I think we had better be seen with my mother as chaperon as soon as possible.'

'Hmm.'

It was one syllable that held a wealth of meaning. 'You do not want to meet her? You must, soon.'

'Yes, of course. I am sure she is delightful, but she will not welcome me as a prospective daughter-in-law, will she?'

'If she likes you, she will accept you whether you are a duke's daughter or a flower seller,' Ashe said with perfect truth. As soon as he said it he spotted the danger. The corollary was, of course, that if Anusha Herriard decided that Phyllida was wrong for her son then she would move heaven and earth to stop the match and the woman beside him was quite sharp enough to realise that. 'And it is no use you play-acting in order to give her a disgust of you. She has seen you and heard enough about you to see through that.'

'I have told you, my lord, I am resigned to my fate,' she said as sweetly and meekly as she had addressed the carriage full of ladies.

And I trust you no more than I do Lucifer, Ashe thought. He would just have to give Miss Hurst something to think about besides plotting to get rid of him.

They conversed with excruciating politeness all the way back across the park to pick up Ashe's groom, then on even blander topics on the drive back to Great Ryder Street.

At a word from Ashe the groom jumped down and went to the horses' heads and he dismounted himself to hand Phyllida out of the curricle. She was relaxed, he saw, confident now that she had arrived home unscathed, probably pleased with the little barbs she had slid under his skin.

He escorted her up the steps, then took her hand and raised it to his lips. That was unconventional enough behaviour these days, he knew, but she accepted it readily enough after a quick glance to ensure that his body hid what he was doing from the almost-deserted street.

Phyllida was wearing short kid gloves. It was the work of a moment to roll the one he was holding down her hand until her palm was exposed to the sweep of his tongue, slow, insinuating, deliberately lascivious.

'Ashe.' She froze, her hand rigid in his, the scent of the jasmine water she had dabbed on the pulse point of her wrist filling his senses as he sucked the swell at the base of her thumb right into his mouth.

'You are mine now, Phyllida.' He rolled the glove back, freed her hand. 'And I hold what is mine and I do not let it go. Remember that.'

Chapter Fifteen

On my own front step... Phyllida stood, her right hand cradled in the left at her breast, staring up at Ashe. Her pulse was thundering in her ears, her whole body felt sleek and tight and as wet as the flesh he had just sucked into his mouth in a blatant erotic statement that she had no answer for. No words at all.

It took an effort of will to unclasp her hands, to reach for the knocker, her eyes still locked with his, to bang it down and then stand there, waiting, waiting until the door opened.

'Clere!' Gregory opened the door wide. 'Do come in.' Despite his tone his eyes were hard.

'Thank you.' Ashe stood aside courteously to let her past. Phyllida made her unreliable legs move, crossed the threshold and went straight into the drawing room and the nearest couch, throwing aside gloves, bonnet, parasol before she collapsed on it, hands over her face.

Behind her she heard the door close and Ashe's voice, pleasant and normal, just as though he had not been wreaking indecent havoc on her nerves a moment before. 'I hope you will be the first to congratulate me, Fransham.'

'Cong… You are marrying Phyllida?' She could almost hear his jaw drop.

'You feel I should have asked your permission first? But Miss Hurst is of age and very independent.' Ashe sounded friendly and not in the least bit apologetic.

'No, no not at all. Delighted.' The relief in Gregory's voice was clear. 'But last night…'

'If a match had been announced last night, then it would have been quite obvious that something untoward had occurred.'

'But it hadn't.' Gregory sounded suspicious again.

'Of course not, but your sister had been at Eldonstone engaged on an activity she does not want to be public knowledge. She *was* found in my arms, her gown *was* disarrayed. People have such nasty minds. Now they will see a perfectly conventional, respectable courtship taking place. I have compromised Miss Hurst, I will marry her—but not with any unseemly rush.'

'Then you have my blessing.' By the sound of it Gregory was pumping Ashe's hand enthusiastically. And no wonder. He would be round at the Millington house immediately, telling them the good news that Harriet would be sister-in-law to a viscount, the heir to a marquess. Phyllida kept her eyes closed and tried to get her unruly body under control.

How could Ashe speak so piously about an *unseemly* rush? Unseemly! What he had just done verged on the indecent and now she wanted more, wanted him, and he knew it perfectly well.

'I must go now. Shall I call tomorrow so we can have a preliminary discussion about the settlements?'

'Yes, certainly. About three suit you?' Their voices became fainter as they went to the front door.

Phyllida lay back against the sofa cushions and tried to work up the energy to be indignant. Gregory did not control her money, she did. If Ashe wanted to discuss settlements, he could do it with her and her lawyer.

But just now she did not feel as if she could add up a simple column of figures, let alone work her way through the complex maze of a marriage settlement— and one she intended to wriggle out of the moment she could.

'Phyll? Are you all right?' Gregory bounded in, full of enthusiasm, and perched on the end of the couch.

'Just tired, that is all. It has been an eventful few days.' Should she tell him what she intended? No, too risky, she thought, studying his open, cheerful face. He would never be able to stop the knowledge colouring his reactions to Ashe.

Her hands lay in her lap, curved palm up, the swell at the base of her right thumb pinker, plumper than the left. The Mount of Venus, they called it on fortune-telling charts. She had thought it just a pretty name, but Ashe had known its sensual potential and had used it ruthlessly. What else did he know that he was prepared to use in her undoing?

There were whispers amongst some of the more daring ladies of erotic pictures and books from the East. Lady Catherine Taylor had confided that she had found just such a volume high up on a dusty shelf in her grandfather's library, but had been too flustered to do more than take a few shocked peeks inside. The next day it had vanished. Others spoke of stone carvings in private collections.

Her imagination presented her with images of Ashe surrounded by beautiful Indian women all highly skilled in the erotic arts, of him studying ancient love texts, viewing carvings, refining his technique…

What would it be like to lie with a man who made love instead of using her bodily brutally for his own gratification?

'Phyll? You are very flushed. Shall I ring for tea or should you go and lie down, do you think?'

'Luncheon,' she said with decision. 'And then I shall do the accounts.' There was nothing remotely erotic about debit and credit columns. 'Tomorrow, please do not commit to anything with the settlements. I would prefer to go through any proposals with my lawyer first.' Old Mr Dodgson could prevaricate for weeks given the slightest encouragement.

'Yes, of course,' Gregory agreed amiably. 'I've enough to do working through all the stuff for my own wedding. I don't imagine for a moment there will be any problem once they realise you are to marry Clere. They want St George's, which is fine with me.'

'And in only a few weeks' time? Until this blew up Mrs Millington appeared very calm about a wedding at such short notice. There must be so much to organise.'

Gregory grimaced. 'It seems Millington simply throws money at it. His secretary could organise the invasion of a small country, from what I've seen of him, and he has hired two lady assistants for Mrs M. who spend all their time planning flowers and drafting lists. I can scarcely get a word with Harriet because she's being fitted for her bride clothes, which is why they are quite relaxed about us exchanging notes.'

'So where will you live?' Phyllida sat down again, all thoughts of luncheon and the accounts forgotten.

'After the visits we are being organised into, you mean? Apparently we will be away for about three weeks and by the time we get back the town house will be transformed.'

'*Our* town house?' No wonder Gregory looked faintly stunned. 'But we rented it to Sir Nathaniel Finch for three years.'

'He has been persuaded that the alternative offered by Mr Millington, at a lower rent and a longer lease, will suit him admirably.'

'What a wonderful father-in-law to have.' It seemed she had succeeded beyond her wildest dreams in finding the right match for her brother.

'He will do anything for Harriet, I think. And it is also very clear that if I am not a good husband my body will be found in several pieces, widely scattered.' Gregory coloured up and regarded his boots with rapt attention. 'Not that I would ever do anything… I mean…I'm in love with her, Phyll.'

'And that is wonderful.' She jumped up and went to kiss him. 'You see—all our troubles are over.' *Until Ashe Herriard realises I have no intention of marrying him.*

The next day's post brought a letter from Lady Eldonstone. She was most grateful to Miss Hurst for offering to handle the unwanted and undesirable items from the country house, she wrote. She wondered if Miss Hurst would care to come and stay for a few days to expedite that and to get to know the family.

It was a charming note, friendly and informal, and

quite definitely an order. That was where Ashe had got his assumption of command, perhaps. Phyllida wrote that she would be delighted to come the next day as Lady Eldonstone suggested and was most appreciative of the offer of the family carriage to collect her and her maid.

Phyllida had thought her poise equal to the most trying social occasion, but she found her hands were trembling as she walked up the steps to the big Mayfair mansion. It would be bad enough if she really had any intention of marrying Ashe, but while she had some scruples about deceiving him, she felt thoroughly guilty over accepting his parents' hospitality.

The Herriards were waiting for her in an airy reception room decorated in cream and greenish-greys. The celadon vases that Ashe had bought at the warehouse gleamed on the mantelshelf, flanking the family group before the hearth.

Lord and Lady Eldonstone were seated, their son and daughter standing beside them. It seemed they had been looking at a book the marquess was holding open on his lap. Lady Sara bent slightly forwards, her hand on her father's shoulder. Ashe was smiling. They looked beautiful, poised, exotic and so at ease with each other that tears came to Phyllida's eyes.

To have grown up in a family like that, with so much obvious love and affection, would have been wonderful. The money and the insecurity would have seemed trivial, if only they had been together like this. She swallowed and blinked hard. What on earth would the marchioness think if she stood there with tears pouring down her face?

'Miss Hurst, here you are.' Lady Eldonstone came forwards, holding out her hands, and caught Phyllida's as she was about to sink into a curtsy. 'None of that, please! This is just a family gathering.' She did not release her, but looked deep into her eyes. 'Is everything all right?'

The blinking had obviously not been hard enough. 'Some dust just now in the street. The wind caught it and it went on my eye, ma'am.'

'Then come and sit with us and I will ring for tea. Oh, you are here already, Herring. Take Miss Hurst's things, if you please, and send in the tea. Now,' she said, hardly waiting until Phyllida was relieved of bonnet, pelisse, gloves and parasol. 'You know my son, of course.'

Of course. 'Lord Clere.'

He bowed as his mother continued, 'And this is my daughter, Sara, and my husband.'

'Lady Sara, Lord Eldonstone.' She attempted another curtsy and this time it was the marquess who took her hand and guided her to a chair.

Ashe's sister sank down on to the footstool beside the chair, as exquisite as a piece of amber with her blond hair, golden skin and creamy yellow gown. 'Sara, please. We are going to be sis… Friends, are we not?'

'I hope so. I am Phyllida.'

'Ashe has told us all about you.' She seemed not to notice Phyllida's blush. 'And he says you worked so hard making a nice room for me at Eldonstone. But he is being very stuffy about showing me what is in the boxes that have been sent down. Are they very naughty?' she asked, low-voiced, as her parents were distracted by the arrival of the tea tray.

'Distasteful, is how I would describe them,' Phyllida said.

'Then Ashe should just have had a bonfire and not made you look at them!'

'Unfortunately some of them are valuable and there were all sorts of things mixed up together, so I had to sort them out. This is a lovely room, Lady Eldonstone. The silks are exquisite.'

'Thank you. I seem to spend all my time throwing things away but gradually a rather fine house is emerging. The silks are one of the things I managed to pack and bring with us in quantity. Which reminds me, Nicholas, we have been invited to a fancy-dress ball the day after tomorrow. We must all go in Indian dress. I am sure we can find something that will suit Miss Hurst.'

'But I have no invitation—it is Lady Auderley's masquerade ball, I assume?'

'And you are not invited? I shall tell her we have a house guest and that you will accompany us.'

'But she... Lady Auderley is one of the hostesses who has never received me,' Phyllida said, wishing the exquisite silk carpet would envelop her.

'Because of your birth,' Lady Eldonstone stated bluntly. 'Well, if she does not receive you, she must have the same objection to me. When I consider some of the rakes and loose screws I have been introduced to in the noblest of houses here, that is completely hypocritical.' Her chin was up, her eyes were sparking like flint struck against iron and she looked ready to pick up a rapier and run Lady Auderley through on the spot.

'I really do not wish to cause you any embarrassment—'

'I will not have anyone in this family—' the mar-

quess cleared his throat and his wife changed tack neatly
'—or who is a guest of the family treated like that.'

'You outrank her, *Mata*,' Sara said with a giggle.
'And she is in love with Papa, so you could arrive on
an elephant, let alone with a charming guest such as
Phyllida, and she will not object.' She turned to Phyllida, who was torn between the desire to sink gently
into oblivion and fascination with the marchioness. 'All
the ladies are in love with Papa,' Sara explained.

'Not with Lord Clere?' Phyllida ventured.

'Papa is safely married. They can flutter their eyelashes all they like, whereas with Ashe their husbands
would become agitated and lock them up.'

'I do not think you have quite grasped how things
work in English marriages,' Ashe drawled. 'The wives
do as they like and the men have duels about it afterwards. Is that not so, Miss Hurst?'

'As an unmarried lady I could not possibly comment,' she said demurely.

'Of course. You will have been living a life of blameless, chaperoned respectability,' he murmured as he
passed her a plate of biscuits.

'Naturally, Lord Clere.'

'We must see what we can do about that,' he replied, making her choke on a biscuit crumb. 'We are
decided, then?' he said to the family. 'Miss Hurst will
join us at the masquerade to give us a tally of three Indian beauties.'

'Shall we find clothes for Phyllida now, *Mata*?' Sara
said. 'She would look lovely in jade green.'

'I think I should start to prepare those items for the
sale room,' Phyllida interjected. 'The specialist sale I

told you about, Lord Clere, is in two weeks' time and, if we delay much longer, we will miss the catalogue.'

'Very true. If you have finished your tea, I will come and assist you, Miss Hurst.'

She could hardly protest that the last thing she wanted was to be in one room alone with Ashe Herriard and a quantity of erotic art, not in front of his mother and sister. 'Thank you,' she said politely and smiled despite the urge to wipe the satisfied expression from his face.

He showed her into an empty room at the back of the house where the crates had been stacked on arrival from Eldonstone. 'The ones of, shall we say, esoteric content are in the boxes marked with an X, according to Perrott, who added a note to say that he did not know what we were paying you, but that it was not enough.'

'When one does this sort of thing for a living one cannot afford to be too nice about it,' Phyllida said prosaically. 'We must list each item and it had better be in my hand as the auctioneer is expecting them to come from Madame Deaucourt and he knows my writing.'

'I will unpack them, call out a description and you can list it.' Ashe set paper and ink in front of her at a desk and went to the first crate. 'Small bronze of a group of satyrs, signed *Hilaire.*'

They began to work steadily, although Phyllida did wonder what on earth any society lady with her ear to the keyhole would make of it.

'...six naturalistic carvings in ivory of phalli, possibly French. Size, improbable.' Startled, she glanced up to find Ashe eyeing one of the objects with scepticism. 'Well, I ask you! Have you ever seen...? No, of course not.' He slammed the lid down on another completed crate. 'This stuff is about as erotic as a plate of boiled cabbage.'

'If you say so.' Phyllida drew a neat line and wrote a new heading for the next box.

Finally Ashe hammered a crate closed. 'That, thankfully, is the lot. I just hope it was worth the work.'

'It will make a thousand, possibly,' Phyllida said, running her pen down the list.

'Pounds?'

'Guineas. Gentlemen will pay high figures for erotica.'

'They'd do better to spend it on flesh-and-blood women.' He sat on the edge of the desk next to her, one booted foot swinging, took the pen and put it firmly back in the standish.

'You do not enjoy looking at it?' she asked boldly, thinking of the tales of Indian love texts.

'Nothing is as arousing as being close to a lovely woman, touching her skin.' His fingers ran slowly over the back of her hand. 'Watching her pupils dilate.' He held her eyes with his. 'Seeing the colour come up under her skin as though an artist has brushed it with the palest wash of rose.' His other hand lifted to caress her cheek. 'That stuff in the boxes is for men who don't have a woman or who are incapable of making love to one if they have.'

'I thought India was famous for its erotic texts.'

'Those are for a man and a woman to use together. In the Far East they call them pillow books. You will enjoy them.'

It was a promise that had the fine hairs standing up all over her body. Phyllida shivered. 'When we are married.'

'Why wait that long?' His fingers slid up into her hair, capturing her, holding her for his kiss.

'Not here,' Phyllida said against his lips. 'We cannot—'

'No,' Ashe agreed. 'Not here.' His tongue, firm and insistent, caressed along the seam of her lips, wanting entrance.

'I mean, not at all. Not until we are married.' It had to be said, but it was a mistake to open her mouth at that moment. The words were swallowed by his kiss and she let herself go with them, unable to resist the urgings of her own feelings, needing to touch him, hold him.

He broke the kiss, not she. And it should have been her, she knew it and could not find it in herself to feel guilty. *He's mesmerised me*, she thought, her hands still fastened on his lapels, her back arched against the chair rail. But, no, she could not blame him. *Persuade, not seduce*, Ashe had said. He was showing her what she wanted, needed as much as he did. It was up to her to resist.

Chapter Sixteen

'Are you frightened of consequences, of becoming pregnant?' Ashe asked with the directness she was coming to expect from him. 'It is such a short time until we will be married that it need not worry you.'

I cannot because I am not a virgin and there is no way I can explain to you why that is so. How would he react when he realised? With revulsion? Would he blame her, think her wanton? It would be hypocritical of him, of course, but men held women to different standards than they applied to themselves.

Might she deceive him into thinking her a virgin? She had no idea how to go about that. Besides, she shrank from the deceit. *I cannot because if I do lie with you now and you believe me a virgin, then nothing is going to persuade you that we must not wed.*

Phyllida rested her forehead against Ashe's shirt-front and tried to find some composure, some strength of will. It occurred to her that, of all the reasons she had for not making love with him, the fact that society would say it was immoral mattered not at all.

'No,' she said after a while. How long had she been

sitting there? Ashe was warm and strong and she could hear his heartbeat and his hands around her felt so good she could stay like this for ever. 'No. I want to. You know that, of course. But, no.'

'Very well,' he said, his voice a deep rumble against her ear. 'I see I must be patient. But you will let me know if you change your mind? There are many things that would give us both pleasure that would still allow you to go up the aisle a virgin.'

'Stop it!' Phyllida pushed back against his chest and he let her go. She swung round and got to her feet, retreating to the far side of the room while he remained sitting on the edge of the desk.

'I am merely trying to persuade you of the joys of marriage,' Ashe said mildly.

'*Marriage* being the operative word! And I do not believe this has anything to do with me and my feelings. You are trying to reconcile *yourself* to the marriage by telling yourself if the physical side is good, then that is all we need to worry about. Your confounded sense of honour is telling you that you must marry me, but you do not want to. Not with your head—*that* knows how unsuitable I am—and certainly not with your heart, because I do not believe for a moment that you are in love with me.'

'Love?' Ashe stood up abruptly. 'Why did you have to drag that into it? Why is it that women must imagine all relationships are about love?'

'I did not drag it in,' she said and felt sick. *Because I am so close to loving you. I didn't know it before, but I do now.* 'It is one factor in a relationship, that is all. Women talk about love because we understand that emotions are important, too. It is not some sinister plot to entrap the entire male population—why should we want to do that when you men are mostly as insensible to your emotions as an illiterate man is to literature!'

She wrenched the door open, stalked out, shut it behind her, remembering just in time that this was not her house and slamming was out of the question, then realised she had no idea where to go. Her room, if she could find it? Back to the salon to face Ashe's family?

'Are you lost, my dear?'

The lightly accented voice made her jump. 'Lady Eldonstone. I was just wondering where I should go now I have finished with those crates.'

'Let me walk with you up to your room. I am sure you would like to get rid of the dust and the ink stains. Then we can go to Sara's room and see what she has found for you to wear to the masquerade.'

'Thank you, I should like that.'

'And it has the added benefit of removing you from my son before you are moved to tell him he is so impossible you will not marry him,' the marchioness said calmly halfway up the stairs. 'Careful, my dear, you will trip.'

'Ashe is… Lord Clere… That is, we had a slight disagreement, but I am sure it is normal.'

His mother sighed. 'Men are sometimes inclined to think with their heads and certain parts of their anatomy first and their feelings a long time later. At the moment Ashe is doing what he believes to be right. I hope you will not take it amiss if I say that it may take him a while to accept that he is doing what he cannot bear *not* to do.'

'I do not take it amiss, Lady Eldonstone, I simply find it impossible to accept,' Phyllida said as they reached the door of her room. Which was a mercy. If he was truly attached to her, then to leave him would hurt him. It was better this way, she had to believe it.

'Ah well, we will see. I had to run away from Ashe's father before he realised he was in love with me. It was quite dramatic—I was dressed as a youth and he dragged me off my horse and kissed me in the middle of a group of very confused Bengali traders.' She sank down on to the *chaise* at the foot of the bed and curled her legs up under her with enviable ease.

'I should imagine that would cause a stir in the middle of London,' Phyllida suggested as she poured water into the basin to wash her hands. But she was going to jilt Ashe, she was determined on that. If he was truly his father's son, he might make that very difficult indeed—but it would be pride, not love, that was going to make him refuse to give up.

'It caused a stir on the banks of the Ganges,' Lady Eldonstone said with a reminiscent smile. 'Shall we go along to Sara's room? I have had a very civil note back from Lady Auderley who will be delighted if you accompany us to her masquerade.'

Phyllida told herself that the more she was accepted, the better it was for Gregory and that she should swallow her pride with good grace. 'Thank you for asking her, I am sure I will enjoy it,' she said politely as her hostess opened Sara's door, then stopped dead on the threshold. 'My goodness, how beautiful you look.'

Sara was twirling in front of the long glass, her skirts flaring out in a bell of shimmering, heavily embroidered golden silk that revealed her legs, clad in tight dark-brown silk trousers, almost to the knee. Her bodice, which left a hand's span of bare flesh between its hem and the waistband, matched the skirts and her hair, covered by a transparent scarf of dark brown, hung in a long plait down her back.

'Do you like it?' She came to a halt and a jangle of golden bracelets fell down her arms to collect at her wrists. Her ankles had bands of little bells tied around them and her earrings gleamed with more gold.

'I think it is stunning. But all that bare skin at your midriff is very daring.'

'I wondered about that,' Lady Eldonstone said. 'I think a jacket over the bodice, Sara, we do not want the ladies fainting away with shock.'

'I was thinking more of the gentlemen having heart attacks,' Phyllida said as Sara put on a jacket that was cut open to expose the front of the bodice and then buttoned tightly from below her breasts to flare over her hips.

'*Mata* will be wearing blue, so I thought this be best for you.' Sara gestured to a pile of green silk on the bed, its colours ranging from darkest fir to palest grass, the embroidery glittering gold in the light from the window. By candlelight it would be spectacular. 'I think we are about the same size.' She held up the bodice for Phyllida to see.

'Try it on.' Lady Eldonstone kicked off her slippers and assumed what appeared to be her favourite cross-legged position on a sofa.

'I'll help you undress.' Sara propelled Phyllida behind a screen and began to unbutton the back of her gown. Unused to having a sister, Phyllida felt almost shy shedding her clothing, especially when Sara said, 'You need to take off everything. Stockings, chemise, the lot.'

'No stays?'

'Goodness, no. The bodice is tight enough to keep everything in place,' Sara said, ruthlessly tying and tweaking.

'Trousers feel very strange.'

'The absence of them feels stranger, believe me,' Lady Eldonstone said. 'I felt positively indecent when I had to start wearing European clothes. And don't forget, skirts were still wide then. I was in constant alarm that the wind would flip everything up.'

'It certainly makes the most of my bosom.' Phyllida peered down at a cleavage she had not known she possessed.

Finally Sara finished. 'No, do not come out. I do not want you to see yourself until the night of the masquerade. *Mata,* do come and look. Doesn't Phyllida look lovely?'

'Exquisite.' The marchioness came round the screen and studied her. 'Ashe will be enchanted. I will find jewellery for you. Now, Sara, help Phyllida change again. The day after tomorrow, in the afternoon, we will turn my bedchamber into the women's *mahal*—the women's quarters in the palace,' she explained.

'All afternoon?' Phyllida turned her back so Sara could lace her stays.

'It will take us hours to get ready. Baths, our hair, the henna for our hands and feet, dressing, choosing jewellery. We will have dinner up here and the men can wait in suspense to see us.'

And we, them, Phyllida thought. She had some idea of how Ashe would look from the subdued Indian costume he had worn at the warehouse. What he might wear for a masquerade, she could not imagine.

* * *

The next day was occupied with finalising the list of items for the specialist sale. Phyllida visited the auctioneer disguised with severe clothing and French accent. Ashe and his father spent most of the day closeted in the study, working on estate papers, and only reappeared for dinner.

Phyllida found herself coming to like the Herriards more and more. They were unconventional, affectionate to each other, intelligent and their outsiders' view of the world she was so used to was constantly entertaining. Sara and her mother treated her as though she was already one of the family and it was all too easy to slip into the comfort of having a sister and a mother after years of fighting to stay afloat with no close female support.

The morning of the masquerade Lady Eldonstone had announced that after luncheon her rooms were to be considered out of bounds to all males.

Phyllida had no idea what to expect, but after half an hour she was convinced that she had strayed into the world of the Arabian Nights. The dressing room was filled with fragrant steam as three baths were prepared, separated by filmy curtains. They wallowed and soaped and scrubbed, then emerged wrapped in towels to have their hair brushed and braided. Once their skin was completely dry, Sara and her mother set to work painting elaborate patterns on palms and feet.

'Will it wash off?' Phyllida surrendered her palm, trying not to flinch as the pen tickled.

'Eventually. It just fades away. This isn't very strong henna.'

Then there was the lengthy process of going through jewellery boxes to select three sets of ornaments. Phyllida tried her best not to gawp at the gold and silver and gems, but she could not resist exclaiming over the set of Burmese sapphires that Lady Eldonstone selected for herself.

'They are very fine, are they not? A bride gift from my uncle, the rajah. Sara, the yellow diamonds for you and for Phyllida, the emeralds, of course.'

'But…Lady Eldonstone, they are far too valuable to lend to me. If I may borrow some bangles and earrings, that would be perfectly adequate, I am sure.'

'You are one of the family, Phyllida, and you will wear the Herriard gems.' Lady Eldonstone quelled her protest with a raised hand. 'It may not be known yet, but you will marry Ashe. Not to dress you accordingly would be to insult you both. Please, humour me in this.'

There was nothing to do but surrender. They ate a light dinner, then, finally, dressed. Phyllida was given sandals to wear, heavy earrings with emerald drops were fixed in her ears, bangles slid up her arms and clasped around her ankles and a gold chain with a single emerald hung around her neck to dip between her breasts. Then the veil was pinned in place over her hair.

'Now you may look,' Sara said, turning her so all three women were reflected in the long pier glass.

'That is not me.' It could not be her, that exotic, bejewelled silken creature with the wide eyes and the curving form.

'Yes, it is,' Sara assured her. 'We would make any maharaja proud, would we not, *Mata*?'

'We would indeed. Now, if this was the women's quarters of the palace we would go and spy on the men through pierced marble screens, move our skirts so our perfume would waft down to tease them, but we must do our best with the staircase.' She handed masks to both young women and slipped on her own. 'Everyone will know who Sara and I are, but you, Phyllida, will be a mystery. Ashe will be so jealous of the admiration you will provoke.'

Phyllida had no doubt Ashe would prove to be exceedingly possessive, but she doubted that his feelings were engaged enough for jealousy, which was a good thing. If he channelled as much energy into anger as he did into passion, he would not be a good man to cross.

'Will they be in the hall?' she asked, wondering how the staircase could give them a secret view of the men.

'Of course,' Lady Eldonstone said with a certain smugness. 'Naturally, we are late.'

They walked to the landing, their sandals making only the softest sound on the carpeted floor. Phyllida found the wide skirts and tight trousers strange and yet liberating to move in. When they reached the banisters Lady Eldonstone put her finger to her lips and leaned over, Sara and Phyllida on either side.

Beneath them, pacing slowly on the marble floor, were the two men. Ashe, his hair loose on his collar, was wearing a golden-brown coat, with tight trousers beneath of bitter orange and a sash of the same colour. As he moved the long line of buttons down the front of the coat glittered gold. Beside him his father wore dark green with black trousers and sash, the spark of green fire from his coat buttons surely that of emeralds.

The marchioness plucked a flower from the vase that stood in an alcove at the stair head and dropped it over the rail. It spun down and landed on the floor between the two men. As one they looked up and smiled and then, in unison, put their hands together as if in prayer and bowed.

'Like this.' Sara showed Phyllida as the ladies turned to go down the stairs. 'We do not curtsy or shake hands. The depth of the bow signifies respect for rank or age.'

It seemed a long way down to the hall and the waiting men. Phyllida hung back to let her companions go first and the marquess came to the foot of the stairs, his hands held out to them.

'How do you manage to look more beautiful every day?' he asked his wife as he bent to kiss her cheek. The emotion just beneath the surface caught at Phyllida. This truly was a love match. 'It is no wonder we have such a lovely daughter.' He smiled at Sara and Phyllida saw he had an emerald stud in his earlobe. 'Miss Hurst. You look—'

'Enchanting,' Ashe finished for him. 'Magical.' Phyllida put her hands carefully together and bowed her head and he did the same, the skin around his eyes creasing as he smiled at her. He had a diamond in his ear and looked, she decided on a wave of longing, indecently glamorous.

'Will we have an armed guard?' she asked, needing to cut the tension that flowed between them. 'We are all wearing the most beautiful gems and jewellery. I imagine we are a footpad's dream come true.'

'We are all armed,' Ashe said.

Of course, he seemed to be able to conceal knives anywhere about his person and his father no doubt did the same. But 'All of you?'

'Naturally. Sara and I have these.' Lady Eldonstone flipped the thick braid of hair over her shoulder and withdrew an ornamental pin that proved to be a long, and probably lethal, skewer. 'Would you like one? I think there is a small one that would be hidden by your hair.'

'Oh, no,' Ashe said. 'You have both been trained to use the things. Phyllida would probably impale a dowager or run an ambassador through, just by turning her head too fast.' He put on his mask and became even more mysteriously exotic. 'I promise to rescue you if you are set upon by footpads.'

Phyllida shivered, partly aroused by the promise in his heavy-lidded gaze, partly in reaction to the potential for violent action in his lean, muscled body.

The carriage was at the door. The marquess began to usher his wife and daughter out, but turned as Ashe said, 'With five of us the ladies' silks will get crushed. I have ordered the chaise and we will follow you.'

'Unchaperoned?' But the marchioness did not appear to find it shocking, or to hear her, and the footman was already closing the door of the larger carriage.

'Do I need a chaperon?' Ashe asked as the chaise drew up.

'Not for you, you wretched man! What if someone sees us arrive?' Phyllida demanded as he handed her in.

'We will be right behind the others, don't fuss so.' He reached forwards and tweaked her veil evenly about her shoulders. 'You are nervous, that is all. Calm down, Phyllida. You look utterly ravishing. No one will know who you are, you can relax and enjoy yourself.'

'Calm down? I am alone in a carriage at night with a man who keeps trying to seduce—I am sorry—*persuade* me to sleep with him. I am laden with a fortune in someone else's gemstones and gold. I am wearing a gorgeous outfit that feels positively indecent for some reason I cannot quite put my finger on and you, you patronising man, you tell me to *calm down*?'

Ashe moved to sit beside her. Phyllida stiffened, but the seat was too narrow to shift away. Through the thin silks the heat of his thigh was like a brand against her skin.

'When I make love to you, Phyllida, neither of us is going to get any sleep,' he promised, his voice like a tiger's purr in the semi-darkness. 'That is a promise. Those clothes feel indecent because wearing them you are more aware of your body and of what your body wants. As for the jewellery, I will protect both you and it.'

'And who is going to protect me against you?' she demanded, trying to keep the quaver out of her voice.

'Why, no one,' Ashe said and lifted her so she was sitting on his thighs. His arms closed around her. 'I want your hands on me, Phyllida. I want to strip those silks from your body and cover it with mine.' She gasped as his mouth found the angle of neck and shoulder and his tongue slid insinuatingly up to the soft skin beneath her ear. 'I want to make love to you until you beg me for mercy.'

They were in a carriage, driving through the streets of Mayfair, minutes away from a crowded ballroom. There was nothing Ashe could do to carry out his threats, his promises, surely? But she wanted him to. With a groan Phyllida ran her hands into the thick silk of his hair and captured his head, holding him as though to prevent the delicious torment his tongue was wreaking ever stopping.

He said something in a language she did not understand, his breath hot, and then his mouth was over hers and she was straining against him, her breasts in the tight bodice aching for his touch, her nipples, without chemise or corset, fretting against the silk lining.

'Ashe. Oh, Ashe, *yes*.'

What she was agreeing to, begging for, she was not sure. If this was madness then she did not care, for tonight they were both mad.

Chapter Seventeen

The jolt of the carriage stopping jerked Phyllida back to reality and sanity. 'I mean, *no*!' she said as she scrambled off Ashe's lap with more haste than dignity.

'Certainly this is neither the time nor the place,' he agreed smoothly as the carriage door opened.

'It will—' The sight of the rest of their party waiting at the foot of the steps choked the words off unuttered. Phyllida fussed with her mask until Ashe was out of the carriage and waiting to hand her down, then descended with a smile fixed on her lips.

Already they were attracting attention. She heard the name *Eldonstone* murmured, saw that the glances from the other guests filing in through the front door were intrigued or approving, and relaxed as much as a woman could do whose heart was pounding, whose knees were knocking and who was mentally castigating herself for an idiot.

If that had happened anywhere but on a short carriage journey, she would have surrendered to Ashe's demands. *Oh, be honest with yourself*, she scolded. *It is not* surrender *and you cannot put all the blame on him.*

You want him, you are simply not strong-willed enough to resist him. Was it inevitable that sooner or later her attraction to Ashe would begin to overcome her fears, her doubts? With the feelings that were growing inside her for him, how could she ever find the strength to deny him?

The great ballroom was already crowded as the Herriard party made its way in. The noise and the conflicting scents and odours and the colour hit Phyllida as a physical blow. She had never been to a masquerade on this scale.

'I almost feel we are back in India,' Lady Eldonstone said with a laugh as a Crusader knight in silver knitted-string chainmail bore down and asked for a dance. 'All this colour and noise! Why, yes, sir, I have this dance free.' And without a backwards glance she stepped on to the floor.

'Curiously liberating, the effects of these masks,' the marquess remarked. 'No introductions, no names. How am I going to keep an eye on our two young ladies?'

'We will use our common sense, Papa,' Sara promised.

'No stepping out on to balconies or the terrace, no little alcoves,' Ashe warned.

'Brother dear, is that what rakes do, lure young ladies into those places?' she asked, all wide-eyed innocence behind her mask.

'It is, as you very well know.'

A tall Pierrott in a skintight costume presented himself in front of Sara. 'Fair damsel, may I have the honour?'

'Lay one wrong finger on her and I'll tear your arm off,' Ashe said pleasantly as his sister took the man's proffered hand. Her partner shot him a startled glance and hastened on to the floor to join a set on the far side.

'May I?' The marquess offered his hand to Phyllida.

'Thank you.'

'Deserted, abandoned,' Ashe said with a heavy sigh.

'You will manage to console yourself, I have no doubt,' Phyllida said sweetly as his father bore her off. She made herself catch his eye and almost gasped. Despite the mock-dramatic tone of his words his expression was not amused, but intense, almost hot. Phyllida followed her partner, feeling as if she had been rescued from a blaze.

Lord Eldonstone was an excellent and amusing partner. Gradually she found herself caught up in the dancing and the atmosphere, swept from one partner to another, relaxing with the anonymity, even though she recognised several familiar faces behind the disguises and was certain she was recognised in turn.

She tried to keep an eye on Sara, but every time she caught a glimpse of her she was behaving just as she ought, dancing in an elegant manner and not romping like some of the young ladies regrettably felt free enough to do. It was hard to miss the Herriards—even in the midst of such vivid and extraordinary costumes and all the jewellery of the *haut ton* they stood out with an exotic glitter. And so did she, she realised as yet another gentleman sought her hand for the dance and she overheard envious whispers from women admiring her costume and gemstones.

And it was bliss to be dancing after so long denying herself the experience. Her feet were beginning to ache, but she did not care. And now it was the waltz, the forbidden dance, the one she had never done in public.

The broad-shouldered Cavalier with the chestnut curls of his wig falling over the velvet of his coat bowed before her. 'Madam, I am honoured that—'

'There you are.' Ashe appeared by her side with a charming smile and more than a whiff of brimstone about him, she could have sworn. His sudden appearance certainly made the other man stiffen. 'Thank you for entertaining my partner, sir, but I must claim her now.'

'But—' The other man eyed Ashe's smile and apparently decided on a strategic retreat. 'My pleasure, sir. Ma'am.'

'That was rude,' Phyllida chided as Ashe took her in his arms.

'It was necessary. Did you see the size of his feet?'

So he was in the mood to jest, was he? It was certainly a relief not to be dealing with his sensual intensity. 'And yours are smaller? And can you waltz? The last time we spoke you had only been having lessons.'

'Simple.' She glanced up at him and realised she was not safe after all. His eyes glinted behind the mask and the smile on his lips was pure sensuality. 'I hold you in my arms and we move together. Rhythmically.'

He was not talking about dancing. Phyllida set her smile into one of bland innocence and pretended not to understand him. 'Excellent. The orchestra is very good, don't you think?'

'When you speak I hear only your voice,' Ashe murmured and swung her into the dance. 'When I breathe I smell only your scent. When I look at a woman I see only you. Do you still believe I am reluctant to marry you?'

'*Ashe.*' He did not mean it, could not, but the dark

honey of his voice, the heat of him so close, the circling strength of his arms, made the passion in the words a physical thing, invading her body, lifting her spirit, bringing tears to her eyes.

They danced as if alone. In silence, in harmony. Phyllida's eyes were closed as though she could trap this moment, hold it, keep it for when she left him and the pretence that they were a couple would be ended for ever.

'Phyllida.'

She blinked and opened her eyes. The music had ceased, couples were chatting as they waited for the orchestra to organise themselves for the next tune of the set. She should chat too, make light social conversation, even flirt a little. But she could not. *I love him*, she thought and swallowed back the tears. *I love him and I could have him. Would it be so wrong of me?*

'Phyllida?' he said again, his voice questioning. 'Am I such a bad dancer?'

'No.' She could have him, but only if she told him the truth, that she might not be able to make love, not fully. Might not be able to give him children.

She found her courage and her voice and laughed. 'You are excellent. But I have longed to waltz and that was magical. Such a beautiful melody, was it not?'

'Beautiful,' he agreed, but his eyes told her it was not the music he was speaking of.

Suddenly shy, Phyllida blinked and looked around. 'What a crush!' On the far side of the room a flash of gold and amber caught her eye. Sara, leaving the ballroom. But the ladies' retiring room was at the other end. 'Ashe, I may be being foolish, but I think Sara just left the room and I can think of no good reason why she should go through that door.'

He turned, frowning, but the glimpse of gilded silk had vanished. 'Are you sure?' But he was already striding off the floor.

Phyllida followed and caught his arm. 'Slowly, do not draw attention.' They reached the door, solidly closed. 'Stand in front and face the room, let me go first, then follow in a minute. The last thing we need is any kind of fuss.'

She opened the door, shielded by Ashe's broad back, and slipped through, to find herself in a narrow passageway. There was light ahead and the sound of voices so she ran along it to where it opened out on to an inner service lobby. She paused, just before the opening. The voices, it became immediately clear, belonged to Sara and the chestnut-haired Cavalier.

'Kindly escort me back to the ballroom, sir. This is not the way to the refreshments and well you know it!'

'Don't pretend you believed that. A little minx like you doesn't parade about, covered in paste jewellery and with her tits hanging out and not expect a man to take an interest.'

'They are yellow diamonds of the finest water, you ignorant oaf. And as for my costume, I would have you know, this is the court dress of Kalatwah!' Sara sounded furious, but not at all alarmed.

'Then let me have a feel—ow!'

Phyllida whipped around the corner to find the Cavalier doubled up, clutching his groin, and Sara pulling the stiletto out of her plait. She tossed the man's elaborate wig aside and tugged off his mask. 'No, put the pin back,' she cautioned Sara. 'I know who he is. It is Lord Prewitt and he is a toad, but we don't want to kill him...'

'Don't we?' Ashe, mask discarded, stalked past Phyllida and seized the gasping Cavalier by his cravat. 'Name your friends, Prewitt.'

'Ashe.' Phyllida tugged at his arm. 'If you call him out, there will be a scandal you won't be able to control.'

He dropped the gasping baron, who fell with a thud and stayed sprawled at his feet. 'You suggest I simply kill him here and now?'

'I suggest you make him very sorry, here and now. Perhaps he would like to apologise first and promise not to say a word of this?'

'Got carried away,' Prewitt gasped. 'Wouldn't dream of mentioning it. Sorry.'

'You will be.' Ashe hoisted him to his feet, waited until the man was standing upright by himself, then hit him square in the mouth. He raised an eyebrow at Sara. 'Enough?'

'Enough,' she agreed. They turned and walked away, back to the ballroom.

In the good light Phyllida saw the girl's face, the unshed tears and the way she bit her lip to stop it trembling. 'Ashe, find your mother, ask her to come to the ladies' retiring room. I think Lady Sara should go home.'

'Of course.'

He vanished into the throng and Phyllida guided Sara down the room, chatting brightly. 'Such a noise, I am not at all surprised you have a migraine. Let us go and sit down quietly.'

'I didn't realise,' Sara whispered miserably. 'I honestly believed he was taking me to the refreshment room.'

'You dealt with him very effectively,' Phyllida consoled her. 'Look, there is your mama.' And Lord Eldonstone, looking like the wrath of God at Ashe's side.

'No harm was done, except to shock her,' she explained as Lady Eldonstone put her arm around Sara's shoulders. 'I do not think anyone has noticed anything amiss and Ashe dealt with the man—he will not dare speak of it.'

'Miss Hurst feels that tearing him limb from limb would be counter-productive,' Ashe said, his voice hard.

'And she is probably correct,' his father agreed. 'Unfortunately. Ashe, will you see Miss Hurst home? I will take your mother and sister now. If some of the party remain, it may quash any speculation.'

Ashe watched them walk away, then took Phyllida's arm and steered her into exactly the kind of alcove that his sister had been warned about finding herself in with a man. 'Are you all right? You were marvellous back there. You dealt with Prewitt, you made Sara feel better, but it must have been a shock.'

'No.' *No, discovering that I am in love with you, that was a shock.* This had all happened so fast that she'd had no time to reflect on just what that realisation would mean, other than that it was certain to be painful. Love him or not, she was not going to marry Ashe Herriard. In fact, loving him made her even more determined. She produced a smile because he was still watching her, his unmasked face serious. 'I am fine, truly, just worried that this might shake Sara's lovely trusting nature.'

'I would have said she was perfectly awake to all the tricks rakes play,' he said ruefully. 'But she is obviously not up to snuff for London society.'

'The unmasking dance!' someone called and the orchestra struck up a waltz.

'Well, Phyllida, shall we be unmasked waltzing in front of everyone? One more step in our public courtship?'

If not here and now, then soon he would move the progress of their wooing further along, push her closer to the moment where she must break her word for his own sake. Break her heart for both of them. And this would give her another perfect waltz in his arms.

'Why not?' she said with a lightness she did not feel. 'It is probably my duty to help you perfect your steps.'

'It was not me treading on my partner's toes,' Ashe said as he resumed his mask and led her onto the floor.

'I never did! What a fib,' Phyllida protested as they passed a small group of matrons, masked and with dominos over their gowns, but otherwise in ordinary evening dress. She saw the quick glances, the exchange of looks, the arched brows and knew she had been recognised, the ineligible Miss Hurst dancing an unsanctioned waltz with the highly eligible Lord Clere. The word had spread that he was courting her, she could tell from the way they were being watched.

It was probably even more entertaining for the gossips than the aborted scandal of their encounter at the inn, for that was an ordinary, squalid piece of tittle-tattle whereas this, if Ashe persisted in his gallant sacrifice, would certainly give the old tabbies something to exclaim over.

'I see we are being watched.' He had noticed them, too.

'I am not surprised. You look quite magnificent in

that attire.' A fact he knew perfectly well, judging by the satirical curve of his mouth.

'Of course. I come from the land of the peacock.' The music began, he took her in hold and launched into the dance.

This time Phyllida kept her eyes open and her wits about her. They might not have been noticed last time, but this time they were definitely under scrutiny. 'There are at least two of the patronesses here,' she said after studying the faces around the edge of the dance floor.

'What can they do?' Ashe asked, executing a particularly ambitious turn. 'Is it like an exorcism and they will stalk onto the floor, sprinkle us with bad claret and pronounce us unfit for Almack's? Or perhaps it will be more military and they will strip off our epaulettes and demote us to the ranks.'

'Idiot!' Phyllida fought the urge to giggle helplessly. 'I think I will just receive the cut direct from them. You, of course, being male and beautiful, will probably be all right.'

'Are you attempting to tease me, Miss Hurst?'

'Me?' She opened her eyes wide at him and he swept her close, far too close for decency, so close that her breasts brushed his chest. Then they were dancing with perfect decorum while she fought to control her breathing and he made unexceptional small talk without the slightest indication of being affected by the woman in his arms.

'Beast,' she muttered. Ashe grinned at her and her heart contracted. She liked this man as much as she loved and desired him. She would adore to be married to him, to have his children, to share the heat and the humour he generated. She had been contented with her

life, accepting of its restrictions, happy with the unconventional freedoms she had created for herself. Now
she felt like a prisoner who had been taken outside the
gates for a while and who must turn and walk back of
her own free will.

The music stopped. All around them partners stayed
close, waiting for midnight. With the first stroke of the
clock Ashe lifted his hand to her mask and she to his.
He bent close and she did not retreat, feeling the heat
of his breath on her lips, watching his eyes, green and
mysterious, still shadowed by the black velvet.

Then the last stroke and he pulled her closer as they
took away their masks. He would kiss her now, in front
of everyone. Claim her. Phyllida held her breath as they
stood like statues in the middle of laughter, cries of
recognition and a pattering of applause as their fellow
guests were unmasked.

'Breathe,' Ashe murmured and stepped back, lifted
her hand in his and kissed her fingertips. 'I am not going
to create *that* much of a stir tonight.'

The party was obviously set to continue into the
small hours. Ashe took Phyllida to find their hostess
and thank her. 'A delightful ball, Lady Auderley. I regret that my parents were unable to take their leave of
you, but my sister developed a severe migraine and had
to return home.'

Her ladyship was gracious, offered sympathy for
Sara's malaise and smiled, only slightly maliciously,
at Phyllida. 'You look delightful, my dear. So many
people have commented on how striking you and Lord
Clere look together.'

'Thank you, ma'am.' Phyllida smiled back modestly.
'But I must thank Lady Eldonstone for kindly lending

me this beautiful costume and her jewellery.' *Remind her she is dealing with the patronage of a marchioness.*

'So gracious of her,' the older woman replied. 'I hope we will have the pleasure of entertaining you here again.'

Phyllida waited until they were back in the carriage before she finally made up her mind. 'Ashe, I must speak with you, tonight.'

As the carriage moved off the flickering torchlight played across his face and she saw he understood her to mean more than speech. 'We will go to the apartment over the shop,' she said and pulled the warm velvet cloak more firmly around her shoulders. 'We will be private there.'

Chapter Eighteen

At last. Ashe said nothing, only pulled the check-string and leaned out of the carriage window. 'Drop us off at the top of Haymarket, we will walk. Tell the staff to lock up and leave the front door locked, but unbolted. They can all go to bed.'

He pulled up the window as they moved off again. Phyllida looked pale, but it was probably only the effect of the heavy shadows. So, she had decided to stop resisting and come to him, to accept that the marriage was inevitable. His body was already primed, heavy with desire, his blood hot with the aftermath of the encounter with Prewitt, the exhilaration of the dances with Phyllida. But there was something more than the prospect of satisfying his desires, of securing her acceptance. Somewhere along the line he had developed feelings that ran deep for this provoking, secretive, unusual woman.

'You have made a decision?' he asked, wondering at the nerves that made him suddenly short of breath.

She raised her head from her contemplation of her clasped hands and said, 'Yes.'

For such a firm syllable it sounded anxious. Nerves, too, no doubt, Ashe thought, deliberately making no move to touch her. He wrestled, briefly, with his conscience. He ought to take her home, send her up to bed with a chaste kiss on the cheek. But instinct was telling him to make certain of her. If she gave herself to him, then she would be committed to this marriage.

It was only a short drive. The carriage pulled up and he helped her down, sheltering her with his body from the bustle that still crowded the pavement. The crowd that was out here, at this time, was no company for a lady. Several women caught his eye and threw out unsubtle lures. They were not called Haymarket Ware for nothing and this was their prime hunting ground as he had learned, very early in his night-time explorations of this new city.

'I should have told them to turn into Jermyn Street,' he said. 'I had forgotten about the quantity of whores that infest this area.' Against his protective arm he felt her flinch. Presumably her forays into the East End had all been in daylight and she had not seen the worst of it, or perhaps the poor drabs who serviced the slums were less brazen and gaudy.

'It doesn't matter,' Phyllida said. 'It was more discreet. Besides, we are almost there.' They turned into Jermyn Street, passing the shutters of the numerous luxury shops, the pavement dimly lit by the light from the apartments above. 'These are mostly lodgings and chambers for gentlemen,' she explained. 'I had thought of doing up the rooms above my shop and renting them out, but I find them valuable for sorting stock.'

He bit back the comment that she could let them out

along with the shop once they were married or sell the lot. Something told him that giving up her business was not going to be easy for Phyllida.

'And last year, when Gregory and I seemed to be arguing about his gambling and parties the whole time, they made a peaceful refuge,' she admitted.

'He has settled down now, with a vengeance.'

'I know. I hardly believed it at first. He said he looked in the mirror, realised he wasn't getting any younger and began to think about what he was doing with his life. He met Harriet at just the right moment and what is so wonderful is that they truly seem to be in love.'

'You had no hopes of that when you were looking for a rich wife for him, though. Why are you so pleased about it now?' A group of young bucks, more than a trifle top-heavy after an evening at their club, were weaving along the pavement towards them. Ashe moved Phyllida into a doorway and stood in front of her.

One of them stopped. 'Hey, look, it's Clere! Come and join us, we're off to find some company, if you know what I mean!' He roared with laughter at his feeble sally, then peered past Ashe into the shadowed alcove. 'Ah, see you've got your own. Good man!'

'Another night, perhaps, Grover,' Ashe said, forcing joviality into his voice.

They reeled off down the road, waving and shouting advice as they went.

'I am sorry about that.' He handed Phyllida down the step again.

'Perhaps every lady should be taken out to the Haymarket at night at least once to see what gentlemen are truly like.' There was an edge to her voice that puzzled him.

'I am not given to rampaging drunkenly through the streets seeking out cheap whores, if that is what you mean.'

'I am sure you are far subtler and have much more expensive tastes,' she responded politely.

'That was not what I meant. I do not court a lady I am not faithful to, nor would I marry one and keep a mistress.'

'Oh.' Then, more softly, *'Oh.'*

Ashe looked sharply at Phyllida, but her face was unreadable in the shadows. Surely that little exclamation had not been one of dismay? Surely no woman *wanted* her husband to take a mistress?

'Down here,' she said, turning into an alleyway before he could put the question into words. She led him into a yard and up to what must be the back door of the shop. 'Wait while I get the key.' She bent, there was a scrape of brick on stone, then she straightened with the key in her hand. 'Ugh. I hide the spare behind a loose brick and I encourage a nice slimy puddle just in front of it to help keep it safe.'

She let him in, shaking her fingers fastidiously as she did so, but turned before the inner doorway and led the way up a narrow flight of stairs and into a room that covered, Ashe estimated, the whole area of the shop below.

'There is a tinderbox on that table. Can you light the candle? I always fumble for ages with it and end up breaking a nail.' Phyllida went to close the curtains and then fidgeted about the room, her jewellery and the golden embroidery on her clothing making her look like an exotic moth in the gloom.

Lord, but she is nervous, Ashe thought as he struck a

spark and nursed the wick into flame. He must be very, very careful, gentle, this first time for her.

The wick flared up and he touched it to the other candles around the room. It was not the bleak storeroom he had feared it might be, but a strangely practical, very feminine den. The walls were hung with tapestries, tattered and worn, but rich with shades of old rose and blue and gold. The curtains at the window were deep-red velvet, obviously salvaged from some grand suite of bed hangings. His feet sank into carpets, spread to overlap and cover the wear and holes.

There was a desk and chair, a deep armchair, a day-bed and a bookcase overflowing with books. 'This is a beautiful room,' he said. 'It reminds me of chambers in my great-uncle's palace, snug, private little caves of luxury.'

'The luxury is threadbare and not all it seems. Few things are what they seem.' There was that bitter note in her voice again, as though she was mocking herself.

'Phyllida, what is wrong? You know I would never force you. It would make me very happy to make love to you here, but if you want to leave, I understand.' Ashe pulled out the desk chair and sat down. Not a gentlemanly thing to do when a lady was still standing, but he did not want to loom over her.

'I need to tell you something.' She sat down on the end of the daybed with an inelegant thump as though her legs would not hold her up any longer. 'You will not wish to marry me once you hear what it is.'

'That I very much doubt,' Ashe said robustly, even as he tried to ignore the stab of apprehension in his gut. *Debts, that was all, nothing to worry about there.*

Phyllida stood up again and this time he rose too,

something in her face warning him that she was serious. Whatever this was, she was not exaggerating its importance to her.

'I am not a virgin,' she said, as though pleading guilty in a court of law.

Ashe blinked. That was not so bad. 'Neither am I, oddly enough.'

Her lips thinned. 'Men appear to set much value on virginity.'

'Are you still involved with him? Am I likely to meet him?' She shook her head vehemently. 'Then, if you can refrain from comparisons which would wound my pride, I do not see it as a problem.' As soon as he said it, he saw the attempt to introduce some humour into the exchange was a mistake.

'Hardly! You do not understand, and I am not explaining it properly.'

'Was there a child?' Ashe struggled to understand, to read the messages her voice, her rigid body, were sending him. He tried to take her hands, but she batted his away.

'No, thank God.'

And then he realised. 'Phyllida. Were you unwilling? *Mere jaan.' My darling.* He caught her in his arms, held on to her despite her attempts to twist free, cradled her against his chest until she stilled and let her head rest against his breast. *'Sahji, jaani.'* He murmured the love-words as he stroked her hair. 'Tell me who it is and I will bring you his heart and his manhood on a platter.'

'It was a long time ago. When I was seventeen,' she said, her voice so low he could hardly make out the words.

Worse and worse, if anything could make it so. So young, so innocent.

Phyllida straightened. 'Let me go, please. I...' He opened his arms and she sat down again, her hands tightly clasped. 'You sit down too, Ashe. I told you because you had a right to know and because I do not think I can make love, not without it all coming back, not without panicking. I am sorry I let you believe that was what I asked you here for tonight.'

He sought for the words to say this right. 'When I kiss you, you respond, Phyllida. In the carriage, when I caressed your breast, that was not feigned, the fire I felt in you. When that man attacked you, hurt you, it would have been nothing like making love with someone who cares for you.'

'I don't... I cannot marry you, not knowing if I can bear that part of it. I should have told you at once, when you proposed this marriage.'

'You did not know me very well. Now, I think, you trust me rather more.' It was not a question, but she nodded. 'You know I would never force you, Phyllida.' That time he did want a response and steeled himself for her hesitation. He had been a rogue, to put it at its lowest. He had done his best to persuade her into his bed, despite her reluctance. Then it had almost been a game, now he was not certain he could forgive himself.

'Of course I know.' She seemed startled that he had to ask and, as she looked at him, her unhappy face softened into a smile of such tenderness that his heart melted. 'But it might come to that, or not have children.'

Ashe got up and walked to the window, needing to move while he absorbed that realisation. An heir. The son to whom he would hand the estate that would be saved from decline, the title he would one day hold. The daughters, the other sons. He had never given them any thought, except in the abstract. Suddenly they were tangible, ghost children who might never become real.

'Then I will abandon persuasion for seduction,' he said. 'We know I can kiss you, hold you, even caress you a little and you are not afraid. It was a terrible wound, but it was not fatal—you will heal with the right medicine. We will take all the time it needs and you will be in control.' He knew he sounded confident. Inside he was unsure, but determined. He had committed himself to this woman and he was not going to abandon her now. Ashe walked back and hunkered down in front of her, took her hands. 'Will you think about it?'

'I will not marry you unless...' She took a deep breath and looked at him. 'I have never been with any other man, you understand, so I do not know if I would be able to make love. I might be creating a problem that does not exist.'

'No one would be unaffected by such cruelty,' Ashe said. 'But if you learn that making love has nothing to do with what happened, then I believe you will be able to separate the two.'

She nodded. 'I did not expect you to be so understanding. I did not know how to tell you, although I knew I had to.'

This was what had been behind the ambiguity he had sensed in her agreement to marry him. She had not decided if she could tell him of this and, being a woman of honour, would not marry him unless she did.

Phyllida leaned forwards and linked her hands behind his neck. 'Shall we try? Make love to me, Ashe.'

He did not answer, simply letting her pull him closer

until he could caress her mouth with his, gently, deeply, increasing the demands of his tongue as she began to melt against him. He pushed just a little ahead of her tentative responses until he felt her relax entirely, begin to tease him a little with nips and sucks and the wandering caresses of her fingers at his nape.

Ashe eased back and unbuttoned his coat, let it fall to the ground, then took her in his arms again and kissed her while his fingers dealt with the fastenings at the front of her tight jacket. She did not resist when he slid it from her shoulders to reveal the swell of her bosom above the constriction of the *choli*, so he kissed across the creamy skin while his fingers caressed her bare midriff.

If she would relax a little he could ease her back on to the daybed, but there was still a tension in her that warned him that might be a step too far. How could he reassure her?

He lay down himself, on his back, and smiled up at her. After a moment she gave a little nod, as though she understood, and bent to kiss him. She was endearingly clumsy, he thought, then realised with a shock when she changed the angle of her mouth and her position on the bed that his reaction was, to put it mildly, patronising. She was thinking too hard, but she was working out what pleased her and, he realised as he fisted his hands in the covers to stop himself grabbing her, she was working out what pleased him at the same time.

Her hand brushed his right nipple, almost certainly by accident, but he was so tense that the sensation shook a groan out of him.

'Ashe?' Phyllida's eyes were wide and dark in the candlelight. 'Did I hurt you?'

'No,' he lied. This was exquisite torture.

'Don't you want to get on top of me?' she worried.

Yes. 'No,' he lied again. He could hear the fear threading through her voice. That bastard would have thrown her down, crushed her with his weight, trapped her. Somehow he had to let her feel in control, as if she could escape at any moment.

'Do you like it when I do this?' He cupped her breasts boldly, let his thumbs find the nipples tight under the silk.

'Oh, yes.' Her lids drooped, her lips parted in a sensual sigh that had his already-hard body almost arching off the bed. He found the ties at the waist of her skirt and loosened them until he could slip his fingers down over the curve of her belly. The delicate skin shivered and twitched to his touch, but she did not fight him. 'Ashe, I...*ache.*'

'Good.' He tugged gently to bring her down to lie beside him and buried his face in the angle of her neck, filled his senses with jasmine and the betraying scent of her arousal. *Slowly*, he told himself. *So slowly.* 'Will you let me pleasure you?'

'How?' She stiffened, curled away from him. 'You won't—'

'No. I won't move from lying here beside you. Just let me touch you.'

He could feel the effort it took her to trust him, to let him brush the nest of curls, to ease one finger between the soft, damp folds. He found what he sought and stroked, just *there*, as her hips came off the bed with the shock of it.

'Ashe!' Phyllida had expected discomfort. Whatever a man did there, however gentle, would hurt, surely? But the shaft of sudden, shocking pleasure lanced through her as if a lightning flash had run from his fingertip to her womb, to her breasts, to every quivering nerve in her body.

'Priya,' he said, his voice husky. 'Sweetheart. Just let go, allow yourself pleasure.'

Allow? She twisted, frantic with not knowing how to deal with the onslaught of delight when she had expected pain, out of control in a way she had never imagined, overcome by her own body's reactions, not his strength. She was aching and needing only the heat of Ashe's body next to her, his arm holding her safe, his wicked, wicked fingers driving her insane.

'I don't know how,' she gasped.

'Let go,' he repeated. 'Your body knows.' And he kissed her and suddenly the pleasure peaked into an almost-pain that made her cry out against his mouth, arch her body hard into his hand to make it last for ever and then she lost herself, utterly, as she clung to him, knowing she was dying, not caring.

'Phyllida?' Ashe's voice, soft and dark as the caress of black velvet, as sensual as sin, as gentle as... *the man I love.*

'What happened?' She was still lying beside him on the daybed. In his embrace, still dressed, although her clothing was disordered. Her body thrummed with a deep, sensual relaxation and quivered with tiny aftershocks of pleasure.

'That was an orgasm.'

She blushed. She knew the word, had even looked it up in a dictionary. 'But that is something men experience.'

'Both partners in lovemaking can experience it.'

He pulled her close, shifting her position so her cheek rested comfortably on his chest.

'But you did not.'

'No. I can wait.'

Phyllida looked down his body. He was clearly aroused. It hurt men to be in that condition and frustrated, she had heard that somewhere. 'Can you?' She put her hand on the hard ridge, the thought of which had so frightened her, and he gasped. She had the power to make Ashe groan, to arch into her hand as though begging her. If he could give her pleasure with a touch, could she do the same for him?

'Let me.' Before Ashe could protest she tugged at the ties of his trousers, slid her hand inside. She had expected the hardness, the heat. She had not realised the skin would be soft, that it would be so sensitive that it seemed to grow as she closed her fingers around it.

She was clumsy, she knew that. Clumsy and shy, but not afraid of him, or of what she was doing. After a moment of resistance Ashe fell back on the bed and let her have her way with him. He moved into her hand, showing her the rhythm he needed, giving her the confidence that she was not hurting him and she could be firmer, bolder. He gasped, his body arched, he thrust hard into her circling fingers and then fell back on the bed as the heat flooded over her fingers.

Phyllida curled into his body, loving the total relaxation, the musky scent, the way the feel of him changed in her hand as his body calmed. After a minute his arm tightened around her and he pulled her close so he could kiss her. 'I'm sorry, sweetheart, that must have shocked you,' he murmured.

'I liked it,' she mumbled into his shirt front, too shy

to meet his eyes. 'Ashe, I think it might be all right after all. When we do it properly, I mean.'

'That *was* properly,' he said and sat up. 'There are all kinds of ways to make love—think of a banquet, lots of dishes. Some great solid roasts, some sweet fluffy concoctions, some rather sinfully sweet, others dangerously spicy.'

He was on his feet, investigating behind a screen. 'Is there water in this ewer? Yes, rather dusty, very cold, but it will do. And a towel.' There was the sound of splashing behind the screen. Phyllida sat up and pulled the coverlet over her bare toes.

'Ashe, do you want to do it again?' That had been wonderful beyond words and the relief of knowing that she could lie in a man's arms, be intimate with him and enjoy the experience, was huge. But whatever Ashe said, sooner or later sex would involve the same act that had taken place in the tawdry room in the Wapping brothel, the act that had taken her virginity. The act she had been paid for by Harry Buck.

Chapter Nineteen

What she had done would brand Phyllida a whore. Any man would say so, she knew that. She had allowed Ashe to think she had been forced, when in fact she had taken money, removed her clothes, lain on that bed and had done nothing to resist. The fact that if she had not then she would have starved, that she needed the money to find her father, to make him come back, or give her enough money to get food and medicine for her mother, food and shelter for all of them, did not alter the fact of the transaction that had removed her claim to be a woman of honour.

It made her angry, that double standard, but that was the way things were. And if she had to do it again, if someone's life depended on it, if Gregory was in trouble and it was the only way to save him, then she would sell herself again without hesitation. Her screams, she had learned in the course of that one bitter night, would only fuel the excitement of the man taking her.

'I only used half the water.' Ashe emerged from behind the screen. 'Do it again? I would like to very much, but not tonight. And the next time, then we will talk about what other dishes on the menu you would like to sample. You choose what we do, when we do it. The control is yours. There is no need to rush anything.'

She shot him a look of gratitude as she passed him, then went to tidy herself. No wonder she loved him. His past had not, she guessed, been blameless—she recalled the amusement with which he had told her he was not a virgin—but he was a decent, honourable man and she was thinking about deceiving him about something he would believe touched on that honour.

Phyllida wrestled with her conscience. She had not meant to make love when she had asked him here, only to confess that she was not a virgin. Ashe's closeness, his response, had overset all her scruples, swept away everything but the desire to be in his arms.

Now she knew how wrong, how weak, that had been. Ashe wanted to marry her out of honour. There were many reasons why she was the wrong bride for him and Ashe believed he knew them all and could make it work despite them. He admitted he was attracted to her. He even knew now that she was not a virgin. His parents and sister seemed to like her and were prepared to welcome her into their family. The benefits to her and to Gregory were too numerous to name.

I love him and I had let myself dream I could marry him. Ashe and love and children. Ashe for as long as we lived.

So, temptation murmured, *do not tell him the truth. How would he be harmed by the secret?*

But shouldn't a marriage be based on honesty and truth? Phyllida argued back as she fiddled with the ties on her skirt and trousers, reluctant to emerge until she had come to some conclusion. If she did not love him, she suspected it would be much easier—never mention her past. But she did love him and so she felt compelled to tell him. If he reacted badly—and what man wouldn't?—she would have lost him for ever.

But I should not be marrying him in any case, she reminded herself with bitter realism. *Marriage is a dream, happiness with Ashe is a dream. Those children will never be born.* Phyllida leaned back against the wall, her hand pressed to her mouth to stifle the sobs that seemed to come from nowhere.

Oh, Ashe, my love. She should never have spoken of children, never have let him be so certain she would marry him. Now, even though he did not love her, she would hurt *him*, not just his pride, when she broke this off.

'Are you all right?' Ashe did not sound impatient.

'Yes.' She found her voice and managed to strike a light note. 'I must admit to feeling a trifle bemused,' Phyllida admitted. Ashe chuckled. He had made her dizzy with his lovemaking. Perhaps that was why it was so difficult to think clearly and logically, to resolve to end this here and now. They were going to make love again, she knew that. It was as inevitable as sunrise.

'Ashe, what is the time?' She made herself come out from behind the screen. It was hard to meet his eyes, although she felt warm and safe with him. Her guilty conscience, she supposed.

'Three. Time to go home. Here is your jacket.' He held it out to her, then stopped and touched one finger to the top of her left breast. 'What is that? A birthmark? I meant to ask when you took off your jacket, but I became...distracted.'

'Yes.' Phyllida squinted down to where his finger

traced the coffee-brown mark the size of a strawberry. 'Luckily it is towards the side so, if I am careful, the bodice of a gown covers it.'

'But why would you want to hide it?' Ashe helped her into the jacket. 'It is a perfect heart. Charming.'

'It is a blemish.'

'Nonsense. It looks fascinating on your white skin, tantalising. Promise me you will not cover it up any more.' He bent and kissed it, then pulled her sides of the jacket together and began to do up the tiny buttons.

'Very well.' It would not be a problem, not with her evening and half-dress gowns and if Ashe liked it she was too flattered to resist. She would only need to remove some of the trim or turn under the edge of the bodice. There were a few days left before she had to end this. In day gowns, with their higher necklines, it would never show in any case.

'Ashe, stop that or we will never get back!' He laughed and ceased tickling between the button holes.

'Come along then. Before you tempt me unbearably.'

Phyllida was sitting sewing with Sara the next afternoon when Gregory called. Lady Eldonstone had insisted that she sit down and rest after a morning supervising the despatch of crates to the auction house and it had seemed a good time to alter the neckline of some of her evening gowns so that the heart-shaped birthmark could be seen.

The lack of logic in doing something that could only inflame Ashe's enthusiasm for lovemaking, and entangle her even more in the deception she was caught in, did not escape her. It was as though she was two people: one sensible, honest Phyllida who should be cold-bloodedly planning the break with Ashe for his own good, the other a dizzy girl in love who could not think beyond the next moment in his arms.

Sara rang for refreshments and Gregory sat down, all long legs, tight pantaloons and gleaming Hessians. 'You are the picture of a perfect London gentleman,' Phyllida teased him. 'So neat and tidy and respectable-looking. And such a smart new crop!'

He grinned at her good-naturedly. 'Harriet likes it. Which brings me to why I am here. You and I have been invited to a family dinner party tomorrow evening, I'm afraid.'

'Afraid? But I thought you got on very well with Harriet's family.'

'I do, but a long-lost uncle has appeared back in town. He's Mrs Millington's brother and a bit of a black sheep, apparently. He's been safely off in Jamaica working as a land agent or some such thing and I suspect they all hoped he'd stay there. Anyway, we've been invited to dilute the family tensions a bit, I suspect. There's a couple of cousins and a great-aunt coming as well.'

'It will be very awkward if he decides to stay, won't it? Or perhaps he has reformed,' Sara remarked. 'Would you care to pour yourself a glass of sherry or Madeira, Lord Fransham?'

'Thanks, I will. Millington was all for showing him the door, apparently, but Mrs M. wants to give him another chance, hence the dinner party.' Gregory went to the decanters while Sara poured tea.

'I will have to ask Lady Eldonstone if it would be convenient. She may have plans for the evening,' Phyllida said. It sounded an awkward situation, but if she could help the Millingtons, she would. Everything was back on course for the wedding and she felt nothing but gratitude to them for their tolerance.

'We aren't doing anything tomorrow night,' Sara said. 'I know because Papa is going to a lecture at the Royal Society and Mama said this morning that it would be good to have an evening at home recovering from all our gadding about.'

Phyllida asked her hostess's leave and, when her brother had gone, went back to removing the lace from the neckline of her dark-green dinner gown. That would do nicely for the Millingtons' dinner. It was a little formal, perhaps, but formality was sometimes a help in sticky social situations.

Ashe was rather less obliging about her plans than the marchioness. 'I had hoped to spend the evening with you in Jermyn Street,' he murmured in her ear later.

'I wish we were,' Phyllida whispered back under cover of a singularly dreary piano sonata. Lady Eldonstone had insisted on attending a musicale that evening. 'I will miss you.'

At seven o'clock the next evening Phyllida emerged from the Eldonstones' carriage outside the Millingtons' house.

She mentally squared her shoulders for a fraught dinner party and wished Ashe was with her. Gregory was concerned for Harriet and she suspected that she would have to spend the time making vacuous small talk to the other relatives, all bristling with disapproval over the return of Mr Phillip Wilmott.

'Oh, do wait a moment, ma'am, that cloak isn't quite fastened.' The maid Lady Eldonstone had lent her was poised in the carriage doorway just as a dark figure strode out of the shadows into the pool of light cast by the door lantern. 'Here, take care, you!'

The man barged into Phyllida, pushing her back against the carriage. *A footpad, so brazen, to attack right on a Mayfair doorstep?* Too shocked to feel fear, she grasped her reticule, ready to strike out at him. The cloak slithered off her shoulders to the ground.

For a moment she thought him a stranger, then, as the light caught his face, she knew him. *Harry Buck.*

''Ello, darling,' he said on a coarse chuckle. 'Thought there was something familiar about you.' She flinched as his eyes went from her face to her bosom exposed by the plain, low neckline of her newly altered gown. 'I remember that. Thought I couldn't be wrong.' Her hand flew to the birthmark, but it was too late, he had seen it.

The maid was screaming for help, the front door flew open as the driver swung down from the box seat, whip in hand. Buck vanished, as abruptly as he had come.

If the carriage door had not been under her hand, she would have fallen, for all the strength seemed to have vanished from her legs. It was her worst nightmare made real. Harry Buck, the man who had bought her virginity, had recognised her, tracked her down.

And then, just as she thought she would faint, the butler was hurrying down the steps. 'Miss Hurst! Are you all right?

Phyllida forced herself to stand straight and think. 'Yes. He must have been drunk. Most unpleasant, but no harm done. Please do not alarm Mrs Millington by saying anything.'

Somehow she reached the house, was announced, greeted. Somehow she managed to get to a sofa and sit before her legs gave way. Apparently her horror and fear were not imprinted on her face, for no one paid her any heed, other than to introduce her to the dubious relative, Mr Wilmott. She kept her face rigidly expressionless and inclined her head, hoping Mrs Millington would simply think her shy in the presence of an acknowledged black sheep.

Mrs Millington had abandoned all correct form for her table setting, apparently anxious to separate the young ladies from her brother. Phyllida found herself making conversation on one side to an elderly cousin who turned out to be a stockbroker and on the other to Mr Millington. She must have made some sense in what she was saying, and apparently she ate and drank in a normal manner, for no one asked her if she was all right.

On sheer will-power she got through the endless meal and back to the drawing room. Gregory, in a brave attempt to support his future in-laws, engaged Wilmott in conversation. Phyllida felt fainter and fainter until eventually she could not stand it any longer. She got up and went to Gregory's side. 'Gregory, I am sorry, but I think I must go back now.'

'Yes, of course. I'll just say goodnight to Harriet.'

She turned on her heel and almost fled to Mrs Millington. 'I am so sorry, ma'am, but I have such a headache. Would you think me very rude if Gregory took me home? I am sorry to drag him away, but—'

'My dear, I will send for your carriage at once.' Fussed over, wrapped up, Phyllida drove back through the darkened streets, shaking with horror.

Ashe was crossing the hallway as she came in, a book in his hand. He grinned at her. 'Good evening. Was it as sticky an evening as your brother feared?'

'Worse.' She looked at him standing there. The man she loved, her lover. The man who still intended to marry her because she had been too weak to end this when she should have done. 'Ashe, I must speak with you.'

'Of course.' He opened the door of the library for her. 'There is no one else at home. What is wrong?'

'I cannot marry you.' As soon as she said it she knew she was right and she should have refused from the first. Now Buck had recognised her she knew she dare not marry and try to keep this a secret from Ashe.

She could not tell him what she had done, could not bear to see his expression change, the liking and the desire ebb away to be replaced by revulsion when he discovered she had not been the victim of some predatory man but had deliberately sold herself. Made herself a whore. She had heard him speak of those Haymarket whores, knew what he, what any man, would think of a woman who did what she had done.

She would have to do what she had always planned once Gregory was settled: leave London altogether and retire to the Dower House.

Ashe became very still as he stood in front of the cold grate. Then he put down the book he had been holding. 'Why not? Is it because of what you told me the other night? Or what happened between us?'

'No,' she lied. 'I was wrong to accept your plan to rescue me from the scandal. I only agreed thinking I would refuse in the end, but I allowed myself to become…more involved than I intended. I can see there is no need for you to protect me any more. The gossip has died down, no one will be the slightest bit surprised if your interest in me wanes. We are completely unsuited to each other and it is foolish to condemn ourselves to a lifetime of an indifferent marriage.'

'Unsuited and indifferent. I see. I had not realised I could be so wrong in my perceptions of either my own feelings or of yours.' He looked as though he was listening to a dry political speech, his face a mask of concentration with no emotion to be seen. 'So making love with me was a way of overcoming your fears?'

'The bad memories. Yes,' she agreed. If he believed she was simply using him, then he would be less inclined to fight, more convinced that he must not marry her.

'I am happy to have been of use.' He raised his eyes to her face and she saw with a shock just how angry he was. Angry, rigidly controlled and dangerous because of it. If she had been a man and had made him this furious he would have struck her, she realised, but she felt no fear, just total misery. Ashe would not hurt her even though he thought she had used him, used his body, in a calculated attempt to deal with her nightmares.

'I will go home first thing in the morning,' she said, striving for a control to match his. 'I will explain to Lady Eldonstone that I realised we would not suit. She can only be relieved.'

'She will be disappointed to have been mistaken in you,' he said. 'As I am.'

'I did warn you, right from the start, that I am unsuitable for you.' Best to make certain, to sever the fragile bond that had grown between them out of desire and liking and what she knew, on her part, to be love. But Ashe did not love her, thank God. He would not fight for her beyond all reason.

'But you had to be noble about it, had to do the honourable thing, even if that overrode your duty to your family,' she added with the intention of throwing oil on the flames.

It worked. Ashe stalked forwards as she retreated before him, until she was backed up against the door with nowhere to go. 'Attempting to do the honourable thing is part and parcel of my duty to my family, to my name,' he ground out. 'And I had thought that I had found a woman worthy of that name, one who would stand by me and my family and fight to bring it, and the lands, back to where they should be. I was wrong.'

He stood back and Phyllida turned before he would see the tears or read in her eyes that her heart was breaking. She left the room without a word and climbed the stairs to her bedchamber. Some foolish part of her was straining to hear the door open behind her, Ashe's voice calling her back. But, of course, it did not happen.

It was quite extraordinary, how much a breaking heart hurt, Phyllida thought as she stood passive while the maid unpinned her hair and removed her gown. Mama, loving foolishly and too well, had died of a broken heart. Her daughter was not going to have even that release, she was going to have to live with the wounds for the rest of her life.

Chapter Twenty

Lady Eldonstone was kind and regretful and exceedingly courteous when Phyllida made her difficult confession that she did not think she and Ashe were suited and that it would be best if they did not meet again. Phyllida was certain that beneath the tranquil poise the older woman was concealing considerable anger that her son was being spurned by someone who had every reason to be grateful to him.

She took herself off before breakfast, back to Great Ryder Street and the news that Gregory was staying with the Millingtons for a few days, presumably to bolster the family while they decided what to do about the return of their prodigal relative.

'You all right, Miss Phyllida?' Anna asked, peering closely at her as she took her valise. 'You look as if you've been awake half the night crying.'

'Nonsense, of course not.' *Just all night, alternating between tears and frozen indecision. What to do? Where to run?* 'I have got a cold coming or something, that is all.'

'I'll make you up my remedy,' the maid said. 'Oh,

and there's a letter for you. I was just about to get Perkin's boy to take it over to you.'

Phyllida picked it up. Not a hand she recognised, ordinary paper, thick, clumsy writing. She trailed into the drawing room and sat down, opened it with no curiosity. A bill, she supposed.

A large engraved card fluttered out and she picked it up from the floor.

Mr Harry Buck's House of Pleasures for the Discerning Gentleman.

Below that was printed in the heavy black handwriting. *Three o'clock this afternoon. Come back to work. Don't be late. I'll need a little sweetener to keep this secret all to myself.*

Phyllida dropped the card as though it had moved in her hand. It lay at her feet, as dangerous as an adder. Overcome by nausea, she staggered to a bowl on a side table and was violently sick.

'Lord love us! What's the matter now?' It was Anna, fussing and anxious.

Phyllida closed her eyes and dragged her hand across her mouth. 'Don't know, something I ate perhaps. I'm sorry, I'll wash the bowl, you shouldn't have to.' In a minute, when she could think, when she had stopped shaking.

'Nonsense. You come up to bed now, my lamb, and I'll send for the doctor and his lordship.'

'No! Not Lord Clere!'

'Your brother, I meant. Now come along, you lean on me.'

'All right. Thank you, Anna. Don't send for the doctor, I will be all right presently. And don't worry Gregory, Miss Millington needs him. But I will lie down for a while, then I have to go out this afternoon.'

'In this state? You'll do no such thing, Miss Phyllida. It's bed for you.'

Ashe ate his breakfast wearing his best diplomatic face while his family pretended valiantly that nothing was wrong, that they'd never had a houseguest and that they were not desperate to know just how affected he was by Phyllida's defection.

He then strode off to Brooks's club, mentally kicking himself when he realised he was averting his eyes from the turning off St James's Street into Jermyn Street.

He already knew enough members to make negotiating the entrance hall and finding a quiet corner to bury himself behind a newspaper a trial, but the club was used to gentlemen seeking peace and quiet after a hard night and no one seemed offended by his curt nods of greeting.

The newsprint swam in front of his eyes, the words meant nothing. *Damn the woman.* He had lost a night's sleep alternating between anger and aching arousal.

Phyllida didn't want him, she thought marriage to him would be a life sentence to unhappiness and she didn't even desire him. Their love-making had simply been an exercise in getting over a traumatic incident in her past.

It was only hurt pride, of course, this sick ache inside. That and unsatisfied lust. He had been used. Used to get her out of a scandal, used to conquer her fears, and now she no longer needed him so she simply walked away. It seemed that her disinclination to marry him overcame his title, his wealth and his prospects.

Ashe folded the newspaper with savage precision and slapped it down on the table beside him. He needed to hit someone. He didn't care if they hit him back, he just needed the outlet of violence.

A waiter came at the crook of his finger. 'Are there any boxing salons near here?'

'Yes, my lord. Quite a few. Gentleman Jackson's is the prime one, of course. I'll give you the direction, shall I, my lord? Or any cabby will take you there.'

'I'll walk.' Ashe took the slip of paper and gave the man a coin. 'Thank you.'

He spent an hour pounding hell out of a punch bag, then sparred with one of Jackson's assistants, the great man being booked for the day. It was some help, the ache of the bruises where punches had landed were a distraction from the internal ache. He ate a hot pie and drank porter in the Red Lion down an alleyway off Pall Mall, making himself focus on the taste and texture of the food as he had on the mechanics of the bout he had fought.

When he had finished he walked north with no fixed idea of where to go, just needing to move.

'My lord!'

He stopped dead and turned. A woman in a plain gown and cloak was hailing him. A maid by the look of her. Then he saw it was Anna, Phyllida's woman.

'Oh, my lord, I was coming to find you.' She panted to a halt beside him. 'Then I saw you cross St James's Square...'

Ashe looked around him and found he was almost in Haymarket. 'What do you want?' he asked curtly.

'It's Miss Phyllida. She came home this morning

looking as if she'd been crying her eyes out, but she said it was just a cold coming on. Then she'd no sooner opened her post than she was casting up her accounts and shaking like a leaf.

'I got her to bed, but she said she had to go out later and off she went, wearing those awful clothes she puts on to go down east. And she'd said she wasn't doing that any more.' Anna took a deep breath and looked him in the face with something very like accusation in her eyes. 'Something's wrong, my lord, and I'm betting it's to do with you because she told me you wouldn't be round any more and bit my head off when I asked why. So what have you done to her?'

'Nothing. Your mistress has decided she wants nothing more to do with me.' He turned on his heel and walked away. He'd be damned if he was going to be interrogated by some maidservant in the public street.

Two yards. *Phyllida crying her eyes out. Well, she rejected me, not the other way round.* Five yards. *Sick, shaking. She deserves it. I feel sick.* Ten yards. *Going east. Into the slums, into the dangerous world of Harry Buck and his ilk.*

Ashe looked back. Anna was standing where he had left her, but when she saw him stop she ran to him. 'My lord?'

'What post?'

'Just one letter. She didn't say who from.'

'Where is it?'

Anna screwed up her face in concentrated thought. 'Don't know. She didn't have it when I took her upstairs. I'll be guessing she dropped it in the drawing room when she took ill.' She put her hand on his arm.

'Please, my lord, do you think there was something in the letter?'

'I don't know, but it is the only clue we have. Come on.'

Anna found the card under the sofa. Ashe read it, once in stunned disbelief, the second time in cold anger. *Come back to work.* She hadn't been raped, she'd been a whore. Phyllida had lied to him, she had hidden this disgraceful secret and only the danger of exposure had forced her to break off their relationship. He could have ended up married to her—and then what would have happened when one of her former clients turned up?

To hell with her, she deserves everything she gets. Ashe ripped the card in half, then made himself look at it again, made himself start thinking with his head and his heart about the real woman, the woman he knew and not the one who had wounded his pride.

Phyllida had been genuinely inexperienced and nervous when he had made love to her. This creature Buck had most likely used her only once. And now he was blackmailing her to get her back to his brothel, into his power.

It would not just be money he'd be after. Phyllida might not realise it, but Ashe could read between the lines and the danger she was in made him cold with fear for her. How she had ended up in this mire could wait for later.

'Have you heard of Harry Buck?' he demanded.

'Yes.' The maid went pale. 'He's a dangerous thatch-gallows, is that one.'

'Where's his brothel?'

She gawped at him, then seemed to realise he was

serious. 'He's got half a dozen of them, so I've heard, but I don't know where they are.'

How long would it take him to scour the slums of the East End of London without help, without local knowledge? Even if he found her brother and explained all this, there was no guarantee Gregory would know where to go. He seemed to have visited the gaming houses, but there was no hint he habituated brothels in such a rough area.

Then he recalled Phyllida asking about his name and whether Ashe was the same as Ashok. She knew an Indian trader in the docks by that name and he, she'd said, was a rogue, but a good-hearted one.

'I'll find her, Anna,' he promised. 'You stay here in case she makes it back without me.' Then he ran.

There was no-one at the Town house as he pushed through the front door, up the stairs to find his pistols and his knives. He went down again three at a time and out into the square to find a cab. 'The docks,' he snapped at the toughest, biggest driver he could see. 'Double your fare if you get me there fast.' He wedged himself in a corner and began to load the firearms. If Phyllida was harmed, someone was going to suffer.

She knew roughly where to go, somewhere in the maze of alleys and courts wedged between Butchers Row, Pillory Lane and New Street where the noise and smells of Smithfield Market did battle with the stench of human waste, over-stuffed graveyards and tanneries. She had stumbled though this area once before, shaking and sore, horrified at what had happened, her fingers cramped around the coins Harry Buck had given her.

It was only later that Phyllida realised that she had been lucky, that Buck had kept his word and used her for that one occasion only and had not simply turned the key in the door and kept her captive to use again and again.

A plump girl with a red shawl, her breasts uncovered almost to the point of indecency, looked a likely person to ask. 'Can you tell me the way to Harry Buck's house?'

'What, looking for a job, are you?' The girl ran a scornful eye over Phyllida's drab gown and brown cloak. 'Prime bit of crack you are, I don't think.'

'Heard 'e needs a cook.' She flattened her vowels, dropped her aitches. 'I'm a good cook.'

'Yeah? Well, his cunny warren's just up there.' The whore jerked her head in the direction of Smithfield. 'The best house, that is.'

'Thank you.' Phyllida made her reluctant feet move. She had no idea how she was going to get out of this, but she had to do something before Buck told the world that the Earl of Fransham's sister was a common whore.

The nausea came back when she saw the house, three storeys of respectable-looking brick turned black by years of soot and grime. The front door was clean, though. Red, glossy and flanked by torchère holders that would blazon its presence to all those seeking it.

Phyllida climbed the steps and banged on the knocker. A panel slid back, a broken-nosed face scrutinised her. She stared back, recognising one of Buck's regular bodyguards. 'Mr Buck asked me to meet him here,' she said.

''E did, did 'e? You must 'ave some interesting tricks if he wants you.' The panel slammed shut and then, with the sound of bolts being drawn, the door opened. 'Come on in then, the boss is along 'ere.'

He peered at her as he opened a door on the first floor. 'You're that dealing woman, ain't yer?'

'Yes,' she agreed as she hesitated on the threshold, summoning enough courage to step into Harry Buck's lair. 'I'm a dealer.' *Not a whore.*

'What's that?' Buck demanded sharply as she walked in. 'What you say, Jem?'

'It's that dealer woman from the warehouse, guv'nor. You know, bought the Chinese stuff when that Indian geezer got lippy with you.'

'Nah, this is a bit of laced mutton, this is.'

Phyllida looked up from the swirling patterns of the Turkey carpet and saw Buck lounging in a chair beside a wide desk.

'What you doing all got up like a dowd, darlin'? You wasn't looking quite so drab last night, off to dinner with your smart friends.'

The bruiser closed the door behind her. Phyllida straightened her spine and looked Buck in the eye. She was not going to give him the satisfaction of seeing just how he made her feel. But the memories kept swirling back like thick, putrid fog to cloud her brain.

You're a pretty one. Think I'll break you in meself. Don't see why I can't have a treat now and again. Thick fingers, unwashed body. Pain and shame.

'I am here. What do you want to close your mouth?'

'Money, darlin', like I said.'

'How much?'

'Hundred.'

She could find that easily enough. But it wouldn't

end there, she knew. 'And that will be that? You will keep your mouth shut?'

'Don't be a silly girl. I'll want that every month. If you ain't got it, you can come 'ere and work for it on yer back. You pay or you work and I stay quiet.' He leered at her. 'You was a scrawny little thing back then, but I remember those eyes, all big and round, just like when you looked at me in the warehouse. That mark like a heart on your tit. I've a good memory, I 'ave. So I had you followed and thought about it 'til I remembered who you was.'

'Blackmail is a serious crime.' And blackmailers were never satisfied—she knew that. Buck would never go away.

'Send me to the nubbing cleat, it would,' Buck agreed, baring his teeth in a grin. 'But who're you going to tell?'

No one, was the answer to that. She needed time to think now she knew what he was demanding, time to find some kind of lever that would counteract his threats. Could she find out something to threaten him with, blackmail him in return? But Harry Buck had probably committed every crime and sin in the book and he was still out on the streets. No one seemed able to touch him.

'I can't find that kind of money all at once. You'll have to give me time to get it together.'

Buck studied her, her gaze sliding like a greasy finger over her face and down over her body. 'Nah. I know that's a lie. So we'll start tonight, shall we? I'll get me hundred out of your body. There's one of me little parties here this evening. They'll like you, my gentlemen will.'

'Oh, no.' Phyllida reached for the door handle, jerked at it and found herself facing Jem's broad chest.

'Oh, yes,' Buck said. 'The lady's staying, Jem. Put her in one of the rooms upstairs and lock the door— don't want 'er straying and 'aving an accident, do we?'

She tried to push past him, knowing even as she shoved at the sweat-stained frieze coat that it was hopeless. Jem picked her up and slung her over his shoulder as easily as he might a child.

The room he dumped her in was quite obviously one used to entertain clients. She wondered, as she stared around at the tawdry red velvet, the huge bed and the mirrors, if this was the one she had been taken to before. It was all a blur, the only real thing in her memory Buck's face above her, his weight, the pain and the sheer helpless terror.

Well, she was not a helpless girl now and she was desperate enough for just about anything. Phyllida pushed up the window and leaned out, hands braced on the filthy sill. She was three storeys up, overlooking a back alleyway. There were no ledges, no drainpipes within reach. This window and the locked door were the only ways out of the room.

She took off her cloak and one half-boot, held the thick fabric in front of the mirror and hit it hard with the heel. The glass shattered into a radiating pattern of long, knife-like shards. Phyllida picked one out at the cost of a cut finger, dragged back the cover from the bed and began to cut the sheet into strips.

Chapter Twenty-One

'You'll do it?' Ashe asked in Hindi.

The tall Indian smiled. 'Of course, my brother. You are the enemy of Buck, he is my enemy. We are allies, are we not? And I do not like that man's dealings with women.' He used a foul word and spat. 'Come, let us hear what my men have discovered.'

Ashe suspected that Ashok—he admitted to no other name—was as much a criminal as Buck. He might not deal in women, but Ashe could smell raw opium, and the heavy locks and the glint of weapons everywhere he looked argued precious contraband hidden in the warehouse that was Ashok's headquarters.

He had been remarkably easy for a man who spoke Hindi to find. The first group of Indian seamen that Ashe saw had been startled to be addressed in their own language by a man dressed in the height of fashion, but Ashe's colloquial speech seemed to win them over and they led the way to Ashok without any further persuasion.

Ashe had explained what he wanted, had swallowed liquid opium from the other man's own cupped palm, exchanged a number of highly coloured items of gossip about Calcutta and was now sitting cross-legged on a heap of silk rugs, drinking sherbet while using all his diplomatic training not to take Ashok by the throat and shake him into urgent action. But this was the Indian's world, his men and, Ashe was acutely aware, his own best and only chance of getting into Buck's headquarters and removing Phyllida.

'Oh yes, my brother, she is still in there. I have the place watched, always, as is prudent with an enemy. Your lady went in—pale, in a dull brown cloak—and has not come out. Now we wait until evening.'

'No. She is in danger. Even as we sit here talking they could be—'

'Wait until evening, then customers come. That's who they want her for. You are just another English gentleman and so the door will be opened to you. My men attack at the back door and others follow you in through the front.' The Indian reached for a sweetmeat. 'When you find Buck, you will have a duel with him?'

'That is for gentlemen.' Ashe slid the knife from his sleeve and delicately trimmed a rough edge on his nail. 'He is not a gentleman.'

'Ah.' Ashok smiled. 'No, he is not. And we do not want the magistrates getting their hands on him, he knows too much about me. Perhaps he will have an accident. While we wait, your lady admired some pearls I have, the last time we did business, but she said they were too expensive for her. Perhaps you would like to look at them?'

My lady. Is she? Ashe pushed aside the thought. The future consisted of whatever time it took to get Phyllida out of there. After that he would try to work out just what she meant to him and discover what he meant to her.

* * *

Waiting was the hardest thing, Phyllida thought as she stood behind the door. The window opposite was wide open, curtains flapping. The posts at the corners of the bed were not part of the structure, she had discovered, merely supports for manacles. With a shudder at the thought of how they had been used, she had tugged one free of the brackets that held it, then jammed it across the window opening before tying the long tail of plaited sheets to it.

The makeshift rope would not hold her weight, she knew, but it served its purpose if it drew her captors to the window and gave her the chance to slip out the door.

It seemed hours before the household began to stir. Footsteps outside had her tensing every muscle, but they passed by. Women's voices, low male replies, a shriek of laughter, the bang of the knocker.

Then, with shocking suddenness, loud shouting, a crash from far below, screams and the report of a pistol. *A raid by the magistrates?* She hardly dared hope.

The door opened without her hearing any footsteps. Phyllida braced herself to run. The man strode towards the middle of the room and as he did so a big black bird landed on the sill with a harsh croak.

'Lucifer!'

The man spun on his heel. 'Phyllida!'

'Ashe. *Ashe.*' She fell into his arms laughing and sobbing.

'Are you all right? Have they—?'

'No. No, just very frightened,' she admitted.

'But not so frightened you could not think,' he said with a glance at the open window, the shattered mirror and stripped bed. 'Clever. That could have worked.'

'You!' Buck burst into the room behind them, blood on his face, a wicked knife in his hands. He waved it at Phyllida. 'You bitch, I'll gut you.'

'You'll go through me to do it.' Ashe drew a long blade from his sleeve. Feet pounded along the corridor, voices shouting in a foreign tongue coming closer.

Buck looked like a cornered rat. He bared yellow teeth at Ashe. 'Some other time. You'll pay.'

He was at the open window in one long stride, threw a leg over the sill and ducked out, his big hands grasping the sheet rope. Lucifer gave a sharp *caw* and flapped away into the alley.

'No! It won't hold,' Phyllida shouted as Buck vanished from sight.

There was a sharp cry from the bird, a scream of 'Get away from my eyes, you—' from below the open window, then a sickening thud.

The room filled with silent, turbaned men. One man leaned out of the window and spoke to Phyllida in a language she did not understand, then, as suddenly as they had appeared, they melted back, leaving her alone with Ashe.

'Oh, God. I've killed him?' She had never meant it as a trap, had never meant to do more than create a diversion.

'You are responsible for nothing. He lived the life he chose and he died of its consequences,' Ashe said harshly. 'If anyone killed him, it was Lucifer. Come on.'

'Where are his men?' She followed him into the corridor and down the stairs.

'Engaged in a battle royal with your friend Ashok and his followers in the basement, by the sound of it.'

She saw the way his eyes went to the head of the

lower stairs, the tension in his body. 'Go. I will be all right here now.'

'No.' He turned away and led her to the front door. 'That is Ashok's fight now. We agreed he would deal with Buck and his men, and he'll take the spoils of that. My part was to find you.'

'What would you have done if Buck had not fallen?'

Ashe took her arm and strode up the street towards Smithfield. A hackney carriage stopped at the top of the road and he hailed it, then turned to look down at her, but he answered only obliquely. 'He touched you, threatened you, put fear in your eyes. Now we get clear of here before someone calls the law.'

He would have killed Buck, she saw it in the cold, hard glitter of his eyes, the set of his jaw, and offered up a silent prayer of thanks that in the end it had been an accident and there was no blood on Ashe's hands.

'Now what happens?' she asked as they sat back on the battered squabs of the carriage and it rattled into motion.

'I take you home and we say nothing to anyone of this. I will speak to Ashok in the morning, make certain everything is tidied up.'

Make certain Buck is dead, you mean, she thought, but did not say it. 'I had not realised that Ashok was more than a trader,' she ventured. It seemed that Ashe was not yet ready of speak of what now lay between them.

'In his way he is as hard and as ruthless as Buck,' Ashe said. 'You will not go into the East End again, too many people have taken notice of you now.'

Part of her wanted to defy him, simply because he was giving her orders, but she knew he was right and she would have come to the same conclusion herself. 'I was going to get a manager for the shop, once Gregory was settled. I will do that now; there is a man at one of the auction houses who I have in mind.'

'And what will you do to occupy yourself?' Ashe asked.

The tiny flame of hope that had flickered into life when he had taken her in his arms in that sordid room wavered and died. Ashe was not going to say they could put it all behind them, carry on as they were before she had met Buck again. But then, how could he? He had learned that she had sold her body, had been prepared to keep that from him at the risk of a scandal that would tarnish his whole family if it came out. And she had always known, deep in her heart, that a marriage was impossible.

'I will do what I always planned, go and live in the Dower House.' There was silence between them, a heavy stillness that felt physically hard to break. After a minute she said, 'I will tell you what happened, when—'

'No. I do not want to hear. It is not my business.' Ashe was looking out of the window as though Leadenhall Street was of abiding fascination.

'You saved me just now. You know what he was going to do.'

'I would have done the same for any woman I knew to be in that danger,' Ashe said politely, as though she had thanked him for rescuing her parasol from a gust of wind.

I love you.

They sat without speaking until the hackney turned into King Street and passed Almack's. They would be in Great Ryder Street at any moment.

'I would not have married you. I never intended to,' Phyllida said hurriedly. 'I knew I could not because of what had happened, how it happened. I was wrong not to have been stronger right from the start, never to have allowed you to kiss me, never to have let this farce of a courtship go on as it has while I let myself dream.

'You will not hear my story and I understand why not. You are very angry and I have put you to a great deal of trouble, let alone embarrassment and danger. But I want you to realise that I would never have compromised your honour by becoming your wife. I could never have married you and kept this a secret from you, even if your honour had not mattered to me.'

Her house key was in her hand now as the carriage drew to a halt. Phyllida pushed the door open and jumped down before Ashe could move. She stood on the pavement and took a last, long look at his face. 'I love you, you see. Goodbye, Ashe.' Then she turned and hurried up the steps, thrust the key in the lock and was inside before she heard his booted feet hit the pavement.

I love you, you see. The door slammed shut. *Goodbye.* That had been final.

'You getting back in, guv'nor, or is this it?' the cabby demanded.

Ashe gave him the address and climbed inside again. *Is this it?* the man had asked. Was it? He should be glad. Phyllida was safe, he was saved from a highly unsuitable marriage, the slums were free of Harry Buck, an unsavoury predator upon women who had met his just desserts.

I love you. She did not mean it, did she? He had not tried to attach her emotionally, she had made no attempt to cling to him, to plead with him. Her eyes as she said it had been dry.

Why had he not let her tell him her story? If she could bear to tell it, then he should have the patience to hear it. Then he realised that it would have taken courage for him to sit and listen, that it mattered to him, more than an abstract story of an everyday outrage. It mattered because Phyllida mattered.

Sara was alone in the drawing room when he walked in. 'Whatever have you been doing? You look as though you have been in a fight!'

'That is because I have been in a fight.' He sank down on the sofa beside her and leaned his aching head on the cushioned back. 'And don't worry Mata by telling her.'

'Of course not. Did you win?'

'I think so.'

'Excellent.' She picked up her embroidery and let him rest.

'Sara, may I ask you something shocking? Something I should not even dream of speaking of to you?'

'Is this something else I should not be telling Mata about? Of course you may.'

Ashe sat up, rested his elbows on his knees and studied his clasped hands. 'What would drive you to sell yourself? To give your body to a stranger, a man who revolted you. Hunger?'

'No!' He felt the movement as she shook her head vehemently. 'I would rather starve.'

'Money?'

'Well, the money would be a reason, otherwise why do it? But...' She fell silent for a while, thinking. 'I would do it if it would save Mata from some awful danger. Or for you or Papa. If one of you were sick and there was no money for a doctor and medicines, then nothing else would matter.'

She said it earnestly, obviously meaning it. After a moment she moved close to him and put her hand on his arm. 'Is that why you were in a fight?'

'Yes. She was very young.'

'Oh, poor thing,' Sara said compassionately. 'Is there anything I can do to help her?'

'No, she's safe now.' *I have broken her heart, but she's safe.* Ashe got to his feet. 'I'm going out, probably won't be home for dinner.'

Fransham, when he finally ran him to earth, was at White's, dozing over a newspaper in a quiet corner of the library. 'Clere! Have a drink.' He waved to the waiter and tossed the paper aside. 'You're looking uncommonly serious.'

Ashe had washed, changed, combed his hair, before he had left home, but it seemed he had not been able to scrub away the darkness in his mind. 'I wanted to ask you something personal, something you probably don't want to talk about. Only it affects Phyllida and I need to understand.' Understand not only Phyllida, not only what had driven her to that desperate act, but himself. How he felt for her, why he ached inside, why he felt worse than he had when Reshmi had died.

'All right.' Gregory sat up and poured a couple of glasses of brandy. 'Ask away, I can always punch you on the nose if you get too personal.'

'Phyllida told me about your parents, why they didn't marry until after she was born. But what happened when your mother died? She didn't seem able to talk about it.'

Fransham's face clouded. 'God, that was an awful time. She told you how unreliable our father was? Well, the time he spent with us got less and less—and so did the money. And then Mama got sick. Consumption, the doctor said. We did the best we could. I was fifteen and I got a job with the local pharmacist, just a dogsbody, really, but he paid me in medicine. Phyllida was seventeen and she ran the house and nursed Mama and kept writing to Papa.

'He never answered, so in the end she scraped together enough money for the stage and set off to London to find him. She came back a month later, looking ghastly, and said he'd died in a tavern brawl. Knock on the head and too much drink. She'd seen the lawyers and they said there was some assets and more debts. I was the earl, and that kept the creditors at bay for a bit, but it was too late for Mama. She died a week after Phyll got home.'

'If she took only enough money for the stage, how had she lived in London?' Ashe asked, knowing the answer only too well. She could have turned around and gone home when she didn't find her wastrel father at once, but she had hung on, kept searching even though she was starving.

'Got some odd jobs, I suppose. I never asked, what with Mama and the news about Father.' Gregory scrubbed his hand over his face. 'I should have thought. She was as thin as a rake, took her ages to put the weight back on.'

So she had sold herself for the money to stay alive while she found her father, because if she did not then her mother and brother would starve. And the world would think—*he* had thought, damn it—that what she had done dishonoured her. And she believed that if she married him it would compromise his honour.

'I have fallen out with Phyllida,' Ashe said bluntly. 'I've hurt her and I doubt she'll open the door to me now.'

'Do I need to name my seconds?' Gregory asked and set his glass down with a snap.

'No. You need to give me your door key and eat dinner out. In fact, I suggest you go and beg the Millingtons for a bed for the night.'

'The devil you say!' But Gregory was pulling the key out of the pocket in the tail of his coat.

'Don't ask and I won't have to lie to you. Thanks.'

'You had better be intending to marry her,' Gregory warned. 'I've been a damned slack brother, but I mean to do the right thing by her now.'

'I can ask. Only Phyllida can accept,' Ashe said and pocketed the key.

Chapter Twenty-Two

Ashe let himself into the house in Great Ryder Street with the care of a burglar. The ground floor was silent, but he could hear the murmur of voices from the basement, the clang of copper pans. Soft-footed, he moved to the top of the stairs and listened. Three feminine voices, none of them Phyllida's.

They were devoted to her, he knew that from observing Anna. Whether that devotion would move them to fillet him with a boning knife or help him, he had no idea, but he could hardly be alone and uninterrupted with Phyllida unless they knew he was there from the start.

'Good afternoon.'

The cook dropped the ladle she was holding and the little maid gave a squeak of alarm. Anna jumped up from the chair by the range where she had been mending and marched up to confront him. 'What did you do to her? You got her away from Buck, I'll say that for you, but she's shut herself away in her bedchamber and she won't talk to me, or come out. If you've hurt Miss Phyllida, you rakehell, his lordship will beat your brains out and we'll cheer him on!'

'I didn't *do* anything to her,' Ashe said and sat down in a chair by the kitchen table, neatly unsettling Anna who did not seem to know how to deal with gentlemen lounging at the table, stealing Cook's still-warm jam tarts. 'I managed to say the wrong things, not say the right ones, and comprehensively put my foot in it with her. So, yes, I've hurt her, but not the way I suspect you mean, Anna.'

He laid the key on the table. 'That's Lord Fransham's, by the way. He knows I am here and he won't be in now until tomorrow.'

'So that's the way it is,' Anna said and sat down too.

'If you're all going to eat those tarts, I'd best put the kettle on,' Cook said, suiting her actions to her words. 'Get the tea caddy, Jane.'

'Are you in love with Miss Phyllida?' Anna demanded. Ashe raised his eyebrows at her tone, but she was not to be intimidated and sat there glaring at him while she waited for an answer.

Am I? 'Do you think I'd tell you before I tell her?' he asked. 'I do not mean her harm, that I promise you.'

Cook passed him a cup of tea and pushed the plate of tarts closer. 'Well, get your strength up. You'll need it,' she added darkly.

She could not stay in her room for the rest of her life. Nor the rest of the day, come to that. Phyllida swung her legs over the edge of the bed and ran out of energy to stand up.

This would not do. Life had to go on and Gregory would be worried and the staff would fret if she hid herself away like a lovelorn adolescent. There was much to be done, that would help. A manager to find for the shop, the Dower House to whip into habitable shape, Gregory's wedding to plan for.

Goodness, she would be so busy she would forget Ashe Herriard in a few days. Oh, who was she deceiving? Not herself, obviously. Phyllida lay down again, curled up into a miserable ball and stubbornly refused to cry. A girl was entitled to mourn for a day when her heart was broken, she told herself with a rather hysterical attempt at humour.

The door opened. 'Go away, Anna. I do not want to be disturbed.' It closed again, but there were soft footfalls, the sound of breathing. 'Anna, *please* go away. Tell Cook I will not be down to dinner and say to Lord Fransham that I have a headache.'

'Lord Fransham will not be in to dinner. He is staying the night with the Millingtons.'

Ashe? Phyllida uncurled and sat bolt upright. 'What the devil are you doing here? I said goodbye and I meant it.' How could he come and mock her like this?

Ashe sat down on the side of the bed. 'I was shocked. I was shaken and I was horrified and above all I was hurting and I had no idea why,' he said abruptly. 'Then I made myself think. No woman sells herself unless she is desperate, or foolishly thinks prostitution is an easy way of life. And you are neither stupid nor wanton. I ought to have had that clear in my head. I recalled what you had said about your father, how your family had been abandoned and so I asked Gregory about the time just before your mother died.'

'You told him what I did?' It would kill Gregory to know she had been driven to that.

'No, of course not.' Ashe scrubbed one hand across his face. 'I might have made a thoroughgoing mess of this, but he has no idea why I asked him. What he told me made sense and I knew why you had no choice. Damn it, Phyllida, if a man fought and killed for honour and to protect his family, then everyone understands, thinks he's a fine fellow. If a woman puts herself through hell for her family, sacrifices everything short of her life, then she is called a whore and is ruined.'

He twisted round to face her fully. 'I should have had that straight in my mind and I should have told you that was what I thought, there and then. What you did for your family was courageous and honourable. When you wanted to tell me about it, I should have listened and reassured you and comforted you.'

He thought her courageous and honourable? He was apologising to her when she had taken advantage of him, hidden the truth from him?

When, lost for words, she simply stared at him, at his beloved face, taut with pain and self-recrimination and regret, he stood up. 'I don't imagine you can forgive me for that. Like an arrogant fool I told Gregory to stay away tonight, that I had been clumsy, but that I would make it right with you and that I would marry you. I was wrong to presume. Insensitive. I am sorry, Phyllida.'

He had his hand on the door before she could find her voice to stop him. 'Ashe, I love you.' His back to her, he stayed where he was, as though he could not turn. 'I would forgive you anything, understand anything. You do not have to marry me and make that sacrifice. Just knowing you understand and do not condemn me for it, that you forgive me for letting this masquerade of a courtship go on as long as it has, that makes so much difference.'

'Why would it be a sacrifice?' he asked and his voice, always so confident, always so strong, was unsteady.

'For all the reasons we have rehearsed before. Sooner or later the strain of that, of my birth, of my secrets, they would crack such a marriage. I would rather not have you than ruin your life.' He had praised her courage just now. This, if he did but know it, was the hardest, most courageous thing she had ever done, sending away the man she loved.

'None of it would matter if I loved you,' he said and turned, his voice quite firm again, his eyes green and calm and certain. 'My family like you, soon they will love you as a daughter and a sister. And, with love, we can face down any whispers about your birth.'

'But you—' Ashe did not lie to her, she felt that deep in her bones. Her heart, so heavy, suddenly became light, the beat so fast she felt dizzy with it.

'But I do love you. It took a lot of pain to make me realise just why I felt the way I did. What I had thought was love before was only a faint shadow of the real thing. You loving me, despite everything, is a miracle I do not deserve. But perhaps our children do.' His beautiful, expressive mouth curved into the first smile she had seen, it seemed, for days. 'Marry me, Phyllida. Let me love you. Shut all your secrets away so they will wither and die in the darkness and come and live in the light with me.'

'Yes. Oh, yes, Ashe.' She found she had scrambled off the bed, all anyhow, her arms held open to him, and he was in them and they held each other so tight she could not breathe, but it did not matter, because Ashe loved her.

Ashe set her back a little and grinned. 'That feels as though a huge weight has just lifted off my heart. Do you want to go and tell Gregory and my family, start to make plans for the wedding?'

'No.' She laughed at the surprise on his face. 'You sent Gregory off for the night. You meant to stay here with me, did you not?'

'Yes, but I already said it was arrogant and insensitive of me to assume that is what you would want.' He was running his fingers over her cheek, tracing her lips, stroking her hair as though he had just found her after a long absence.

'It is exactly what I want,' she murmured and stood on tiptoe to kiss him. 'I want to show you how much I love you. I want to feel how much you love me.'

'You are not afraid?' Ashe murmured into her hair.

Phyllida swallowed. 'A little. Parts of it will not be... will hurt, I know that.'

'No, they won't,' Ashe said with complete confidence. 'For a start, no one has ever made love to you before and, even if they had, they were not me.'

'Of all the arrogant creatures!' she protested, laughing uncertainly as he attacked the fastenings of her crumpled gown.

'Not at all. I know what I am doing—don't frown at me like that. There have been other women, but you are the last one. The last and only.' Her gown fell to her feet, her corset dropped away. 'As I was saying, I have been learning to *make* love so I could pleasure the woman I *do* love.'

Ashe shrugged out of coat and waistcoat together,

yanked off his neckcloth and pulled his shirt over his head. 'There is a time and place for leisurely undressing, but this is not it. You, my darling, need sweeping off your feet and that is precisely what I am going to do.'

His boots went flying, his breeches were kicked off, Phyllida clutched rather desperately at the front of her shift as she found herself confronted by a naked, fully aroused, man. 'Oh, my.' Her eyes felt wide as saucers.

'All yours, indeed.' Ashe said as he stripped the shift from her, deposited her on the bed and straddled her hips. 'This is the frightening bit, I imagine. I promise I won't squash you.' He slid down her body and she felt her legs opening instinctively to cradle him. He took his weight on his elbows and looked down at her. 'All right?'

'Yes. Yes, perfectly all right.' And it was. There was no point of resemblance at all to how it had been with Buck. This was Ashe and he loved her and he was going to pleasure her. She reached up and freed his hair from the tie, ran her fingers through the silky weight of it, gasped as he bent his head and let the ends tease across her breasts.

He kissed her mouth, a fleeting caress, then slid down her body until he could kiss her breasts, nibbling the tips until she gasped and then sucking and swirling with his tongue until her hips lifted off the bed and she writhed against him, her fingers laced into his hair as though she did not know whether to hold him captive there for ever or push him away to end this exquisite torture.

'Ashe. Oh, please…'

He moved to the other breast, shifted his weight so he could slide one hand down between her thighs where she ached and throbbed and needed him, needed him desperately to do those wonderful things that he had the other night.

When Ashe left her breasts she gasped in protest, but he only murmured, 'Sweet, so sweet,' and possessed her mouth again while his fingers slid and teased and pressed and she panted into his mouth, so close to the bliss, so close.

Then his weight and heat had gone, leaving her reaching for him. She opened her eyes and saw his dark head where his hand had been, his hair fanned out over her thighs, startling against the white skin. He pushed firmly but gently to open her and then kissed her there, even as he slid two fingers into her. Shocked, she tensed. It would hurt, she had known it would…

'Oh.' It was a murmur, a gasp. Instinctively she tightened around the intrusion, arched up against his mouth, sobbed wordless pleas that he would never stop, never, because it was almost there, that wonderful sensation that transcended reality.

He moved, too fast for her to protest at the absence of his lips, his hand. He was over her, holding her, whispering what she knew were love words although she did not know the language. His hips moved in the cradle of her thighs and he filled her in one long stroke and she shattered, broke, heard her own voice crying out.

Phyllida came to herself to find the pleasure was not waning, only changing. Ashe moved within her, his body part of hers, his gasps of pleasure hers as well as his. She curled her legs around his hips, tilting up until he was as deep as she could take him, and clung to the broad shoulders, slick with sweat, kissed him wherever she could reach and heard her own voice, 'I love you, I love you', as he groaned and went rigid in her arms.

They lay locked together in a hot, sticky, blissful knot on top of the tangled sheets. Phyllida kissed the angle of Ashe's neck, the only place she could reach. 'You were not arrogant at all,' she told him. 'Very modest, in fact.'

He pushed up on one elbow and smiled down at her. 'I'm glad you think so. Does that mean that you have not changed your mind?'

'It does. I intend making an honest man of you, my lord.' She wriggled out of his embrace and surveyed the room. 'Just look at this! Your breeches are hanging from my dressing-table mirror, there is a boot in a hat box and that dreadful brown gown will never be the same again. And to think that before you came in I was lying here trying to convince myself that no one died of a broken heart and that somehow I could get over you.'

'Do you think you might?'

'Get over you?' Phyllida placed her index fingertip in the middle of her chin and assumed a pose of deep thought. 'I suppose I could possibly become tired of you. To be on the safe side you had better ask me in, say, eighty years' time.'

'I will make a note in my memorandum book,' Ashe said seriously. 'I do love it when you pretend to be serious and prudent.'

'Well, make the most of it.' Phyllida ran one fingernail down the middle of his chest, down to the flat belly with its intriguing trail of hair, and tickled into Ashe's navel. 'Because I fully intend to be scandalous, frivolous and utterly naughty.'

'Excellent,' Ashe murmured, submitting to her

hands. 'I will do my very best to survive eighty years of this, my love, but I warn you, we had better practise as much as possible.' And then he ceased to be able to say a coherent word for the next half-hour.

* * * * *

REQUEST YOUR FREE BOOKS!

 HARLEQUIN® HISTORICAL:
Where love is timeless

2 FREE NOVELS PLUS 2 **FREE GIFTS!**

*Jeannie Lin takes you on a journey of
discovery, temptation and passion in her brilliant
new title THE SWORD DANCER.*
The thrill of the chase! How far would you go for love?

"A private bath, thief-catcher?" she remarked lightly.

His eyes snapped open and he started, sending a cascade of water splashing onto the floorboards.

"Wen Li Feng," he choked out. His hand gripped the edge of the tub and his muscles tensed all up his arm and throughout his body.

There was something both vulnerable yet undeniably virile about the sight of Han naked. Her tongue cleaved to the roof of her mouth. She attributed the warmth creeping up the back of her neck to the steam that surrounded her, dampening her skin. Needless to say, she was no longer thinking about battle scars.

She worked to keep her gaze on his face. "Your work must be quite profitable."

His breathing had quickened and he fought to regain his composure. "You should be careful of your reputation, Miss Wen. Everyone will assume you are here to provide me with an intimate service."

Men's bodies weren't unknown to her. Li Feng had lived in close quarters with other performers. Before that, she'd been isolated on a mountain sparsely inhabited by monks. She may have lost her first kiss along with her virginity recently, but even before that she'd simply never learned to be shy. Despite having had a lover in the past, it was still a shock to see thief-catcher Han's naked form.

The two of them had wrestled, fought and had so much physical contact that now the sight of him unclothed completed the picture. Her knowledge of his body was nearly as intimate as a lover's.

She moved to stand over him. All that shielded him from her

view was a layer of bathwater and the haze of steam. Neither the water nor the steam was clouded enough.

An unwelcome heat flooded her cheeks. She hoped it wasn't accompanied by a blush that Han could see. Li Feng had chosen this particular location to confront him so she could finally have the thief-catcher at a disadvantage, and she hated the thought of losing her edge.

"You should know that I can track you as easily as you can track me."

Han made no effort to curl up his knees to hide that part of himself. "You are relying on my sense of modesty to prevent me from capturing you right now," he said as he started to rise.

With a flick of her hand, she unsheathed the short sword hidden beneath her sleeve and pressed the tip to his chest. "I'm relying on this blade."

His gaze remained on her, unflinching, but he did sink back into the tub. "Have you ever killed anyone, Miss Wen?"

She cocked her head. "You can be my first," she said with a smile.

His eyes darkened at that and the air thickened between them. She suddenly wished she had brought a longer blade. The length of the sleeve sword kept her too close to him. The point of it remained over his heart, pressing firmly against flesh without breaking skin. He seemed unafraid. She, by contrast, was suddenly very afraid. Not of him, but rather the skip of her pulse.

Relentless thief-catcher Han sees life—and love—as black-and-white. But when he finally captures the spirited Li Feng, she makes him question everything he thought he knew about right and wrong. Will Han betray the elusive sword dancer he is learning to love, or trust his long-disregarded heart and follow her to dangerous, tempting rebellion?

Look for Jeannie Lin's THE SWORD DANCER. Available in Harlequin® Historical June 2013.

TEMPTING THE PREACHER'S DAUGHTER

Plain preacher's daughter Violet Benson is always the wallflower—until charismatic gambler Cade Foster takes her under his wing. Suddenly the men of Morrow Creek start looking at her with new eyes—and the women with envy—but Violet is only interested in one man: Cade.

Agreeing to be his "lucky charm," Violet becomes embroiled in the gambler's thrilling world. With her newfound confidence, she is determined to uncover the secret sorrow behind the eyes that smolder beneath his Stetson, and prove to this fascinating man that he can take the biggest gamble of all…with his heart.

Look for

The Honor-Bound Gambler

by Lisa Plumley in June 2013.

Available wherever books are sold.

COMING IN JUNE 2013

Reforming The Viscount

BY FAN-FAVORITE AUTHOR

ANNIE BURROWS

TO REFUSE HIM ONCE WAS A MISTAKE—TO REFUSE HIM TWICE WOULD BE MADNESS!

Viscount Rothersthorpe can't tear his eyes from Lydia Morgan any more than he can calm the raging fury coursing through his veins. Is there no end to the irony? Come to town to find a wife, only to be taunted by the past?

Furtive glances across the ballroom are not helping to ease Lydia's state of shock—the man who once uttered a marriage proposal as one might remark upon the weather has returned. But when he stuns her with a second outrageous—but now wickedly delicious—proposal, it is clear that, despite the rumours, the rake from her past has not reformed!

Available wherever books are sold.